The Musician and His Art
Essays on Hindustānī Music

The Musician and His Art
Essays on Hindustānī Music

Deepak S. Raja

With a Foreword by
Daniel Neuman

DK
PRINTWORLD
Publishers of Indian Traditions

Cataloging in Publication Data – DK
[Courtesy: D.K. Agencies (P) Ltd. <docinfo@dkagencies.com>]

Raja, Deepak, author.
The musician and his art : essays on Hindustānī music / Deepak Raja; with a foreword by Daniel Neuman.
pages cm
"This book is a collection of lectures and essays I have presented/written over the last five years" – Preface.

1. Hindustani music – History and criticism. I. Title.

LCC ML338.R35 2018 | DDC 780.954 23

ISBN: 978-81-246-0955-2
First published in India in 2019

Printed and published by:
D.K. Printworld (P) Ltd.
Regd. Office: Vedaśrī, F-395, Sudarshan Park
(Metro Station: ESI Hospital), New Delhi - 110015
Phones: (011) 2545 3975, 2546 6019
e-mail: indology@dkprintworld.com
Website: www.dkprintworld.com

Dedicated

to the memory of

Prof. Sushil Kumar Saxena

and

Prof. Ashok Da Ranade

Foreword

It is with a deep sense of honour that I write these few words on Deepak Raja's remarkable collection of essays and lectures. Remarkable because I know of no other author or thinker on Hindustānī music, at least in the English language, who engages as wide a compass and delves as profoundly into questions concerning Hindustānī music as does Deepak Raja.

Consider depth. Who else has even engaged the subject of generations of teacher/performers and their musical influence through time and mapped these out as Deepak has done over a period of more than a century? He means here the periodicity of paradigm shifts as they seem to appear in this music tradition. He follows this section with a study of YouTube views of individual artists and the *gharānā*s they represent and charts the *gharānā* viewership as a ranking of aesthetic obsolescence! This example alone demonstrates the new questions he asks and the new methodologies he employs.

Another example is his article "Amplification, Recordings and Hindustānī Music". It is not that aspects of this have not been considered previously. Deepak Raja's insight, however, is the first to illuminate the non-obvious but profound ramifications these new technologies have had for Hindustānī music in the twentieth century. Knowledgeable readers will find his analysis of Faiyyaz Khan's and Kesarbai Kerkar's strategies for voice production in the preamplification era, for example, quite illuminating. These strategies had important musical aesthetic consequences for later artists as well.

This is all another way of saying that this collection of essays is brimming with such jewels, large and small throughout. This work is a highly valuable contribution to our knowledge of Hindustānī music and adds to the significant corpus that Deepak Raja has published in his previous books.

For anyone who wants to learn many things new about Hindustānī music, musicians and its unparalleled culture, this work is a signal contribution. It needs to be in the collection of anyone who has a genuine interest in Hindustānī music.

September 2018

Daniel M. Neuman
Professor, Executive Vice Chancellor & Provost Emeritus
University of California, Los Angeles, USA

Preface

This book is a collection of lectures and essays I have presented/ written over the last five years. Some of them have appeared on my blog (http://swaratala.blogspot.in), while some of them have been filmed during delivery and uploaded on YouTube. Some have appeared in print, but in media of restricted reach. But, some have not yet appeared on any print or online medium at all.

Only one of these essays, which I have chosen as the title of this book – *The Musician and His Art* – has been published earlier in my last book (*The Rāga-ness of Rāgas*) as "The Rāga-ness of Musicians". This repetition was necessary because the perspective deserved attention independently of the context in which my previous work included it. In addition to this, it provides an appropriate meta-theme for the contents of this book.

The lecture titled "Perspectives on Rāga-ness" delivered as the 4th Kumar Gandharva Memorial Lecture revisits, consolidates and crystallizes several ideas on the subject introduced in my fourth book *The Rāga-ness of Rāgas*. With this effort, I hope the ideas have achieved a greater clarity of thought, and transparency of communicative intent.

I habitually prepare a disciplined text version of a lecture before I present it. This is, occasionally, also a requirement of the hosts. However, it has been my practice never to actually "read" a written paper at a lecture or a seminar. I find it more useful to relate to my audiences, and speak off my PowerPoint slides. In the process, many newer/unplanned ideas and telling details emerge during the delivery and the interactions which follow.

I then have the opportunity to enrich the written text after the delivery and offer it as an easy reference for interested readers in a printed medium.

A lecture, as delivered, often also resorts to the use of Indian languages in order to relate episodes and conversations. This limitation of reach can be circumvented by offering a text version, written in English, with translations, where necessary. This makes the written text more valuable than the video version for those who do not understand Hindi, the most commonly used diversion from a basically English presentation.

Besides these practical considerations, I also have a personal affinity for the print medium. I have spent a substantial part of my working life in the newspaper industry. In a world that is fast turning away from the print medium, I still attach a great deal of sanctity to it. In this context, I recall the words of one of my mentors, Prof. Ashok Ranade:

> Writing a book is very different from writing for a periodical. A book addresses posterity. You have to write it with the awareness that your work could be read for at least two decades after it is published; and should still make sense.

As is to be expected, the thematic canvas of this book is wide. Some ideas do get repeated in the various chapters. A perfectly "logical" sequencing of the essays/papers has not been possible. Despite my efforts at presenting a coherent flow, this infirmity remains, imposed largely by the nature of its contents. I trust it will be overlooked.

It is with these considerations that I conceived this enterprise and was encouraged to do so by my publisher. I trust it will prove its value, as anticipated.

Mumbai
12 September 2018

Deepak S. Raja

Acknowledgements

I acknowledge a debt of gratitude to:

- Śrī Vighneśvara for permitting this endeavour to reach fruition.
- Śrī Naṭarāja and Mā Sarasvatī for giving me access to the knowledge of music.
- My parents for supporting, in every respect, my pursuit of music and musicology for over 65 years.
- All my *Guru*s for guiding, inspiring and mentoring my pursuit of music.
- My life-long mentors in the pursuit of musicology – Prof. Susheel Kumar Saxena and Prof. Ashok Da Ranade.
- All the eminent contemporary musicians, who have spared valuable time and effort to help my understanding of musicianship beyond my own limited experience.
- My cousin and dear friend, the late Chandu (Chandrakant) Kapadia, for convincing me, as long back as the 1980s, that I was destined for a life in music.
- The editors of *SRUTI* magazine (Chennai), for encouraging me to pursue critical writing on Hindustānī music.
- Lyle Wachovsky, Managing Director, India Archive Music Ltd., New York, for discovering and mentoring the musicologist in me.
- The scholars of Hindustānī music and ethnomusicology in various parts of the world, whose friendship has enabled

me to keep in touch with the academic environment outside India.

- The luminaries of the music world, who contributed thoughtful Forewords to my first four books on music – Pandit Shivkumar Sharma, Pandit Ulhas Kashalkar, Pandit Arvind Parikh and Vidushi Ashwini Bhide-Deshpande.
- Shri Ashok Vajpeyi, Managing Trustee, The Raza Foundation, New Delhi, for challenging my capabilities repeatedly with opportunities to publicly address various critical issues.
- The organizations have conferred honours upon me for my contribution to musicology over the last five years – The Vasantrao Deshpande Pratishthan (Pune), The Gujarat Rajya Sangeet Natak Akademi (Gandhinagar) and The Music Forum (Mumbai).
- The hosts of the various lectures and seminars at which the papers I presented find a place in this book.
- Prof. Keshavchaitanya Kunte, for kindly scrutinizing the drafts of two essays included in this book.
- My publisher, Shri Susheel Mittal of D.K. Printworld, New Delhi, for being a loyal ally, and accepting unconditionally every book that I decided to offer him for publication.
- Dr Daniel Neuman, an eminent musicologist, for contributing a Foreword to this book, and adding generously to its stature.
- Ms Vaishnavi Anand, artist, Carnatic musician and dancer, Singapore, for granting me the permission to display her illustration of Mā Sarasvatī in the Kerala graphic style on the cover of this book.
- All those unnamed supporters of my work in musicology, for having patronized an unworthy beneficiary.

Contents

1

Prof. S.K. Saxena
The Pioneering Aesthetician of Hindustānī Music

I was 16 when Prof. Saxena first walked into the Philosophy class at Hindu College in 1964. Except for a brief period, I have not lived in Delhi since my graduation in 1967. I was 65 when his last letter reached me in January 2013. He stepped into the sunset soon thereafter.

On every facet of Dr Saxena's persona, there are people more competent than me to pay him tribute. I merely recall with gratitude my experience of having been touched deeply by his presence over a period of almost 50 years.

I have attended possibly 70 of his classroom lectures over a year, and thereafter exchanged ten or fifteen letters, and met him and spoken to him over the phone as many times. The Superior Man, as portrayed in Taoist literature, does not require great frequency of interaction to influence lives. He does so merely by being what he is.

India was a different country when Saxena Sahab taught my class at Hindu College. Philosophy was not considered a "useless" subject pursued only by boys ineligible for admission to profession-oriented courses and by girls merely to qualify for the matrimonial market. The Cold War was at its peak and ideology wasn't dead yet. Herbert Marcuse, Jean-Paul Sartre,

---

The 2013-14 issue of *Vageeshwari*, the journal of the Faculty of Music and Fine Arts, University of Delhi, was dedicated to the memory of Prof. Sushil Kumar Saxena. This is a reproduction of my contribution to the commemorative volume.

Karl Marx and Ayn Rand – all had fanatical followings among the youth.

In class, Dr Saxena inspired enquiring minds to pursue philosophy as a cultivation of the human personality, independently of the professions they might choose. Like many of his students, I pursued a career in business, performing a variety of roles, before turning to musicology. With Saxena Sahab as my foundation philosopher, I have found myself as happy – and perhaps as effective – being a man of action in the world of thought as being a man of thought in the world of action.

My training in Hindustānī music was my special bond with Dr Saxena. He thought I should have pursued post-graduate studies in aesthetics under his supervision; but that was not to be. But, when I did finally take up work in musicology, he became my guiding angel. He regularly sent me personally inscribed copies of his books and papers on musical aesthetics. Whenever my critical essays appeared in *SRUTI* (of which he was a contributing editor) or elsewhere, he would phone or write to me with comments and encouragement.

In 2004, I sent him the manuscript of my first book on Hindustānī music for his opinion. He promptly called up his publisher, Susheel Mittal, and recommended its publication. Susheel asked him if my work was significant and similar to his own. He replied that it was significant precisely because it had the diametrically opposite perspective. With that introduction, he bequeathed to me a relationship which is now into its fourth project, with a fifth on the anvil.

When my second book on Hindustānī music (*Khayal Vocalism: Continuity within Change,* 2009) appeared, Dr Saxena volunteered to review it for the Journal of Sangeet Natak Akademi. The tenor of the review is immaterial; his signature below it was an honour. In his last work, *Hindustani Music and Aesthetics Today,* his acknowledgments refer to me as an "eminent musicologist".

I could have died of embarrassment. But, I chose to regard it as a mentor's parting challenge to a ward with unrealized potential.

Amongst modern scholars, if Bhatkhande is credited with establishing the theoretical framework for music performance, Dr Saxena can be credited with developing the conceptual framework for its aesthetic appreciation. But, the awareness-altering quality of his writings invites what he himself wrote about Ustad Ameer Khan.

> His music, at its best, was rarely a dazzle. It would be rather an influence, an atmosphere, which would just be with us till long after the recital. – Saxena, 2010

For several days after reading his monumental work – *Hindustani Music and Aesthetics Today* – I found myself moving around in a trance-like state under its intoxication. The supra-intellectual appeal of this book has no peer within my knowledge.

Inevitably, I interacted with Dr Saxena at a personal level, too. It is impossible, therefore, to remember him selfishly, merely as a mentor and benefactor. I had occasion to encounter in him a consummate homeopath, an outstanding composer of dhrupad bandiśes and a man of very deep spirituality.

In my memory, all of this dwarfs in comparison to the sense of indescribable peace one felt in his company. His was a presence that exuded love. And, here I allude to Erich Fromm's argument (*The Psychology of Ethics*) that love is not the quality of a relationship; it is the character of a person.

Astrologers have said that I have an exalted *guru* in my birth-chart. I doubt if anybody's guru can be more exalted than this.

2

Prof. Ashok Ranade

A Rare Guru

For more than a decade now, my search for superior wisdom has led me repeatedly, and always fruitfully, to the doorsteps of Prof. Ranade. Irrespective of the context of interaction – from the most formal to the totally personal and informal – Prof. Ranade has always enriched my thinking with insights and perspectives which are unique to him.

It would be impossible to enumerate the many ways in which he has contributed to my intellectual life. The best I can do here is to highlight his methods of guidance, and the manner in which he has shaped my perspectives as a writer on music.

In him, I have found an intellectual guide who forces his wards to think, both vertically and laterally. To achieve this aim, he is capable of using a wide enough range of devices to put the most inscrutable Zen master to shame. One day, he can casually throw a profound concept at you and ask you to think about it. On another day, he may provoke you by stating the most outrageous proposition – a proposition he himself might not be able to defend, if pushed to the wall. Irrespective of the device he deploys, he leaves his wards with much more than the answers they sought – he imparts to them the ability to find their own solutions.

His intellectual canvas is vast, beyond imagination. But, like a majority of people who seek his guidance, I have sought his

---

This essay was written on 22 December 2007. It was intended for a felicitation volume on Prof. Ranade's 75th birthday. The publication, however, could appear only posthumously as a commemorative volume.

help on matters related to Hindustānī classical (art) music. To him, art music is not merely about art music; even music is not about music alone. Art music, he insists, must be understood against the backdrop of the multiplicity of musical traditions, including the tribal, folk, devotional, martial and popular. Likewise, he urges his students to view musical issues as just one element in the entirety of the cultural process. He is not satisfied with figuring out of what a piece of music is. He drives untiringly towards an understanding of why it is what it is. Such a brief leaves almost no branch of knowledge untouched.

In handling the two facets of enquiry – the "what" and the "why" – Prof. Ranade emphasizes the need for Indian musicology to remain "Indian". His concern is particularly significant because a large part of contemporary writing on Hindustānī music – including mine – is in English and addresses, at least partly, an audience lettered in Western musicological concepts.

He is all for the study of Western scholars who have written on Indian art music, as much as he champions the study of Bharata's *Nāṭyaśāstra* and Śāraṅgadeva's *Saṅgīta-Ratnākara*. But, as writers, he believes, we must protect Indian musicological concepts against the risk of losing their "Indian-ness". If this necessitates the coining of new words and phrases totally unknown to Western musicology, he encourages me to be fearless in doing so. He considers it important that, even when rendered in a foreign language, the concepts remain anchored to the Indian musicological tradition, and faithful to the quality of the relationship between the Indian artist and his art.

I have steadfastly resisted the temptation of asking him what constitutes the "Indian-ness" of Indian music because his reply could well send me off on a lifelong chase for an answer, well beyond my ability to figure out.

My work as a writer on music has also been inspired by Prof. Ranade's enthusiasm for instrumental music as a mature and sophisticated art, deserving of greater musicological enquiry, and his insistence that the task must be spearheaded by trained instrumentalists like me.

In this context, he laments the traditional notion of instrumental music as an "inferior" art form and regrets the continued inability of critical writing to step out of the shadow of vocal music in terms of musicological concepts. With stunning validity, he points out that the musical experience delivered by instrumental music differs radically from that of vocal music. Consistent with their technologies of sound activation and melodic execution, different instruments have even evolved their own genres (*rāga* presentation formats), which no longer require a reference point in the vocal tradition. Considering that instrumental music now matches – and perhaps even surpasses – vocal music in terms of stature and popularity, the time is ripe for it to spawn its distinctive set of musicological concepts, and an independent body of musicological literature under Indian authorship.

Describing a *guru*, who derives immense satisfaction from seeing his wards pursue their own distinctive competencies, strive towards originality while remaining rooted in the tradition, and become self-dependent, might seem like a tautology. In theory, every *guru* is expected to fit such a description. In reality, however, such a *guru* is rare, because only a *guru* supremely secure in his knowledge can exhibit such qualities. As one who has partaken greedily of Prof. Ranade's wisdom, I wish for him the satisfaction of having guided a worthy beneficiary.

3

Perspectives on Rāga-ness

I HAVE chosen today to discuss various perspectives on *rāga*-ness. By "*rāga*-ness", I mean every idea that makes a *rāga* a *rāga*. In Sanskrit or in Hindi, we would call this the *rāga tattva* or *rāgatva*. I am restricting my observations to Hindustānī music, because that is the only music I have studied.

The eminent musicologist, Prof. Ashok Ranade held that there is something uniquely Indian about a musician's relationship with his art. He encouraged me to explore how, and to what extent, this relationship is shaped by the phenomenon of the *rāga*. I am sharing my explorations today, despite the limitations of time and context. The subject is worth discussing because of its centrality to Hindustānī music and to Kumar Gandharva's music.

The various perspectives are undoubtedly related. But, I am drawing upon several disciplines to explore the territory. A sequential flow of ideas is therefore not possible. The best I can do is present a collage of perspectives in the hope that the connections between them remain transparent.

Rāga as a Melodic Entity

A *rāga* is a set of *rules governing the selection, sequencing and intonation* of *svaras*. (Here, I need not deal with all the dimensions of intonation relevant to *rāga*-ness.) This definition validates

---

The text is a version of the 4th Kumar Gandharva Memorial Lecture, hosted by the Raza Foundation, New Delhi, in July 2017.

several derivative descriptions. The eminent aesthetician, Prof. S.K. Saxena has referred to a *rāga* as a *melodic matrix* governing composition and improvisation. Some Western scholars have referred to a *rāga* as a *partially composed melody.*

Defining the *rāga* as a melodic entity, however, does not encompass its aesthetic dimensions. The *rāga* phenomenon is inseparable from its emotional potency – the notion of *rasa.* However, *rasa* is, in itself, an inexhaustible subject and is better handled separately.

Rāga as a Melodic Representation of an Emotional Idea

Interestingly, the word *rāga,* in itself, has no melodic meaning at all. It is derived from the Sanskrit verb *rañjana* = to colour or to tinge. It is rarely encountered in isolated usage. It is generally encountered as a part of emotionally potent words like *anurāga* and *vairāgya.*

Mataṅga says in the *Bṛhaddeśī* (800 CE):

> A *rāga* is born from the act of colouring or delighting: this has been said to be its etymology. That which colours or delights the *minds of the good* [emphasis mine] through a specific *svara* (interval) and *varṇa* [intervallic transitions] or through a type of *dhvani* (sound) is *known by the wise* [emphasis mine] as *rāga.*

These observations have two implications: First, that a *rāga* is a melodic representation of an emotional idea. Second, that the melody delivers its emotional charge through the artistic prowess of the musician, and is accessible only to the "good" and the "wise". In this context, Prof. Saxena observes that the "goodness or excellence that is needed for being delighted is aesthetic sensitiveness and not moral purity".

The *rāga*'s communicative efficacy is thus attributed to the receptivity of the listener, as much as the competence of the performer. So, a *rāga* is a rule-based system of sounds, used by its adepts for communicating emotional ideas to those who are cultivated in the interpretation of the sounds as emotional stimuli. When a medium of communication restricts its usefulness to a well-defined community, it qualifies as a language.

For various reasons, experts in linguistics will not grant the status of a language to music. This is understandable because we are looking at a different kind of language – a specialist language for the *pleasurable communication of emotional ideas*. If it is a different kind of language, it can have its own conceptual framework, which need not conform to the framework applied to spoken and written languages such as English or Hindi.

Rāga Music as a Language

For the purposes of this presentation, I will focus on those features that permit us to consider music a language and a *rāga* a particular kind of linguistic statement.

A language is a voluntary means of interaction between members of a community. Being voluntary, it is used for a purpose – eliciting a response. In a rather simplistic formulation – the response to any communication may be in the nature of, (a) accepting/rejecting *information*, (b) confirming or altering *belief*, (c) activating a *feeling*, and (d) triggering *action*. In this context, *rāga* music may be considered a specialist language for activating an emotional trigger amongst those capable of interacting through the medium of *rāga* music.

A language can support several genres of literature (e.g. short story, novel, and poetry). A user can create entirely novel genres/structures and yet be understood. This is true of *rāga* music.

The precise process by which a user learns a language is one of the inscrutable areas of cultural anthropology. Despite this, a language can be analysed in terms of its own conventions of usage. Hence, a person who knows one language can learn another. I state this feature with some caveats.

Languages are, by definition, "parochial" or "vernacular" in the sense that their knowledge defines a distinct community – even an identity. Likewise, all art music traditions are considered "parochial", though some traditions may be more "parochial" than others. Languages do function as barriers against unwelcome cultural intrusions. Likewise, it appears to me that the phenomenon of *rāga*-ness has been an access barrier to the essentials of our musical culture for the music community cultivated elsewhere.

To paraphrase Noam Chomsky, an immensely influential voice in linguistics, a language fulfils its communicative purpose through statements of finite length (sentences/statements) incorporating a finite number of patterns (vocabulary) assembled from a finite set of sounds (alphabets/phonemes), arranged in a predictable sequence (syntax).

In this sense, every *rāga* may be defined as a "statement", because it uses a finite set of *svara*s to construct a finite set of patterns and arranges them in a consistent and predictable sequence to fulfil its communicative purpose.

Where, then, is the problem with recognizing *rāga* as a linguistic statement? The issue concerns the theory of meaning.

A language is an arbitrary system of communication, relying for its communicative function in the "habitual" association of sounds with their meaning. Linguistics theory recognizes four levels of meaning for a statement:

a. *Acoustic/phonetic meaning* – the meaning delivered by the sounds.
b. *Lexical meaning* – sound patterns (words/phrases).
c. *Syntactical meaning* – the meaning delivered by the arrangement/sequence of sound patterns.
d. *Referential meaning* – meaning derived by implicit/explicit reference to statements other than itself.

These criteria are sufficiently met by *rāga*s.

The main hindrance to the acceptance of music – any music – as a language rests largely on the proposition that music does not support the notion of "lexical meaning". In the present context of *rāga*-ness, this objection can be questioned. Each *rāga* qualifies almost entirely as a linguistic statement and is understood by the members of the *rāga* music community – just as a statement in any spoken language is understood by its "native" ethnic-linguistic community.

Having said this, we can still accept that a dictionary of the emotional meaning of *rāga*s is not even a remote possibility, while the dictionaries of English or German are useful guides to meaning. But are they more than guides? Any dictionary provides a number of meanings for each word, which may, in different contexts, have different communicative intent. So even lexical meaning cannot be said to deliver 100 per cent correspondence between a communicative intent and its comprehension.

I am suggesting that the difference between lexical meaning of a spoken language and *rāga* music is probabilistic in nature. A statement in English made to an English-knowing person may have, say, 80 per cent chance of being understood precisely as intended. In comparison, a *rāga*, performed competently for a *rāga*-knowing audience may have a far lower chance of achieving its communicative intent. This "far lower" has to exceed 50 per cent; otherwise, it cannot remain in circulation.

In scientific language, a high probability relationship between cause and effect is called a "theory", while a moderate/indeterminate probability relationship describes a "hypothesis". Therefore, a statement in English or Spanish is the product of a psycho-linguistic "theory" of communicative efficiency. Even a pre-composed piece of music is a "theory" of communicative value. But, a *rāga* can only be considered a "hypothesis".

This brings us to the consideration of a *rāga* as a "psycho-acoustic hypothesis".

A Rāga as a Psycho-acoustic Hypothesis

The hypothesis is plausible because it represents society's accumulated and collective experience of associating certain sound patterns with certain emotional ideas. Even in an exact science, a hypothesis is not arbitrary. It is supported either by critical observation or astute speculation. In science, every hypothesis invites/attracts conclusive evidence of predictable outcomes and aspires to become a theory. A *rāga*, however, never intends to become a theory. It remains perennially a hypothesis, tested uniquely each time it is performed.

The question then arises – from where does a *rāga* accumulate the evidence to accomplish a high probability of an emotional response? A simple answer is – it draws on the cultural memory. My view is that, the associations of the sound patterns of a *rāga* with their meaning reside in the collective unconscious, just as the associations of words in a spoken or written language reside in memory of the culture in which the language has evolved.

What, then, is a performance of a *rāga*?

A *rāga* is a formless form – formless because it represents only a possibility of an aesthetically coherent and emotionally satisfying manifestation. And, a form because it has distinct and recognizable contours. A performance of *rāga* music is an attempt by the musician to draw upon the "formless form" of the *rāga* resident in the cultural memory, and translate it into a communicable form with the aim of maximizing the probability of eliciting the emotional response latent in its melodic structure.

Each time such an attempt is made, the total inventory of melodic ideas within the recognizable boundaries of a *rāga* is being altered – some ideas are added while some are deducted. Thus, while each performance is governed by a *rāga*, it also shapes/reshapes the *rāga*. From this phenomenon, we derive the notion of a *rāga* as a dynamic consensual melodic entity.

A Rāga as a Consensual Entity

The consensual personality of a *rāga* is the sum total of the melodic ideas that have been deployed in the attempt to communicate the emotional charge latent in the formless form to listeners. It is like a bank from which a musician draws while performing, and which he replenishes in the process of performing.

It is interesting to compare this feature of *rāga*-ness to the behaviour of the stock market.

The investment value – the price – of a stock is being determined and redetermined constantly by the trading activities of individual investors. However, the investment value – as reflected in the price – is also constantly determining and redetermining the trading decisions of individual investors. This is a circular argument; but it is true to the behaviour of the stock market, and of the melodic personalities of a *rāga*. One of the world's most influential investors, George Soros, describes this as "auto-reflexivity".

"Auto-reflexivity" is a phenomenon characteristic of interactions between a multiplicity of independent intelligent beings. We have often heard it said – "the market has a mind of its own" and, indeed, it does. The market is credited with an independent intelligence despite being merely a collective expression of investor trades. Likewise, the *rāga* can be seen as an independent intelligence, despite being a collective expression of individual melodic interpretations of it.

The dynamics of a *rāga*'s consensual personality are also driven by the economic interests of the participants in the process. A musician is an economic being. He draws upon, and contributes to, the consensual personality of *rāga*s in a manner that enables his music to remain aesthetically relevant to contemporary audiences. This is comparable to the economic interests of an investor, who wants to remain relevant as an investor.

The metaphor can be stretched further. But, it is not necessary to do so in the present context.

There is, of course, also a divergent view – that a *rāga* is an autonomous entity. This view is reflected in the "commanding form" proposition favoured by Prof. Sushil Kumar Saxena with reference to Hindustānī music. The proposition draws on the work of Susanne Langer, the American philosopher of art.

Rāga as the Commanding Form

In the context of Western art music, Langer accords the status of the commanding form to the composition, because it is the composition which determines the entire process of invention and elaboration. Prof. Saxena argues that, in Hindustānī music, the *rāga* rightfully occupies this status.

He denies this status to the composition (*bandiś*) because, even the composition has to be in conformity with the *rāga*. In terms of the musician's attentiveness, too, the *rāga* shapes the totality of performance more comprehensively than the specific detail of the *bandiś*.

This idea invites some reservations. There cannot be more than one commanding form. So, the commanding form proposition has to choose between the *rāga* and the composition. Without detailing the reservations, it is unlikely that the music community will accept such an either/or proposition relating *rāga*s to *bandiś*es.

A reconciliation of these divergent views emerged during my conversations with Ustad Vilayat Khan.

The Rāga as a Transcendental Entity

I once prodded Khan Saheb into sharing his vision of *rāga*-ness. According to him,

> A *rāga* is much bigger than the collective imagination of all

> the musicians who have ever lived and will ever be born. We struggle all our lives to catch a glimpse of a *rāga*. May be, once in a lifetime, on a day when God is smiling upon us, we may get a fleeting glimpse of it. And, on that day, we can feel that we have validated our lives as musicians.

If a *rāga* is so vast, where are the boundaries of each *rāga*?

> The limits of a *rāga*'s personality are drawn only where the boundaries of another *rāga* are breached.

In these observations, Khan Saheb makes the connection between the consensual melodic personality of a *rāga* and its formless form. The formless form has an autonomous, and virtually divine, existence which a musician constantly aspires to access by penetrating/transcending the consensual personality of a *rāga*. A *rāga* performance is thus a contemplative act and the relationship of the musician with the *rāga* is essentially reverential.

The influential German composer, Karlheinz Stockhausen probably refers to this feature in his book *Towards a Cosmic Music*, when he says:

> When a musician walks on stage, he should give that fabulous impression of a person who is doing a sacred service. In India ...; when a group of musicians are performing, you don't feel they do it to entertain you. They do it as holy service. They feel a need to make sounds, and these sounds are waves on which you ride to the eternal.

Stockhausen describes the sense of awe with which the Indian musician undertakes the task of performing a *rāga*. The spirit of reverential surrender is articulated in the *Rāgavibodha* of Somanātha (1609 CE) (Ayyangar, 2017):

> That is called *rūpa* (form) which by being embellished with sweet flourishes of *svaras* brings a *rāga* vividly before one's mind. It is of two kinds – *nādātma* (one whose soul or essence is sound), and *devamaya* (one whose soul or essence is an image

incarnating the deity), of which the former has many shapes, and the latter has only one. – 5.11

Being a "formless form" and the object of contemplation, the *rāga* is viewed as a divinity to whom the musician prays, entreating it to descend into its melodic form. This idea is entirely consistent with Hindu thought – that humans can access the *nirākāra/nirguṇa* (formless / free from attributes / the Divine) through an intense engagement with the *sākāra/saguṇa* (the manifest form / the one possessing attributes). *Rāga* music can thus be viewed as a form of melodic polytheism.

The notion of a *rāga* as a transcendental entity, possessing an autonomous existence in the cultural memory, encourages us to consider the notion of archetypes in modern psycho-analytical thought.

Deities, Rāgas and Archetypes

I was intrigued by a recent news item that archaeologists had discovered a 3,000-year old sculpture of Lord Viṣṇu in an ancient temple in Cambodia. The immediate question that arose in my mind was – how did they identify Lord Viṣṇu? I found the answer in the same news item – the image had four hands, respectively holding *śaṅkha* (conch shell), *cakra* (rotor blade weapon), *gadā* (mace) and *padma* (lotus).

I infer from this that a four-armed human-like form with *śaṅkha*, *cakra*, *gadā* and *padma* has constituted the identifying feature of a Hindu divinity for at least 3,000 years. He may have had different names in the past – we do not know.

Over these 3,000 years, millions of artists have portrayed Viṣṇu with these identifying features, adding to them their own notions of other attributes. The idea of Viṣṇu has a 1,000 attributes (*śrī viṣṇusahasranāma*). But, Viṣṇu is not Viṣṇu without these four attributes.

Viṣṇu is a (probably) timeless image deeply embedded in the

Hindu psyche, which elicits a predictable response appropriate to the associations which are etched in the cultural memory. Viṣṇu is an archetype in the sense in which Carl Jung expounded the idea. And, so are other deities, with their identifying physical attributes and personality traits.

Like deities, *rāga*s possess identifying features which connect with their emotional associations embedded in the cultural memory. *Rāga*s in Indian classical music exhibit similar characteristics and can be viewed as archetypal entities in the Jungian sense.

Superficially, it might seem that deities and *rāga*s are different because one is visual, while the other is aural. This is not a significant issue. First, the archetype is formless and can manifest itself aurally or visually. Second, there is a well-established phenomenon in Hindustānī music of *rāga*s being "visualized". And, these tendencies may well have some universal/ physiological basis – modern neuro-science is tending to suggest that, the visual and aural faculties are intimately connected.

In confirmation, we have *rāga-dhyāna* verses; we have Rāgamālā paintings, and we also have articulated linkages between the aural and visual contemplations of *rāga*s.

Ustad Vilayat Khan often said:

> There is an eye sitting inside a musician's ears, and ears sitting inside a musician's eyes.
>
> A *rāga* should be so performed that you can see it standing there, right before you.
>
> – Quoted by Namita Devidayal in *The Music Room*

What Are Archetypes?

The word "archetype" derives from the Greek noun *archetypos*, meaning that which is "first moulded". It signifies a model or a type after which other similar things are patterned. The idea of archetypes goes back to Plato. The cultural ramifications of the notion have entered academic discourse since Carl Jung dealt extensively with them.

In Jungian thought, archetypes are collectively inherited ideas, or primordial images, patterns of thought that are universally present in the human psyche. They may manifest themselves as recurring symbols or motifs in dreams, literature, painting, iconography, music, mythology and legends, sharing similar traits. Jung treated archetypes as psychological organs, analogous to physical ones, in that both are morphological constructs that arose through evolution.

Archetypes do not have a well-defined shape, but acquire a definitive form "from the moment they become conscious, namely, nurtured with the stuff of conscious experience". Basically, an archetype is an empty nothing, pregnant with an innate tendency of shaping things.

The usage of archetypes in art helps the work to win widespread/universal acceptance. This is because audiences can relate to, and identify with, the underlying themes both socially and culturally.

The features of the archetype I wish to emphasize in the present context are:

a. They are primordial images.
b. They are formless forms.
c. They manifest themselves variously without losing their identity.
d. They are collectively inherited by a culture/universally.
e. Their "meaning" is understood unconsciously/intuitively.

These characteristics of Jungian archetypes permit us to view *rāga*s as archetypal entities.

Archetypes as Cultural Forces

Literature on archetypes is not unanimous about whether

archetypes are universal or culture-specific. With respect to *rāgas*, my view is that they are, essentially, culture-specific archetypes. Here I draw upon the crucial distinction between the *rāga* as a "consensual melodic entity" and the *rāga* as an "archetypal entity". I refer obliquely also to the distinction between the neuro-acoustic processing of sound signals and their psycho-linguistic interpretation.

For their aesthetic coherence and elegance, the consensual melodic entity can appeal to musically sensitive persons cultivated in other cultures. But, the entire gamut of associations inherent in the *rāga* archetype is accessible only to persons rooted in Indian culture. When you take either a cultivated north Indian musician or a cultivated north Indian audience out of the picture there is a substantial "de-contextualization" taking place and the communication loses some of its access to the cultural memory. The result is some loss of meaning.

I would support this view with some examples:

Easily understood examples relate to time theory of *rāgas*. In this I include the concept of seasonal *rāgas*. It has adequate textual support in classical musicological literature. The theory has often been dismissed as fanciful and arbitrary by Western musicologists. It is essentially a musical expression of our relationship with nature as experienced in northern India.

It is interesting that Carnatic music has no sympathy for these prescriptions, and for good reason. Being closer to the equator, the peninsular south does not experience as marked a fluctuation in temperature and humidity across different parts of the day/night or between the different parts of the year as the sub-Himalayan north does.

Extend this logic to a musician or audience in Japan or Sweden, and the entire notion becomes meaningless. But, it remains meaningful to Hindustānī musicians because they infuse into their music that something – tangible or otherwise, consciously or otherwise – which connects with the cultural memory.

First, I consider the example of *sandhi prakāśa rāga*s – those prescribed for performance around sunrise and sunset. The defining feature of these *rāga*s is the use of *komal* (flat) *re* (2nd) and *komal* (flat) *dh* (6th). This family of *rāga*s is treated as solemn by the Hindustānī music community. Why?

The sun remains the primordial deity in Vedic religion – the all-powerful Gāyatrī-Mantra is to be recited at sunrise, noon and sunset. In a rural-agrarian society preceding the advent of electricity, every facet of life was governed by sunlight. The traditional Indian family gathers around the family alter at sunrise and sunset for the *āratī*. In several Indian languages, these time zones are called *godhūli belā* – the time when the cows kick up clouds of dust on the village roads, going out to pasture and returning home. Sunset is the time when homes – even homes with refrigerators – in several parts of north India light a lamp near the earthen water pitcher in the kitchen with the sentiment that the spirits of departed ancestors could be thirsty and might visit home to quench their thirst. The lamp indicates the location of the pitcher and is a symbol of welcome. The cultivated Indian musical mind is unconsciously attuned to these associations of *rāga*s like Rāmakalī or Śrī. These ideas are uniquely Indian.

Consider the associations related to particular melodic phrases. I cite the example of *nī dh nī sā* (*komal nī, śuddha dh, śuddha nī, sā*) both deployed – though slightly differently – as the signature phrases of Bahār and Malhār. I find it significant that Bahār is a *rāga* of spring, heralding relief from the severe north Indian winter and Malhār is the *rāga* of the rainy season, heralding relief from the oppressive north Indian summer.

In both these seasons, nature renews itself and justifies expressions of euphoria. What explains the euphoric connotation of this phrase? Nothing, except that a *rāga* is our language and statements in our language mean what they mean – only to us. Any musician or listener in the world can relate to the consensual melodic personality of Bahār or Malhār. But, Indians effortlessly imbue this phrase with the entire community's experience of the seasons.

Examples of a different kind are *rāga*s named after deities. Consider Śaṅkara or Durgā. Both are formidable deities. Their consensual melodic personalities are easily accessible to any musician or listener anywhere. But, only a Hindustānī musician can visualize and communicate the awesome attributes of the archetypal Śiva or Durgā with an appropriate treatment of poetry, melody and rhythm.

According to an impeccable source, Naseer Ameenuddin Dagar stated at a seminar many years ago that a good *dhrupad* singer has to be a devotee of Lord Kr̥ṣṇa. *Dhrupad* poetry, as you know, is replete with the mythical romance of Lord Kr̥ṣṇa and his paramour, Rādhā. For a Muslim musician to make this statement publicly could have taken some courage of conviction. We do not need to agree or disagree with this statement. But we can appreciate the point he was making.

In my view, *rāga*s are culture-specific archetypes. What is accessible to musicians and listeners outside our culture is, at best, the consensual melodic entity and its aesthetics. We may concede that the *rāga*s possibly have a component that is universally appealing. But, their archetypal associations have a cultural meaning, which is not accessible in its entirety to musicians or listeners nurtured in a different culture.

I consider it appropriate to contrast the archetypal notion against the strictly melodic notion with which I started my presentation.

Melodic vs Archetypal Notions

I find it impossible to imagine that a mathematician sat down one day, worked out all the permutations and combinations of twelve *svaras*, derived an astronomical number of ascending–descending patterns, and called them *rāgas*. If this was so, there would have been at least 5,000 documented *rāgas*, even if not all were performed at some time or the other.

The evolutionary history of *rāgas* suggests an organic evolution. Without going into the history, and quite independently of it, it seems fair to assume that *rāgas* evolved from songs.

I define a song as a stable construct incorporating poetry, melody and rhythm, which is a self-sufficient piece of music, requiring no validation beyond its direct appeal to a listener's heart. Songs are not composed. They are spontaneous emanations, which "compose themselves".

The primordial sources of *rāgas*, the songs, acquired this appeal by achieving a perfect congruence between the emotional suggestions of the melody, the cadences of the rhythm and verbalized thematic content of the poetry. And perhaps by accident, more than by design, this congruence connected the music with cultural archetypes and activated the cultural memory of pleasant emotional experiences.

Over a period, learned people observed that many of these songs were "more or less" similar in their melodic patterning and emotional appeal. They clubbed them together, extracted from them the features that unified them as aesthetic typologies. The purpose of so doing was to make their aesthetic appeal replicable by all musicians. The cultural archetypes, the formless forms that we recognize today as *rāgas*, owe their evolution to such progressive abstraction. This abstraction gave *rāgas* a stable anchoring in the "primordial image", the "archetype".

I now have the conceptual foundation for relating *rāga*-ness to Kumar Gandharva's music.

Kumar Gandharva and Rāga-ness

Under the patronage of Mughals and, later the princely states, *rāga*-ness had become abstract enough to impart to Hindustānī music a definite intellectualism – what the distinguished critic, Mohan Nadkarni called a "formal aloofness". I break down this phrase into two components – formalism and aloofness. With the arrival of the microphone, the radio and the gramophone recording, the time was ripe for Hindustānī music to shed its intellectualism. Kumar Gandharva achieved this by rethinking *rāga*-ness and reintegrating it into the cultural process.

He took Hindustānī music closer to its origins in the Song (with a capital S) – the Song in all its facets: the poetry, the melody and the rhythm. The Song, as the origin of *rāga*-ness, and the most direct access to the archetypes that populate the Indian consciousness.

By circumventing the *rāga* as the "commanding form" of performance, he freed his music from the "formal aloofness" of the major *gharānās*, all of which were the products of the colonial–feudal–elitist era.

Kumar Gandharva's "song-orientation" was also significant because it restored poetry to its place in Hindustānī music at a time when the ascendant *gharānās* of his era – primarily Kairānā – were tending to relegate the lyrics to musical insignificance.

When he performed a *khyāl* in a mature *rāga*, he treated the *bandiś* like a Song. Here I draw, once again, a distinction between a Song and a *bandiś*. A Song is a self-contained piece of music which requires no validation outside of itself. A *bandiś*, on the other hand, is composed as an enabler and facilitator of the *rāga vistār* protocol established in *khyāl* vocalism.

His *khyāl* renditions did, indeed, respect the consensual melodic personality of *rāgas*; but not always. His renditions did indeed feature the improvisatory movements typical to the *khyāl* genre, but not necessarily in the orthodox sequence. He did not permit the appeal of his Song to become subservient to the demands of *rāga* grammar, or to the intellectualism of *khyāl* architecture.

He found greater freedom to express his music as a Song in the *rāgas* he "discovered" from the folk/regional melodies of the Malwa region. Here he was reenacting the process by which *rāgas* came into being and making direct contact with the archetypes which imparted a soul to those melodies. In his *Dhun-Ugam Ragas*, he was bound neither by established notions of *rāga*-ness, nor by traditional compositions in them, nor by established architecture of *khyāl* presentation.

Kumar Gandharva freed himself even from the notion of *rāga*-ness in his *bhajans*, which remain in wide circulation even today. A *bhajan* is a Song; and he knew how to access the soul of a Song better than anyone of his era. His special contribution to *bhajans* was the revival of interest in the secular saint-poet Kabīr, with whom he shared a special spiritual connection.

In all his music, we observe a calculated carelessness, which has often been attributed to his involvement with folk music. I see this feature as a conscious primitivism, totally consistent with his rejection of the formal aloofness of Hindustānī music and his intuitive connection with its archetypal nature of *rāgas*.

Because of his comprehensive rebellion against the values that dominated Hindustānī music at that time, he could have been dismissed as an insignificant maverick. But, it was impossible to deny his musicianship and the impact he made with his uncanny access to the soul of *rāgas*. His music was not easy to understand. His following remained small. But, he influenced the aesthetic values of successive generations.

This is why the notion of *rāga*-ness cannot be meaningfully discussed without reference to the contribution of Kumar Gandharva. I trust I have done reasonable justice to the memory of a landmark musician of the twentieth century.

4

The Musician and His Art

Ashok Ranade believed in the uniqueness of the Indian musician's relationship with his art, and that we should develop a uniquely Indian way of understanding it. The proposition is significant because, in Hindustānī music, the musician makes such a large number of choices – either consciously or otherwise – during his musical life and pertaining to each performance that the resultant musical experience can only be explained by what the musician is.

Pursuing this line of thought, an attempt is made here to derive a meaningful notion of personality types from the character of Hindustānī music and to relate the resulting typology to widely acknowledged motivational and personality types.

I would like to believe that, in addition to representing an acceptable interpretation of theoretical constructs, the ideas presented here enjoy the benefit of six decades of my pursuit of Hindustānī music as an aspiring performer and almost three decades of interacting closely with a wide spectrum of musicians as an analyst and interpreter of their music.

The Nature of Hindustānī Music

Literature on musical aesthetics is found frequently to debate two supposedly rival propositions.

1. Music is an expressive art.

This essay was published earlier under the title "The Rāga-ness of Musicians", in my book *The Rāga-ness of Rāgas* (2015).

2. Music is a communicative art. I will argue that these propositions, even if applied together, would not be sufficient to describe Hindustānī music. A satisfactory description obliges us to add a third proposition.

3. Music is a contemplative–meditative art. Inclusion of this third dimension is warranted by the "formless form" called the *rāga* which presides over the entire process of music making. The act of performing Hindustānī music is synonymous with translating and manifesting the "formless form" into a communicable form. The process governing this manifestation is contemplation/ meditation.

   Entries against "contemplation" and "meditation" in *Shorter Oxford English Dictionary* (5th edn) reveal a considerable overlap. They are therefore considered together. Contemplation/meditation is a process of profound (spiritual/religious) reflection upon a subject, aimed at exploring its possibilities and purposes. Thus, contemplation/meditation, as an element in art, can be seen as a manifestation of an artist's humility and receptive surrender before the majesty of the ultimate source of beauty.

Expression

By lexical connotation, "expression" is an act of pressing or squeezing something out, thus implying a purposive, voluntary effort. It produces a manner or mode of symbolizing or manifesting character, quality of feelings, sentiments or intentions. In other words, the act of expression involves drawing upon one's thoughts, beliefs, feelings and intentions to produce sensory emanations in the nature of symbols or signs. Thus, expression, as an element in art, is to be seen primarily as a manifestation of the artist's sense of selfhood and an awareness of himself as the generator of aesthetic value.

Communication

By lexical connotation, "communication" is a process of conveying, imparting, transmitting and exchanging something intangible with the result of succeeding in evoking an understanding. The word also connotes the sharing in, partaking of, or enjoying in common, with the purpose of making or maintaining social contact. In other words, communication involves making one's self-understood with the purpose of relating meaningfully to others. Thus, communication, as an element in art, can be seen as a statement of an artist's seeking of integration within society.

While these three descriptions seem adequate to describe the process of music making in Hindustānī music, there is a popular notion of creativity/creation that can interfere with conceptual clarity on the subject. It helps, then, to examine it for its relevance or otherwise in the present context.

Creativity

The word "creativity" derives from the Latin verb *creare* = "to make something from nothing". Implicitly, creativity is the production of something which expresses one's original genius or talent. In classical thought, creation was regarded as the exclusive province of God or the gods. Only the Creator can create. Humans, having themselves been created by the Creator, can only imitate. Works of imagination were considered products of the Divine–human relationship. Their aesthetic value was attributed to this relationship. Even after the arts got secularized, artists continued to regard themselves as acolytes of some quasi-sacred mystery.

It is only in the modern period that the notion has gained currency of the creator of great works as being a unique individual, who wrestles not only with the materials of his art but also with his own spirit. Once their individuality was mirrored, defined and fulfilled in their work, artists began to establish an attitude to their art – to its actuality, its theory, its present and to its marketplace (McLeish, 1993).

Against this perspective, it would appear that the notion of creativity in art began as a suggestion of artistic humility, contemplation and meditation, and drifted – in the modern period – towards the dominance of expression, representing an assertion of the artist's individuality. For the purposes of this discussion, I wish to put this notion aside as being unstable, ambivalent and redundant.

The Musician Personality

Any significant performer of Hindustānī music will have a certain minimum level of command over all the three processes – the contemplative/meditative, the expressive and the communicative. Therefore, when we consider personality types and their relationship with their art, a certain hierarchy of orientations needs to be acknowledged, because the issue deals with the introversion–extroversion dimension of the human personality. After all, the three are distinct, though connected, activities. Contemplation is an introverted activity. Expression is partly introverted and partly extroverted. And, communication is extroverted.

Even amongst acknowledged maestros, we can identify contemplation-dominant personalities, expression-dominant personalities and communication-dominant personalities. With any of these orientations becoming dominant, the remaining two will take a backseat in varying degrees. And, obviously, each personality type will deliver music that is qualitatively different from that of the other two personality types and will tend also to attract different categories of audiences.

With specific reference to Hindustānī music, then, we may consider three types of musical personality:

1. Contemplation-dominant,

2. expression-dominant, and
3. communication-dominant.

We may now consider the possibility of correspondence between these categories and broader frameworks for classifying personalities or motivational traits.

Jung's Personality Types

Psycho-analyst Carl Jung published his work *Psychological Types* in 1921. Although several alternative typologies have emerged since then, his work has remained immensely influential, and has gained widespread use in clinical testing for sixteen personality types representing a refined measurement of the introversion–extroversion dimension of the personality. The system is known as the Myers–Briggs Type Indicator (MBTI).

The MBTI framework identifies the "artist" as one of the sixteen types. We are, however, looking for a subclassification of artist into three dominant tendencies. The MBTI description of the "artist" can therefore remain the core of our classification, with other indicators of personality suffixed to the classification.

THE MBTI ARTIST

The primary mode of living is focused internally, where everything is dealt in accordance with one's emotional response and consistency with the value system. The secondary mode of living is external, where the five senses guide behaviour in a concrete and literal fashion. Original and independent. Need their own space. Have no desire to control or be controlled by others. Unusually gifted at creating things which affect the senses. Willing to rebel against anything that does not conform to their values and goals. Takes life very seriously, constantly evaluating various value systems in search of clarity and underlying meaning.

THE CONTEMPLATION-DOMINANT PERSONALITY
(Artist-Idealist)

We may now consider which of the sixteen MBTI types may be suffixed to the MBTI artist to define the contemplation-dominant Hindustānī musician. The MBTI "idealist" suggests itself to me as the closest approximation for this purpose.

The MBTI idealists' primary goal is to find out the meaning in life and to make the world a better place for people. They are on a constant mission to find the truth and underlying meaning in things. Every piece of knowledge is evaluated through the idealist's value system for its potential for defining or refining his own path in life. They will cover every possible detail with determination, when working on a particular "cause". Focus on feelings. Averse to, or suspicious of, theoretical constructs and impersonal judgements.

THE EXPRESSION-DOMINANT PERSONALITY
(Artist-Performer)

Of the sixteen MBTI types, the expression-dominant personality may be approximately described by suffixing the MBTI performer to the MBTI artist.

The MBTI performers live in the world of here and now, and relish excitement and drama. Spontaneous and optimistic. Very sensitive and sympathetic to other people's well-being. For them, the entire world is a stage and they love being the centre of attention. They would love life to be an unending party with themselves as hosts. Hate structure and routine, preferring to go with the flow, and improvise in any situation.

THE COMMUNICATION-DOMINANT PERSONALITY
(Artist-Giver)

Of the sixteen MBTI types, the expression-dominant personality may be approximately described by suffixing the MBTI giver to the MBTI artist.

The MBTI "giver" is a highly people-focused individual. Understands and cares about people and has special talent for bringing about the best in them. Makes things happen for others, and derives satisfaction from it. Very sensitive to criticism. Such artists get under people's skins and get the reactions they seek. Their motives can be unselfish, but often manipulative. Tend to define their life's directions and priorities according to other people's needs and place them above their own. Can be expressive and open, but more focused on being responsive. Uncomfortable with impersonal reasoning, or having to deal with logic and facts.

Maslow's Hierarchy of Needs

Between 1943 and 1970, Abraham Maslow developed a theory of human motivation based on a hierarchy of human needs, starting from the lowest (biological) to the highest (transcendence). The hierarchical arrangement of these needs argued that human beings could be motivated to seek progressively higher satisfactions from life, as their lower level needs were satisfied. Though Maslow proposed this as a theory of motivation, it also serves as a classification of the human personality by defining the dominant driving force of human behaviour at a given point in time. The hierarchy serves equally well as a mapping of the evolutionary path for musicians, as for people in other walks of life.

The Maslow framework is especially relevant in the present context because, in Hindustānī music, a performance is a unique product of a musician's art, its totality governed by the entirety of forces incumbent on the performance, but representing primarily the driving force operating in the musician's personality at that time.

Maslow's Hierarchy of Needs (the Lowest to the Highest)

1. *Biological and physiological*: air, food, drink, shelter, warmth,

sex, sleep, etc.

2. *Safety*: safety from elements, security, order, law, stability, etc.
3. *Love and belongingness:* friendship, intimacy, affection, etc.
4. *Esteem*: self-esteem, achievement, mastery, independence, status, dominance, responsibility, etc.
5. *Cognitive needs*: knowledge, meaning, etc.
6. *Aesthetic needs*: appreciation of form and balance, search for beauty.
7. *Self-actualization*: realizing personal potential, self-fulfilment, seeking personal growth and peak experiences.
8. *Transcendence*: helping others to achieve self-actualization.

Contextualization of Maslow to Hindustānī Music

The *contemplation-dominant personality* is driven in its musical endeavours primarily by the four highest level needs: cognitive needs, aesthetic needs, self-actualization needs and transcendent needs. This describes an essentially introverted personality, concerned with the external world only to the extent that it has taken upon itself the responsibility of guiding others towards their own self-actualization.

The *expression-dominant personality* is driven primarily by the need for esteem, rooted in the sense of selfhood. If it exhibits some concern for the higher level cognitive or aesthetic needs, it is only to the extent that such concerns might support its seeking of esteem.

The *communication-dominant personality* is primarily extroverted and is driven primarily by the three lowest needs: the need to belong and be loved with the implicit aim of achieving the satisfaction of the needs for security and biological sustenance.

The Three Modes of Existence

Hindu philosophy defines three modes of existence *(guṇas)* – *sattva, rajas* and *tamas* – which pervade all things and beings in the universe. The balance of the three in each thing or being differs, and it is this balance that determines its behaviour. From these three Sanskrit nouns are derived the three adjectives – *sāttvika, rājasika* and *tāmasika*.

The word *guṇa* has been variously translated through its various probable etymologies. The connotations include: elementary property, quality, character, habitual behaviour, invisible essence, attribute, classification, addressing/attitude and enumeration. Collectively, these connotations permit the use of the concept as a classification of personality types and also to define a person's relationship with a particular facet of his life. In the present context, both these dimensions of classification are appropriate and intended. The qualities associated with the three classifications are as follows:

1. *Sāttvika*: The quality of harmony, balance, goodness, purity, universalizing, holistic, creative, building, peaceful, virtuous.
2. *Rājasika*: The quality of passion, activity, neither good nor bad and sometimes either, self-centredness, egoistic, individualizing, driven, moving, dynamic.
3. *Tāmasika*: The quality of imbalance, disorder, chaos, anxiety, impurity, delusionary, negative, dull, apathetic, lethargic, violent, vicious.

This threefold classification of human personalities/tendencies is summarized thus in the *Bhagavadgītā* XVIII. 23-25:

> "An Action, which is a rightly regulated by one undesirous of fruits, without attachment, without liking or disliking; that is called *Sāttvika*. But, the action done for the satisfaction of desires, or with an egoistic sense, and with an inordinate efforts; that is declared as *Rājasika*. The action initiated under

delusion without regard to one's capacity, consequences, loss or injury (to others); that is said to be *Tāmasika*" (Aurobindo, *The Bhagvadgita*).

Using this conceptual framework, I submit the following propositions for consideration:

1. The *contemplation-dominant personality* in Hindustānī music is a *sāttvika* personality, and has a *sāttvika* relationship with his art.
2. The *expression-dominant personality* in Hindustānī music is a *rājasika* personality and has a *rājasika* relationship with his art.
3. The *communication-dominant personality* in Hindustānī music is a *tāmasika* personality and has a *tāmasika* relationship with his art.

The Musician and His Art: Sāttvika, Rājasika, Tāmasika

I now examine how this classification, based on the three modes of existence, will tend to be reflected in the music. Two facets of performance will most significantly be influenced by the personality type:

1. The approach to the *rāga*.
2. The approach to the architecture of performance.

THE APPROACH TO THE RĀGA

Because the *rāga* is the presiding deity of Hindustānī music, the quality of musicianship is substantially understood through the relationship between a musician and the *rāga*. To appreciate this perspective, it is necessary to view the *rāga* as a multi-tiered entity.

Tier 1: The formless form

Tier 2: The consensual form

Tier 3: The qualifying form

The *sāttvika* musician relates to the *rāga* as a formless form, pregnant with infinite possibilities of manifestation. Acknowledging the *rāga* as a virtual deity, the *sāttvika* musician acknowledges his own insignificance as a seeker of its munificence. The *sāttvika* musician's music is an entreaty addressed to the presiding deity of the *rāga* to descend into its melodic form and to reveal its emotional secrets to the seeker. The music of a *sāttvika* musician is therefore imbued with a spirit of reverential deliberateness, humility, serenity, joy, enlightenment and transparency of musical ideation.

The *rājasika* musician relates to the *rāga* with the aim of commanding it. Command can only be achieved over something that is finite and whose boundaries are known. The *rājasika* musician therefore masters the consensual form of the *rāga*, consisting of all the facets that have been hitherto explored. His musical energies are focused on command and mastery. He will not fritter them away on the exploration of the unknown.

The *tāmasika* musician relates to the *rāga* merely in terms of fulfilling its minimum qualifying demands. His treatment of the *rāga* barely qualifies him as a performer of art music. He has no familiarity with the *rāga*'s melodic personality beyond the seven or eight phrases that constitute its skeletal phraseology (the *Chalan*). His handling of the *rāga* may even descend to the level of treating it as a mere scale, breaching or ignoring its distinctive melodic contours.

APPROACH TO THE ARCHITECTURE

Like architecture, *rāga*-based music is an experiential art to be appreciated cumulatively through the exposure. The building arts metaphor is therefore relevant to Hindustānī music. Architecture is known to have three facets. The first is the plan, which represents the functional organization of spaces. The second is the sculptural aspect which defines its broad visual contours – the way the artefact looks. The third is the ornamental aspect – the way the artefact seeks to please.

In relation to Hindustānī music, it appears that the distribution of musical effort between these three facets will reflect the personality of the musician and his relationship with the *rāga*.

The *sāttvika* musician relates to the *rāga* in a spirit of reverential deliberateness. The *sāttvika* quality is associated with serenity and orderliness. It explores the *rāga*'s formless form for its manifestation possibilities in logical order and the revelations emanate from him in logical sequence. The music of the *sāttvika* musician is dominated by neatness of organization, in which his musical thought becomes transparent. Because of this quality, the effect he creates with his music is elevating.

The *rājasika* musician relates to the *rāga* in a spirit of conquest of known melodic territories. There is no exploration to be done. His musical energies are therefore focused on the technical perfection and elegant execution. His forte will, therefore, be sculpture. The ideation component of music making will tend to be translucent. Consequently, his organization of musical material may be less than neat. The overall stance of such music – at its effective best – will tend to be authoritative. In some cases, it may even come through as intimidating.

The *tāmasika* musician relates to the *rāga* in a casual and apathetic manner. Ideation is assumed to be non-existent. The organization of musical material will tend to be chaotic and even frenzied. The emanation of emotional stimuli from his music can be only accidental. Such music may have no way of holding audience interest except through ornamentation and titillation.

Conclusion

Because of its well-defined, culture-specific connotations, the framework based on the three modes of existence represents my preference for dealing with the relationship between the Hindustānī musician and his art.

The entire argument of this chapter can be summarized thus in Tables 4.1-2.

The superimposition of alternative frameworks from the behavioural sciences upon my tri-dimensional description of musicianship does not deliver perfect congruence. And, this was neither intended nor expected. A broadening of perspectives is, however, achieved.

Post-Script

After this argument was first made public, some valid queries have been raised, which deserve a considered response.

One query was whether a pyramidal graphic representation would not be a more appropriate for the *sāttvika*, *rājasika* and *tāmasika* categories. My view is that a pyramidal representation would imply a hierarchy of human tendencies, with *sāttvika* at the upper end and *tāmasika* at the lower. A hierarchical view is not warranted because society is not homogeneous and encompasses people with a wide range of needs and expectations from classical music. Even the same person could have different needs and expectations at different times or at different stages of life. The variety of musician personalities and musical orientations exists simultaneously on the concert platform precisely because of this reason.

Every category of music is legitimate as long as it commands an audience, because it satisfies a certain category of need and is, therefore, socially valuable. The maker and buyer of Rolls Royce cars cannot, by any defensible yardstick, be considered "higher" or "lower" in social value than the maker and buyer of Piaggio scooters.

The second query is whether the three categories should be seen as mutually exclusive, watertight, categories. My answer to this is: No. The human personality and classical music are both far too complex to be pigeonholed into watertight categories. By

Table 4.1: Typology Matrix

Musical Personality	*Myers–Briggs Type*	*Maslow's Need Hierarchy Levels*	*Three Modes of Existence*
Contemplation-dominant	Artist–idealist	Cognitive Aesthetic Self-actualization Transcendent	*Sāttvika*
Expression-dominant	Artist–Performer	Esteem	*Rājasika*
Communication-dominant	Artist–Giver	Biological and physiological Safety Love and Belongingness	*Tāmasika*

Table 4.2: Musical Features

Mode of Existence	*Attitude Towards Rāga*	*Rāga Form in Focus*	*Ideation*	*Architecture*	*Aesthetic Impact*
Sāttvika	Reverential	Formless form	Transparent	Neat and orderly	Elevating
Rājasika	Command	Consensual form	Translucent	Relatively informal	Authoritative
Tāmasika	Apathetic	Qualifying form	Opaque	Disorganized or chaotic	Titillating

and large, most eminent musicians, whom we would classify as maestros, could fall in the *rājasika* category. But, there will be many who will be borderline cases. Some will tilt towards the *sāttvika* and some others to *tāmasika*. And, this is, indeed, the nature of conceptual frameworks and behavioural models. They are an aid to understanding broad patterns of occurrence of certain phenomena. Nothing more, nothing less.

5

Bhakti (the Devotional Spirit) in Hindustānī Music

Recently, an influential aficionado of Carnatic music publicly expressed the view that Hindustānī music is lacking in *bhakti*. There was more than a suggestion that Hindustānī music has abandoned the transcendentalism fundamental to the Hindu artistic tradition. Such perceptions appear to be widely shared amongst members of the Carnatic music community. Hence, the need to address them.

These perceptions arise evidently from the fact that the lyrics of mainstream Carnatic music are predominantly devotional, while those of Hindustānī vocal music tend to feature a wider variety of themes with a bias, perhaps, towards "Śṛṅgāra Rasa" (the romantic/erotic sentiment). Without getting into the philosophical niceties of the *rasa* theory, I attempt to examine whether the pattern warrants the inferences evidently drawn.

Understanding Musical Genres

Every genre of vocal music features lyrics (or some other form of articulation), melody and rhythm. But, at any given time, an artist's musical energies – however one may define them and to whatever we may attribute them – are limited. They cannot possibly be directed equally towards delivering the aesthetic satisfaction of all the elements in one rendition. Therefore, each

---

This essay was published in the 400th Special Anniversary Issue (January 2018) of *Śruti* magazine.

genre is designed to focus a musician's energies on a different facet of the musical endeavour.

Even if a musician's energies were unlimited, a variety of genres would emerge because a multiplicity of genres would fulfil the needs of society more efficiently. Audiences represent a diversity of tastes; even the same listener welcomes different aesthetic satisfactions at different times or in different moods or even on the same concert platform. This is why the culture supports different genres of music – each specializing in the delivery of a different category of aesthetic satisfaction. The focus of musical energies, and the consequent delivery of aesthetic satisfactions, form the basis on which genres of vocal music may be classified.

1. *Svarāśrita* (melody dominant), where primary target for musical energies is the treatment of melody.
2. *Padāśrita* (composition dominant), in which the composite target of musical energies in the totality of the pre-composed melodic–rhythmic–poetic entity.
3. *Layāśrita* (tempo dominant), in which the determining factor in the delivery of musical value is the tempo of rendition, which forges a distinctive relationship between the melody, rhythm and the lyrics.
4. *Arthāśrita* (interpretative), where the musical endeavour is focused on the musical interpretation of the lyrics.

The last classification of vocal music recognizes the interpretation of literary meaning as a musical endeavour qualitatively distinct from the one characteristic of the *padāśrita* genres. Interestingly, this category covers the semi-classical genres because it is dominated neither by *svara*, nor by *laya*, nor by the *pada*.

These are not mutually exclusive categories, but indications of dominant tendencies. Some genres qualify for a dual classification. And, indeed, the individual musical personalities of musicians may also tilt the balance of musical energies in one genre towards those characteristic of another, without necessarily prejudicing the essential character of the genre.

Svarāśrita and Padāśrita

Considering the features of the dominant genres in practice today, Carnatic music may be described as predominantly *padāśrita*, while the comparable mainstream genre of Hindustānī vocalism may be described as *svarāśrita*.

Both traditions feature pre-composed and improvised elements. Both traditions conform to *rāga*-grammar disciplines. And, both engage intricately with *laya* and *tāla*. But, they differ in their fundamental orientation. The "commanding form" (to use Susanne Langer's concept), which drives the entire rendition in the *padāśrita* Carnatic tradition, is a pre-composed poetic–melodic–rhythmic entity; it is even referred to as a "Song", thus making its aesthetic intent transparent. On the other hand, the commanding form in the *Svarāśrita* Hindustānī tradition (as argued by S.K. Saxena) is the distinctive arrangement of *svaras*, which is the *rāga-svarūpa*.

In a *padāśrita* tradition, the entirety of the poetic–melodic–rhythmic entity is intended to act as an integrated whole to deliver its aesthetic satisfaction to the listener. Compositions are deemed to represent a perfect aesthetic congruence between the lyrics, the melody and the rhythm. This explains why the *padāśrita* Carnatic tradition places a high premium on the devotional literary content of its classical music repertoire and treats the composition as inviolable in every melodic–rhythmic detail. Interestingly, even instrumental music of the Carnatic tradition renders compositions written for vocal rendition, implying that if the melodic–rhythmic shell is faithfully rendered, the listener will "fill in" the lyrics which remain unarticulated. Such a musical tradition, driven predominantly by the devotional lyrical component, reflects its moorings in

Hindu polytheism – the idea that by an intense absorption in the manifest forms of the deities (*sākāra/saguṇātmaka upāsanā*), man may transcend the manifest form of the chosen deity and attain union with the formless Divinity (*nirguṇa/nirākāra*).

Understanding Bhakti

To fully comprehend the issue, we need to understand *bhakti.* The word *bhakti* is an abstract noun derived from the Sanskrit verb *bhaja* (to serve). The essential stance of the one who serves is a surrender to the Master's wishes. So, the essence of *bhakti* is *śaraṇāgata-bhāva* (the spirit of surrender), or the total annihilation of selfhood, along with a total acceptance of man's insignificance before God (if you are a theist) or in the overall scheme of the universe. The *sākāra/saguṇātmaka bhakti* of a *padāśrita* tradition aims at this transcendence of the human psyche – pushing the listeners' mind to the region of consciousness that lies between the *sākāra* and the *nirākāra*.

I humbly suggest that the Indian mind has access to the same process through an alternate musical route – the *svarāśrita* route, which Hindustānī music takes.

In a *svarāśrita* tradition, the hero of the musical endeavour is not a deity (*sākāra/saguṇa*), but a *rāga* (a "formless form", a *nirākāra ākṛti*). The entire musical endeavour is an attempt to translate/interpret/manifest the formless form of the *rāga* into a communicable form.

We may pause here to appreciate that, in essence, a *rāga* is not different from a deity. Just as Viṣṇu is identified by *śaṅkha, chakra, gadā* and *padma*, a *rāga* is identified by its distinctive arrangement of selected *svaras*. Viṣṇu has been visualized differently by millions of artists over the millennia – but never without *śaṅkha, chakra, gadā* and *padma*. Likewise, Rāga Mālkauṅs/Hiṇḍolam is visualized and projected in sound pictures in millions of ways, but never without its identifying attributes – such as may be acceptable from time to time.

Deities and *rāgas* are, in fact, both formless forms (*nirākāra ākṛti*) and meditating upon the attributes of either of them will lead one into the same region of consciousness on the border between the *sākāra* and the *nirākāra.* If the essence of *bhakti* is *śaraṇāgata-bhāva*, the *padāśrita* and *svarāśrita* traditions both appear to qualify.

There is textual support for this view in the Indian musicological tradition.

> It (the *rāga-rūpa*) is of two kinds – *nādātma* whose essence is sound and *devamaya* whose essence is an image incarnating the deity. Of the former, there are many shapes; but the latter has only one. – Ayyangar, *Rāgavibodha of Somanātha*

William James, the father of American psychology, defines the "Divine" as an unfathomable vastness, leaving man with no option but to accept his own relative insignificance, and to plead for grace.

> The "divine" mean(s) ··· such a primal reality as the individual feels impelled to respond to solemnly and gravely. ··· The personal attitude, which the individual finds himself impelled to take up towards the divine ··· shall have to confess to at least some amount of dependence on sheer mercy. ···
>
> – W. James, 1961: 47

From this perspective, one may view performance in the Hindustānī tradition as a prayer to the Divine form of a *rāga* – entreating it to descend into its melodic form.

Lyrics in Khyāl Vocalism

This perspective does not, admittedly, resolve the issue of *khyāl* lyrics, which are allegedly biased towards "Śṛṅgāra Rasa". It is necessary, here, to consider whether the evident poetic inclinations of a *svarāśrita* genre can be considered fundamental to the aesthetic intent of music; whether the lyrics are intended to perform a literary function at all, and whether they are germane to the delivery of the aesthetic satisfactions characteristic of the genre. Metaphorically, I am asking whether a person can be convicted in India for a crime committed under the laws of Botswana.

Khyāl is not a *padāśrita* genre. No less a scholar than B.C. Deva described a *khyāl* composition as "a mere peg on which to hang the *rāga*". He did so possibly with disapproving intent, but with stunning realism. *Khyāl* lyrics are not composed as carriers of literary meaning, though they do possess meaning. Their thematic content is musically insignificant compared to the value of the texture (vowels and consonants) they provide for the delivery of the melodic idea. They constitute the platform for the exploration of the *rāga* form (the *nirākāra ākṛti*).

This may, incidentally, be the reason why the *khyāl* genre tolerates lyrics of mediocre literary value. This may also be the reason why *khyāl* lyrics, written in the Braj Bhāṣā dialect of Hindi, are performed throughout the Hindustānī music region – including Pakistan and Bangladesh – in the same language. In extreme cases, the tradition tolerates even a virtual rape of Braj Bhāṣā lyrics in their articulation, because their musical function is faithfully performed without the comprehension of literary meaning.

In his book, *Indian Musical Traditions*, Vamanrao Deshpande, amongst the most respected critics, recalls a brief flirtation (revolt?) the *khyāl* attempted with lyrics written in Marathi, rather than Braj Bhāṣā. Maharashtrian vocalists soon discovered that the textural musical value uniquely offered by the original Braj Bhāṣā lyrics had been lost and the experiment was abandoned.

A similar affirmation of the musical (rather than literary) value of lyrics comes from the introduction of *sargam* (solfa symbols) articulation into *khyāl* vocalism – evidently an import from the Carnatic tradition. In the *padāśrita* Carnatic genre *sargam* articulation is a *svarāśrita* diversion. In the *svarāśrita*

Hindustānī genre, however, it has an entirely different presence. It functions as a *svarāśrita* embellishment, or a textural relief, in what is already a *svarāśrita* genre. Therein lies its conceptual and aesthetic significance.

The *sargam* is, by its very nature, a set of meaningless consonants, devoid of literary meaning – as meaningless as isolated alphabets in a written language. The *sargam*'s effortless – though not universal – admittance to *khyāl* vocalism supports the view that the communication of literary meaning has only negligible relevance, if any, to the delivery of aesthetic satisfactions of the *khyāl* genre.

Deshpande has argued that the *khyāl* genre has liberated melody and rhythm from poetry, and hence raised Hindustānī music to a level of "pure music". And this, he believes, represents the highest achievement of Hindustānī music so far.

The Spiritual and the Devotional

It is in this light that the issue of *bhakti* in Hindustānī music has to be viewed. To regard devotional lyrics as the exclusive flag-bearers of *bhakti* in music is a misrepresentation of the character of music as an art, as well as *bhakti* as a human aspiration. The liberation of music from poetry does not, in any manner, dilute its transcendentalism.

The transcendentalism of the *khyāl* is "spiritual", when it focuses the musician's meditative attention upon the *nirākāra ākṛti* of the *iṣṭa rāga*. This transcendentalism cannot, by any reasonable logic, be considered inferior or less elevating than focusing "devotional" energies upon a *sākāra ākṛti*. In fact, it is reasonable to argue that, at its highest level of intensity, *sākāra* is only a pathway to the *nirākāra*, signifying man's emotional experience transcending all classifications. It can only be described as "bliss" or "delight". Eduard Hanslick, the esteemed nineteenth-century Austrian music critic (*The Beautiful in Music*, 1891) was much maligned perhaps for saying precisely this. This is why *Taittirīya Upaniṣad* says: *raso vai saḥ*. The experience of *rasa* is a mystical/religious experience.

Even at a purely philosophical level, however, art remains in *śaraṇāgata-bhāva* mode as long as the artistic endeavour remains an acknowledgement of man's insignificance in the overall scheme of Creation. This is the essence of Hindu thought.

Acknowledgements: The author is indebted to Dr. Milind Malshe, Dr. Padma Sugavanam and Mrs Meena Bannerjee for their contribution to the development of this argument. Their agreement with it may not, however, be assumed.

6

Amplification, Recordings and Hindustānī Music

IT IS an honour to be delivering the annual lecture in the memory of Pandit V.N. Bhatkhande. Bhatkhande was the intellectual father of the twentieth-century movement that brought our music out of aristocratic patronage and scholarly vaults, and made its knowledge accessible to the public.

Two parallel developments of great significance were taking place in the music world while Bhatkhande was making his epic contribution. One was the missionary work of his contemporary, Pandit Vishnu Digambar Paluskar in making music education available to a large number of aspirants all over the country. And, the second was the pace at which amplification and recording technologies were enlarging the audiences for classical music – bringing it to every neighbourhood, every home.

Musicianship, scholarship and connoisseurship – the three pillars of a musical culture – all owe their vibrancy to the conceptual and theoretical foundations Bhatkhande laid. I salute his memory and attempt to share my views on the subject at hand.

I do not claim technical knowledge of sound engineering or of recording technologies. So, my observations will be conditioned largely by what I have observed. What little I now understand is the gift of a few friends engaged in concert hall sound management and recording. I shall therefore focus

---

Bhatkhande Memorial Lecture, Dadar–Matunga Cultural Centre, Mumbai, 22 October 2016.

attention on the musical, artistic and cultural aspects of the subject.

Amplification

The common understanding of amplification is that it enhances the volume of the sound – so it travels farther and reaches more people. This is, indeed, true. But amplification does more than this. First, it enhances pitch-perception – the pitch of the generated sound is more accurately perceived and the melodic contours are more clearly heard. Second, amplified sound is richer in harmonics – so the timbre (tonal quality) of the sound is truer to the sound actually produced – assuming it has not been electronically manipulated. Third, amplified sound has longer sustain than unamplified sound – it remains captured in the enclosed space of the concert hall for a longer period.

All these effects of amplification are, of course, conditioned by the acoustic environment in which the music is being performed. What the microphone captures depends on the acoustic design of the concert hall and what the audience receives as speaker output also depends on the same reality. The electronics involved in the process are equally important – the microphones used to capture the sound, the amplifiers used to magnify it and the speakers used to deliver the magnified sound to the audience.

To understand the implications of amplification for Hindustānī music, we need to go back to the strategies adopted by Hindustānī music to cope with the unamplified environment for performance. Understandably, loudness, or the throw of the voice to the maximum distance were the main concerns. Several examples come to mind. These examples are from recordings of the 1930s and of musicians trained in the early years of the twentieth century, before the arrival of either recordings or a widespread availability of concert-hall amplification.

THE PRE-AMPLIFICATION ERA

Faiyaz Khan cultivated a throaty, guttural style of vocalization which enabled a louder output. Because the environment did not support refined melody, he adopted a bold, almost staccato, style of intonation, delivering sharp, angular melodic contours. For the same reason, his tans were simple in construction, and his *bandiś*es were rhythmically clever. And, because the sound had a very short audible life, he sang his *vilambit bandiś*es at a considerably quicker tempo of about 38-42 beats per minute, than his main contemporary rival, Kesarbai Kerkar, who sang them at 25-33 beats per minute.

How did Kesarbai manage? Her strategy was different. Though endowed with a high-pitched voice, she cultivated a masculine breadth in her voice. She could deliver much more refined melodic detail in her music by adopting the *śuddha ākāra* (the AA vowel) form of articulation as her mainstay. This gave her music a greater continuity of musical effect even at a much slower tempo in an environment that did not support the sustenance of vocalized sounds.

Then, consider the Gwalior Gharānā singers. Their strategy was entirely different. They sang their *vilambit bandiś*es at about the same tempo as Kesarbai (25-30). But, to suit the fluidity and simplicity of their style, they cultivated a phenomenal range, with a strong bias towards melodic action in the upper registers. Vocalization in the upper registers enhances the brightness factor that throws the voice farther.

Abdul Karim Khan also a product of the pre-amplification era, took yet another route. The Kairana brand of elaborate and ornate melodic exploration required a slower tempo (14-20 beats per minute) than any of their contemporaries had attempted. He adopted a needle-sharp singing voice, low on harmonics, which could travel faster and hence farther without additional lung power.

In instrumental music, the *sitār* and *sarod* for instance, early twentieth-century music was heavy on stroke craft and dazzling speed of execution because the environment did not sustain the sound for long. On the *sitār*, fretwork dominated the melodic elaboration of the *rāga* because the environment would not deliver the nuances of string-deflection. Compositions for the *sitār* and the *sarod* were rhythmically clever because melodic artistry would not reach the listener.

Thus, different lineages of musicians adopted different strategies to cultivate and service the largest possible following within the limitations of the acoustic environment in which they were placed. The advent and the growing penetration of amplification brought noticeable changes in music.

THE TRANSITION TO AN AMPLIFIED ENVIRONMENT

With the advent and progress of amplification, reach ceased to be the primary concern of musicians. The timbre – the pleasing quality of the sound – became important. The art and science of voice culture became a concern for vocalists. Because every melodic detail of music would be captured and magnified, technical perfection became important. Implicitly, vocalists also began to enjoy a wider choice of stylistic directions and this enabled the migration of musicians from one stylistic lineage to another.

It is my personal view that the dramatic change in the stylistic landscape of vocal music starting from the 1940s can be attributed substantially to the spread and growing sophistication of amplification. This could, for instance, explain the sudden decline of the aggressive, masculine Agra style and the rise of the melody-oriented styles like Kairana and Jaipur. A similar picture is visible in *dhrupad* vocalism. Around the time of independence, *dhrupad* vocalists of several *gharānās* had a significant presence. Within two decades thereafter, the melody-oriented Dagar Bani reigned supreme, while the aggressive styles – Darbhanga and

Bettiya – had been marginalized.

With the arrival of amplification, *khyāl* vocalism permitted ladies to compete with men for a place on the concert platform. Early twentieth-century recordings of lady vocalists suggest that their presence was confined largely to semi-classical musical genres. Once amplification made the *khyāl* physically less demanding, ladies could compete and come to the forefront of the classical music platform. Understandably, they emerged primarily under the influence of the modern melody-dominant styles – rather than the older masculine styles.

The more fundamental change in the music-scape came in the form of the opportunity for instrumental music to challenge vocal music for the elaborate sophistication of *rāga* presentation. The human voice could be trained to address 100/200 people without amplification. Most instruments of the pre-amplification era, however, could not address more than 30/40 people at a time. Amplification gave the string instruments – *sitār, sarod, rudra viṇā* – the incentive to re-engineer and fully exploit the opportunity and contend for centre stage. The *sitār* and the *sarod* were re-engineered in the 1930s and 1940s, while the *rudra viṇā* was re-engineered in the 1960s. The rest, as they say, is history.

Amplification also facilitated the entry of the newer and low-volume instruments like the *santūr* and the Hawaiian guitar. The flip side of the coin is the decline of outdoor instruments like the *śehnāī* and its accompanists – the *tāśā* and the *naqqārā* – which could not face a microphone and produce a pleasant sound.

These responses to amplification technology had necessarily to alter the sociology and economics of music performance.

THE SOCIOLOGY AND ECONOMICS

As concerts began to service audiences of 700/800 people instead of the 100/150 numbers typical of the pre-amplification era, concert hall architecture emerged as a significant participant in the musical culture. By putting a microphone in front of the musician, a certain psychological distance had already been created. Concert hall design added to this distance by creating a physical distance between the musician and the audience. A musical tradition that had evolved as an collaborative/interactive effort between artists and their followers, experienced a loss – or at least a substantial dilution – of the intimacy.

The loss of intimacy was significant not only as it isolated musicians from their audiences. Its consequences were equally significant for the relationship between members of the audience. The concert hall seating transformed an informal, actively consultative engagement between knowledgeable listeners into a passive shoulder-to-shoulder relationship. This deprived the musical culture of a process which had contributed substantially to the evolution of a connoisseur class. In the pre-microphone era, this connoisseur class was an integral part of a complex "quality control" mechanism which rated musicianship and determined the profession trajectories of musicians. The arrival of the microphone commenced the dissipation of this important segment of the Hindustānī music ecosystem.

In addition to the creation of a psychological and physical distance, concert hall music also created a status barrier. In most cases, the concert stage itself elevates the musician above the level of the audience for distance visibility and places a passage between the stage and audience seating. But, I suggest that the status barrier created by amplification is more subtle than this.

Loudness itself is a distance builder and a status creator. For instance, I do not have the right to speak to my father in a loud voice; but he has the right to do so. That defines his status. By giving the musician a unidirectional access to a large audience, amplification created a status differential between the artist and the audience. This was perhaps the beginning of the "Star" system because it subtly projected the performing musician not only as a master of the art, but almost as a "superior" human being.

The emergence of the modern concert hall was the first step also towards classical music ceasing to be a process and becoming a product.

Conceptually, when a producer is isolated from the consumer in time and space, a market can be said to have been created. In this case, the isolation takes place only in space, not in time. But, another feature of a market does raise its head. Somebody has to build/own/hire a hall, pay for the sound system and ensure an audience. Thus was born the intermediary. Indirectly, capital also entered the picture as the investment made on the concert hall and the sound system. With capital in the picture, the return on investment became a factor. It did not matter whether there was a profit motive or whether the consumer paid. A commercial ecosystem had taken shape. And, rightly or wrongly, the size of the audiences started being perceived as a measure of artistic value. The foundation for the "Star" system had been laid.

The drift towards a classical music market crystallized through the emergence of recordings as a significant, and later the predominant, interface between the musician and the audience. Commercial recordings brought all the features of a marketplace into full-fledged action. There was the artist (the produce/designer/creator), the manufacturer (the recording company), the distributor (the wholesale and retail trade) and the consumer (the listener).

Commercial Recordings

THE 78 RPM ERA

The 78 rpm disc permitted a recording of only 3.5 minutes. In that era, a normal *khyāl* performance on stage had a duration of 30/35 minutes, a *ṭhumrī* presentation was 15-20 minutes and a *rāga* rendition on the string instruments was about 20 minutes long. So, the 78 rpm demanded a substantial compression. An admirable amount of planning took place to deliver the satisfaction of a *rāga* rendition. The acoustic quality was poor in the early days, but it improved steadily as electronics began to play a role. The musicianship on display was often great, but the totality was still unsatisfying because of the duration. It was, at best, a bonsai of a banyan tree. It took off because it made a vast resource of musicianship available, for the first time, to listeners at large, and because there was nothing else – radio receivers were yet to become a household product. It enabled music lovers to identify musicians whose radio broadcasts they should look out for – public concerts were too few. In the process, it opened up a large middle-class market for classical music.

The success of the 78 rpm disc enthused the community of musicians – they could see aristocratic patronage coming to an end, and the need to promote themselves to a larger constituency on a national scale. This is why we find that the early recordings were primarily of ladies from the courtesan districts. They lived a life of anonymity and ignominy in a servile relationship with their agents and patrons. To them, recordings came as a means of establishing their identity as musicians and liberating themselves from an existence that denied them self-esteem.

But, of course, most significant musicians also recorded as they could also see the advantages of reaching a large national audience and cultivating a following beyond the reach of radio. Even the legendary Abdul Kareem Khan reportedly recorded 36 discs with 72 items. Only a handful of musicians resisted recordings initially, the most notable being Faiyaz Khan and Kesarbai Kerkar. Initially, these two luminaries even shunned the radio. Faiyaz Khan relented under orders from his royal patrons and Kesarbai never relented.

There were several reasons for this. Their personal stature and financial comfort were so high that they had no need to take far-sighted decisions. The second reason was a combination of elitism and arrogance. They could all along afford to be selective about the audiences they would sing for. It was not easy for them to accept the idea of a faceless audience qualified to hear them merely by parting with a few rupees. The third was insecurity. In a concert situation, a few errors or liberties would be forgotten. But, on a recording, even the slightest blemish would be heard repeatedly, be gleefully maligned by professional rivals and tarnish reputations. Ultimately, as we know, both recorded a significant number of 78 rpm discs. Their egos probably did the trick. They needed to ensure their place in history as, respectively, the Emperor and Empress of the concert platform.

All I have said about 78 rpms above is valid in general. But, if you ask me to identify the greatest triumph of that era, I will name two. The first is D.V. Paluskar. In his times, a classical musician was not taken seriously until he was 40. Paluskar, however, died at the age of 35. Left only to radio broadcasts, he would have died virtually unknown. In later years, several of his radio concerts were published on concert-length media. His 78 rpm recordings were sufficient to establish him as one of the greatest vocalists of the twentieth century.

The second triumph of the era – though in a different sort of way – is Bhimsen Joshi. A 13-year old Bhimsen stood one day outside a record shop in Kundgol village (Karnataka) listening to music he could not afford to pay for. By some design of destiny, the music he was hearing was a 78 rpm disc of Abdul Kareem Khan. In those three minutes, he decided he had to sing like the Ustad. That fateful night, with just the clothes on his body, and without a rupee in his pocket, Bhimsen Joshi left home in search of a *guru*. The rest is history.

Towards the tail end of the 78 rpm era, there was a brief EP (Extended Play) era, which delivered 7 minutes of music on one side. Some great music was published on EPs. But, its technological and commercial life was too short to be historically significant, as the Long Playing (LP) era with 22 minutes of music per side speedily pushed the EP into history.

THE LONG PLAYING ERA

The LP offered near-concert length durations. By this time, electronics had vastly improved the acoustic quality of sound capture and processing. Magnetic tape recording had arrived, thus making splicing and editing possible. Stereophonic multiple-track recording had become possible. The end product of the recording industry on the LP was acoustically, artistically and aesthetically more satisfying than anything the music world had heard. Interestingly, the LP era commenced around the time when All India Radio (AIR) began to shrink the share of classical music in total broadcast time. Of course, it cannot be called a replacement because radio broadcasts were free and LPs cost a good deal of money. In its totality, however, I regard the LP as a major inflection point in the history of Hindustānī music.

A durable impact of the LP was to open up the south Indian and international markets. Without a satisfying display of *rāga* presentation architecture, Hindustānī music could not have created an empathy with audiences cultivated in the radically different aesthetics of music. The beginning made by the LP has flowered into a widespread appreciation of Hindustānī music in southern India and abroad.

The aesthetic leap required of Western audiences was even greater. At a time when Hindustānī music was hardly known in the US and Europe, the LP introduced cross-culturally sensitive music lovers to the monophonic, entirely improvised world of *rāga*s and the architecture of their rendition. It was the LP that made it possible for the Senior Dagar Brothers, Ravi Shankar and Ali Akbar Khan to shape a vast international constituency for Hindustānī music, followed by several others thereafter. The impact of this development on the *dhrupad* genre was greater than any of the other segments of Hindustānī music, since *dhrupad* was then a dying art, which survives today largely on the patronage of Western audiences.

In the domestic market, an important contribution of the LP was to enable the ascendancy of the romanticists of *khyāl* vocalism. Romanticism is to be interpreted here as a conscious revolt against the formalism and the aloofness of demeanour characteristic of orthodox *khyāl gāyakī*. Though the roots of romanticism could be traced to earlier musicians, categorical romanticism is represented primarily by Kishori Amonkar, Kumar Gandharva, and to a lesser extent, by Jasraj. They brought to the *khyāl* an explicit sentimentalism which Hindustānī music had hitherto heard only in semi-classical, folk and popular music. This feature could be understood and accepted as "classical" only because it was embedded in the established presentation protocol of *khyāl* rendition. A 3-minute 78 rpm capsule rendered in their style would have been dismissed as insignificant and no different from a film or folk song.

Of course, it is also significant that the arrival of the LP coincided with the entry of the first post-Independence generation of audiences into the market. A new liberal/ liberating/liberated consciousness was taking charge of the cultural process and was in search of a new fragrance in traditional music. The romanticists appeared to satisfy that need and the LPs of the romanticists appear to have encashed it.

The LP era was also the beginning of the "Star System" in Hindustānī music. The phenomenon is understandable from the recording companies' point of view. In the preceding 78 rpm era, the market was merely being "seeded" with a suboptimal product. The number of musicians offered had to be large and the repertoire of each musician also had to be large to cover the risks of an ill-defined emerging market.

The LP was almost a "revolutionary" product, offering a high level of customer satisfaction, handled by a better organized marketing network. It suited the recording companies to publish more and more of any musician who sold well, promote him more heavily, push up his market rating and reap the profits. An FMCG (fast moving consumer goods) corporate culture became viable, as big consumer brands could be built. And, naturally, dealing with twenty highly-profitable artists was administratively more attractive than dealing with a relatively untested 200. An oligopolistic recording industry found it convenient to create an oligarchy in the classical music business. This, of course, had its effect on the concert market, where the performance fees of the stars outpaced inflation several times over, leaving less and less money to support the entry of fresh talent.

A natural consequence of this was the unleashing of a powerful homogenizing force into the musical culture. It expressed itself in two ways. The first was a "standardization" of *rāga*-grammar and a shrinkage of the *rāga* universe. In the 78 rpm era, several variants of each *rāga* could be heard on discs of various musicians. The LP era steadily shrank the number of musicians visible on the horizon. As a result, many *rāga*s went out of circulation, and the variants of the *rāga*s performed by "star" musicians became the "standard" by which *rāga*s began to be recognized. In some cases – as in the case of the Rāga Mārwā recording of Ameer Khan on an LP – the *rāga* almost changed its fundamental character. My personal view is that this consequence was unfortunate for the tradition. I am not sure we should be happy about *rāga bibhās* with *komal dhaivat* going out of circulation just because Kishori Amonkar's *śuddha dhaivat* version was hugely successful.

The other unhappy consequence of the oligopolistic phenomenon was the corrosion of the stylistic diversity engendered by the established *gharānā*s of music. Once concert-length, mature music was available to aspirants to musicianship, there was no incentive left for them to imbibe the distinctive ideologies of music making cultivated by the different *gharānā*s. Soft options became available. They could either memorize and perform complete recordings of the leading musicians or pick up appealing ideas from various sources and integrate them using their own (undeveloped) sense of aesthetic coherence. As a result, whether in vocalism or in instrumental music, only two *gharānā*s are discernible today – The Xerox Gharānā and The Cocktail Gharānā. This is a well considered academic observation, even if it might appear frivolous in its choice of words.

The LP revolution triggered a significant rise in the status of accompanists. On a 3-minute recording, there was no scope for the melodic and rhythm accompanists to display their musicianship. On a 22-minute LP, their role could be noticed and also enhanced to add to the richness of the musical experience. This possibility was most advantageous to percussionists who could rise to the level of being virtual partners in music making – particularly with the plucked/struck instruments like the *sitār, santūr* and the *sarod.* The LP benefited accompanists also in a different manner.

A brilliant accompanist like a Ramnarayanji could release a couple of solo recordings and almost single-handedly create a global market for the *sāraṅgī* as a solo instrument. In perhaps a similar development, the *tablā* accompanist also rose in personal stature to an extent that it triggered off something of a revival in the *tablā* solo as a performance item – a phenomenon that had begun to recede after the demise of the two soloist giants: Ahmed Jaan Thirakwa and Ameer Hussain Khan. The "Zakir effect" is now a celebrated phenomenon in Hindustānī music.

THE AUDIO-CASSETTE ERA

Scaling up from 22 minutes per side, the audio-cassette made, in most cases, a duration of 30 minutes available on each side. This added momentum to the forces that had been released into the music world by the LP. This particularly helped the publication of live concert recordings held in private collections. Obviously, they were of inferior acoustic quality, having been recorded by amateurs in uncontrolled environments with amateur equipment. But, by this time, some acoustic restoration was possible. Consumers were happy with the additional access to great musicians available through LPs, but also to some great musicians who had been relatively ignored in their lifetimes by the recording companies during the LP era.

The most interesting aspect of the audio-cassette business was its economics. It was a low-cost business in terms of capital requirement as well as material costs. The cost of producing 500 copies and 5,000 copies was virtually the same on a per-copy basis. Almost anybody could turn a producer. And, indeed, a large number of new recording companies did emerge during that period, threatening the monopoly of the music majors. Many new artists were launched into the market challenging the sparkle of the LP era stars. Many of the artists launched during the audio-cassette era are amongst the leading musicians of today.

THE CD ERA

The CD (compact disk), using digital technologies, further multiplied the forces unleashed by the LP and the audio-cassette. There was a quantum jump in the acoustic quality of studio recordings as well as live concert recordings. The CD had the advantage of being even more attractive in terms of the producer's economics. Anybody with a computer could turn producer. The CD technology came with the additional advantage that a digital copy was acoustically identical to the original, while analog copies on the magnetic tape medium suffered some generational loss in duplication. So, the minimum viable print order for CDs could be much smaller than on audio-cassette.

Most importantly for the CD, the availability of 75/78 minutes of recording (in WAV format – Waveform audio file format) made it possible for musicians to undertake some daring experiments, and producers ready to risk their capital on them. I can cite the example of two such attempts by Ustad Vilayat Khan Saheb. He recorded two CDs of Bhairavī and two of Khamāj for India Archive Music, New York. One of the two in each *rāga* had only a 75/78 minute *ālāp-joḍ-jhālā* and the other had only *bandiś*es. The Khamāj *bandiś*es CD featured seven *bandiśes* in a row.

I was doubtful about the commercial wisdom of these decisions. Who would want to buy a 78-minute *ālāp* either in Bhairavī or Khamāj? And, who would want to buy seven Khamāj *bandiśes* strung together, with none of them individually complete in terms of *rāga* presentation protocol? I did query Khan Saheb on this. His reply was simple – he said he had spent his entire lifetime exploring these two *rāgas*; he thought it was time for him to share his vision of them with the music world. In effect, he admitted to having produced an academic presentation of encyclopaedic scope, almost as a textbook for aspiring musicians.

Of course, there were other musicians of Khan Saheb's generation, who could not re-imagine their presence on recordings in a way that would exploit the duration available on a CD. I have studied recordings of one such musician who felt obliged to play one *rāga* for 75 minutes, did not have the melodic resources to back the decision and rendered a boringly repetitive Gorakh Kalyāṇ. Not all musicians knew how to handle the expansive canvas available on a CD.

The Business Side

The recording industry is more than a century old. I thought it was time to look at it from the consumer's perspective. The first enquiry had to be in terms of the price of music to the customer.

Since we are talking of different time periods, it was necessary to apply an inflation adjustment factor to the retail price to arrive at a fair judgement. Table 6.1 shows the results of my computations, based on my own memory of prices, and the recall of my seniors by age.

The price per minute of music to the consumer, in inflation adjusted terms, has been coming down steadily, with every change of storage media. The consumer can have no legitimate complaint on this account. He can only complain about the truly great musicians of the LP era, who did not receive as much support from the recording companies as they deserved. A few examples that come to mind are Ameer Khan, Hirabai Barodekar, Sharafat Hussain Khan. There could be several others in this league. These are, however, minor issues in the totality of the phenomenon.

We may assume that this volume-driven pricing policy would have been profitable for the recording companies. But, as for the size of the market – it is reliably known that the classical music market had remained stable at about 1per cent of the total recordings market for several decades up to 1990, i.e. before the Internet explosion began. Could the pricing policy have helped enlarge concert-hall audiences? In fact, an inverse relationship is evident between the two. After the arrival of LPs, classical music actually lost concert hall audiences. Did people reduce concert attendance because recorded music of high quality was available at home? It is impossible to answer this question.

It seems fair to state that the recording companies serviced three generations of increasingly satisfied customers with consistently attractive prices and created a massive treasure for the musical culture, while making its targeted profits. They conducted efficient businesses, as their owners expected them to do. Their presence, however, had cultural consequences which need scrutiny.

Table 6.1: Consumer Economics of the Recording Industry

Year	*Format*	*Duration (Minutes)*	*Unit Price (Rs.)*	*Price (Rs.) Per Minute*	*Inflation Adjusted(Rs.)* 2015
1958	78 rpm	7	3.50	0.5	12.62
1963/64	LP	44	22.00	0.5	9.96
1967-68	Cassette	60	20.00	0.33	4.12
2000	CD	74	90-300	0.25-0.82	1.2-1.49
2015	CD MP3	840	90.00	0.10	0.10

Cultural Intervention

The intervention of amplification, coupled with that of recording technologies, changed the basic character of Hindustānī music. Some aspects of this change have been discussed earlier. There are a few other ways of looking at this issue.

Hindustānī music is a process and not a product. It is a process to be undertaken uniquely each time and by each musician, during performance. The moment a performance is captured and widely distributed, it becomes a product. This aids the destruction of the uniqueness of each subsequent performance by every other musician attempting to undertake the same process.

Hindustānī music has no existence, except in performance. The essence of performance is the contemplation upon the formless form of the *rāga* in order to interpret and present it in communicable form. This is ensured by enjoining upon the musician the dual role of composer and performer. Any force that aids or encourages the separation of these two roles, or deprives performance of its contemplative dimension, damages the fundamental character of Hindustānī music.

Hindustānī music has evolved on the principle of continuity within change. Any force that imposes a permanence or continuity upon any musical experience or militates against evolutionary change is disruptive of its basic character. Every piece of performed music is unique. The moment it is captured on storage media, that uniqueness acquires a date. And, anything with a date attached to it, comes with an expiry date. The concept of an expiry date runs contrary to the cultural intent of a tradition based on continuity within change.

The emergence of recordings as "virtual *guru*s" is an unfortunate consequence of the abundant availability of recordings. The art of Hindustānī music is intended to be perpetuated by oral transmission. A musician performs what he does during his lifetime and his music dies with him. What remains after him are the principles of music making that he has imparted to his students. Even in the worst case scenario of a musician who intends his disciples to become his clones, the effort cannot succeed. This is because of three human imperfections – imperfect perception, imperfect retention and imperfect reproduction.

These three imperfections together make it impossible for the oral tradition to spawn "Xerox *gharānā*s". The traditional system of art transmission was designed to ensure that each musician becomes a spokesperson of his generation and addresses an audience of his generation. How else would he make a living? By preserving the performed music of great musicians, the recording industry not only made cloning possible, but encouraged it.

By providing readymade models of mature music, recordings encouraged aspirants to abandon their roles as composers and focus their endeavours entirely on performance. An exceptionally talented vocalist of 25 can memorize a recording made by Ameer Khan at the age of 50 and deliver a convincing performance. Under such conditions, he has no need to delve into the mysteries the *rāga*, which is the fountainhead of Hindustānī music, with its contemplation being the primary purpose of music making. The result is unidimensional music – effective in execution, but blank on individuation and ideation. Such a result does not qualify for classification within a living artistic tradition.

In its totality, I believe, commercial recordings aided by the sophistication of amplification and sound processing, disconnected Hindustānī music from its source as well as its destination. The source of the music is the *rāga* which is being steadily consigned to irrelevance. Its destination is the audience, which now stands isolated in time and space and cultural context. Any artistic manifestation that has lost its moorings in the source and also its engagement with its destination creates its artefacts in a vacuum, and cannot sustain a vibrant culture.

The crucial issue is whether it was the recording industry's job to sustain the fundamentals of the musical culture. The answer has to in the negative. It is the music community's job to preserve its culture. The music community had to find ways of dovetailing its musical assets into its fundamental concerns for evolutionary change. Instead, the community enjoyed the fruits of the recording industry's efforts and neglected the deployment of its output as an aid to its objectives. As a result, an archival treasure spanning over a century of recorded music continued to corrode the fundamentals of the musical culture until the online media came along to alter the picture.

Everyday, we come across evidence of the growing influence of the online media over the classical music world. Their penetration is growing steadily along with Internet penetration. It is probably too early to conceptualize the pattern emerging as a result of this technological intervention. The evidence of their impact is yet scattered; but, it appears to affect all facets of the music world – music as performed, music as studied and music as traded/shared.

Assessing the impact of this intervention becomes even more difficult because it coincides with the arrival of second post-Independence generation of Indians as the dominant cultural force. In earlier and later essays, the significance of this has been discussed in some detail. On reasonable evidence, and based on sound socio-economic reasoning, Hindustānī music appears to be on the threshold of a paradigm shift. How the recording-era treasure of Hindustānī music fits into the emerging picture remains to be seen.

Acknowledgements: The author is indebted to recording engineers, Avinash Oak and Manohar Kunte for their technical inputs for this lecture.

7

Abstraction in Our Times

THERE is a fundamental difference between the way the visual arts and Indian classical music view abstraction. In the visual arts, abstraction is seen as a degree of departure from representational images and a proximity to a relationship between the basic elements – form, colour and texture. In classical music, we view abstraction from the opposite end.

Our reference point is abstract. Our primary focus is the interaction between the basic elements – melody, rhythm and poetry. Abstraction is viewed as degree to which the experience of their interaction is conditioned/moderated/diluted by the manner in which it manifests itself in performance. Therefore, while the visual arts can be discussed in terms of "degrees of abstraction", classical music needs to be discussed in terms of "degrees of dis-abstraction". The difference will become clearer, I hope, as I proceed.

Classical music and the visual arts are both arts. They must, therefore, have some meeting ground. I will attempt to explore that meeting ground.

Abstraction

At the outset I must share what I understand by abstraction. *The Oxford Dictionary* defines abstraction thus:

> The act of considering something independently of its associations, attributes, or concrete accompaniments/a thing

---

Paper presented to a workshop for art critics, Roop-Aroop, organized by the Raza Foundation, New Delhi, on 19 February 2018.

so considered/a thing that exists only in idea/freedom from representational qualities.

With reference to art in general, I understand abstraction as the seeking of a reference point outside of the artist, the subject as well as its audience. With reference to music in particular, I have two ways of understanding abstraction:

- Music has three dimensions – the contemplative, the expressive and the communicative. Abstraction is that territory in which the contemplative dimension dominates the expressive and the communicative dimensions.
- With specific reference to Hindustānī music, I have found it helpful to draw on the notion of "commanding form" enunciated by Susanne Langer, and interpreted by S.K. Saxena.

The Notion of a Commanding Form

In the context of Western art music, Langer accords the status of the commanding form to the composition, which determines the whole subsequent process of invention and elaboration. India's eminent aesthetician, Saxena (2001) argues that, in Hindustānī music, the *rāga* rightfully occupies this status.

But, a *rāga* is merely a set of rules governing the selection, sequencing and treatment of selected *svaras* (tones). Can it be considered a "form" at all? Saxena answers in the affirmative because, it is possessed of a distinct shape which makes it identifiable and distinguishable from others. A *rāga* is, indeed, a "form", but a "formless form".

It is the task of the musician to translate/interpret/render the "formless form" as a "communicable form". What, then, is the territory of abstraction in Hindustānī music? It is the territory in which the communicable form remains rooted in its source, the formless form.

What does it mean to interpret a formless form as a

communicable form? It means giving it a structure. And, for communicability, the structure has to be familiar. This process, which Ashok Ranade described as "ritualization", involves casting the *rāga* into a genre.

"Ritualization" is, in effect, a process of dis-abstraction. This dis-abstraction varies in degree, depending on the genre in which the formless form of the *rāga* is cast. So, the tradition gives us a choice of various genres, each involving a different degree of dis-abstraction.

The Classification of Genres

With specific reference to Hindustānī music, a genre may be defined as a distinctive hierarchy of melodic, rhythmic and phonetic (where relevant) elements, with one of the three constituting the primary determinant of aesthetic satisfaction and the remaining two being supportive to it. This hierarchy is reflected in the "architecture" of each genre – the specific features of the different movements and their sequencing. In terms of their specific features, the movements constituting a genre may themselves be classified as predominantly melodic, rhythmic or phonetic.

In an earlier chapter, I have outlined my classification of the genres in Hindustānī music. Though these categories appear to pertain only to the genres of vocal music, they are applicable to instrumental music also, because instrumental genres derive their basic architecture from one or more of the vocal genres.

The Inverse Hierarchy of Dis-Abstraction

THE SVARĀŚRITA GENRES

The *rāga* is a melodic entity. Therefore, the inverse hierarchy is defined by the extent to which the ritualization imposes a dis-abstraction on the commanding form. By this criterion, the *svarāśrita* genres rank highest in their "abstraction quotient".

They are *dhrupad* and *khyāl*.

THE DHRUPAD GENRE

The *dhrupad* genre imposes the lowest degree of dis-abstraction on the formless form of the *rāga*. It does indeed feature *svarāśrita* as well as *padāśrita* movements; but treats them separately, the *svarāśrita* movement allows interpretations of the commanding form – the formless form – as abstractly as the musician's imagination will permit.

THE KHYĀL GENRE

The *svarāśrita khyāl* genre comes next in the inverse hierarchy of dis-abstraction. The genre integrates *svarāśrita, layāśrita* as well *padāśrita* movements; but it is designed to devote the highest importance to the *svarāśrita* movements.

THE LAYĀŚRITA GENRES

In this category, we may classify *ṭappā*s and *tarānā*s. They come lower in the hierarchy because they deploy rhythm for forging an engaging relationship between the phonetic and melodic elements. In this process, they permit only a limited exploration of the formless form.

THE PADĀŚRITA GENRES

The *padāśrita* genres, focused on the totality of the composition, present a limited perspective on the *rāga*, with only negligible scope for its exploration beyond the pre-composed form. In this category, we may include *bandiś-kī-ṭhumrī*s and *bhajan*s.

THE ARTHĀŚRITA GENRES

These genres are concerned entirely with the interpretation of literary content and not governed by the *rāga* form at all. These genres may more accurately be described as poetic genres presented musically.

What Trends Do We Observe Today?

IN THE SVARĀŚRITA GENRES

The movements devoted to the exploration of the formless form are shrinking in terms of duration and attention to the contemplative process. The movements devoted to rhythmicality are gaining prominence. There is also a growing presence of phonetic elements – poetic as well as non-poetic.

THE LAYĀŚRITA GENRES

These genres, which have traditionally had a minor share of performance, are gaining in popularity and frequency of performance.

THE PADĀŚRITA GENRES

These genres are also gaining in terms of frequency of performance on the concert platform and as determinants of the popularity of musicians.

THE ARTHĀŚRITA GENRES

There is a virtual explosion of the *arthāśrita* genres evident in the last two decades. They do not require an anchoring in the *rāga* as the commanding form. They may, however, conform to definitive commanding forms in poetry and informal/minor melodic forms.

The Trends: In Summary

Of the three elements of Hindustānī music — melody, rhythm and poetry/articulation – it is the melodic element that is receding from prominence, while the rhythmic and poetic/ phonetic elements are gaining prominence. The aggregate "abstraction quotient" of art music available to the listener is shrinking.

This proposition can also be stated in terms of the creative process. Currently predominant tendencies in Hindustānī music suggest that the contemplative dimension of the art is shrinking and being progressively subordinated to/replaced by the expressive and communicative dimensions.

Stated in this fashion, Hindustānī music becomes comparable to other arts. Art distinguishes itself from other voluntary and pleasing human endeavours by the dominance of the contemplative dimension over the expressive and the communicative.

In music, I would ask the question – how much can you dilute the contemplative genres and movements before you are obliged to call it entertainment? In the visual arts, you would probably ask – how much loss of abstraction can an artwork accept before you are obliged to call it interior decoration?

I have the impression that Hindustānī music and the visual arts are both being obliged to answer these questions today. If this is so, the roots of the phenomenon must be traced to the larger cultural process determined by socio-economic realities. I would have reason to believe that the visual arts would also need to look at the same realities for clues to the hospitability (or the lack of it) of their markets to abstraction.

The Cultural Process

The hospitability of the musical culture to abstraction needs to be viewed from three angles: the socio-economic angle, the demographic angle and the technological angle.

Hindustānī music is a legacy of the feudal-agrarian culture that dominated India right up to the end of colonial rule. After Independence, that music was transplanted to the urban–industrial–commercial culture of the metropolitan cities. Aesthetic values are governed largely by the predominant means of livelihood in a society. Different means of livelihood subject man to different relationships with time and space – both fundamental to the shaping of aesthetic values. To this extent,

Hindustānī music had to undergo a transformation to satisfy the musical needs of its new patron class.

It is also important to acknowledge the role of growing sexual freedom in shaping aesthetic values. The relative anonymity of urban–industrial–commercial societies grants much greater sexual freedom to its members than feudal–agrarian societies did. Superficially, these two might seem unrelated. In reality, however, they are intimately connected. Art and sexual activity both belong to the pleasure principle in human nature. Art represents the sublimation of the pleasure principle, while sexual activity represents man's proximity to the animal kingdom.

The investment of emotional energies and intensity of the induced pleasurable experience may be equally great in art and in sexual activity; but the two differ substantially in the speed with which they build and release tension. Orgasm-directed sexual activity delivers a speedy build-up and release of tension. Art, on the other hand, delivers a gradual build-up and release of aesthetic tension. In this sense, the Indian aesthetic tradition, inspired by tāntric thought, is "an-orgasmic" in its fundamental orientation. (I make here a distinction between "an-orgasmic" and "anti-orgasmic".) The two pleasures mentioned fall at different – and indeed, very distant – points of the pleasure-seeking spectrum of human behaviour.

The greater sexual freedom characteristic of the urban–industrial–commercial environment shapes what may be called a culture of extended adolescence. Though we must grant hormonal activity its legitimate due in this reality, adolescence – as a cultural force – is not merely an age group. It is a heightened awareness of physicality and a subdued awareness of emotionality. It is, in effect, a culture of cerebral and emotional lethargy. The contemplative dimension of art demands exactly the opposite – the cerebral and emotional engagement, and interpretation of the manifest form in terms

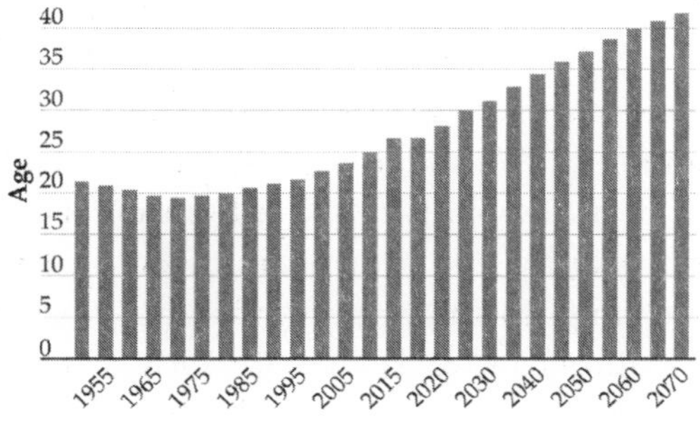

fig. 7.1: Median age of the Indian population: Historical and projected

of its formless source.

In the Indian context, the notion of "extended adolescence" is unnecessary for defining the culture. The demographics of the country make adolescence almost literally a here-and-now reality. India's median age is 27. Statistically, half of India's population is below 27. That is adolescent enough. Impelled primarily by biological forces, and aided by socio-economic realities, today's culture dominated by the 25-30 age group can only be inhospitable to abstraction as a significant presence in the arts.

India is a "young country", but not for long. The median age will be touching 30 by 2025 and 35 by 2045. Birth rates are falling; but death rates are slowing faster. Demographic trends point towards increasing life expectancies and the emergence of a "counter culture" or a "subculture" shaped by the "grey generation" (60+). This is a generation outside the realm of sexual activity and hospitable to abstraction as a significant presence in the arts.

I find it interesting that the pre-Independence high of median age around 22 comes down for about 30 years, before it rises and crosses 22 again in the year 2000, a time span of 53-55 years, conforming to the cyclicity indicated by the Kondratiev model and the generational perspectives of the modern Spanish thinker, José Ortega Gasset.

What appears to be a polarization of society in terms of generations – and implicitly aesthetic values – may well be the germ of a new cultural paradigm emerging from the nascent demography. India appears to be on the threshold of a radical change in the pattern of interaction between co-existing generations. I shall review the Ortega and Kondratiev propositions later in the paper. Both these are also discussed in greater detail in a later chapter.

The third issue is technological. The explosion of recording, storage and distribution technologies has isolated the musician from the audience in time and space. This isolation has played a major role in replacing the "process" of music with the "product".

Unlike the visual arts which are created in the absence of its audience, Hindustānī music is interactive and relies on the presence of its audience for shaping the musical endeavour. Hindustānī music requires the musician to simultaneously perform the roles of a composer and a performer in real time during a performance. It can therefore be said that Hindustānī music does not exist except in performance. Implicitly, it acquires an existence only in the presence of the audience, with the audience being a participant in the music-making process.

The "absence" of an audience affects the contemplative dimension of the endeavour more than the expressive and the communicative. In fact, this results in a hyper-activation of the expressive and communicative dimensions at the cost of the contemplative. As recordings became the primary vehicle for delivering music to its audiences, the contemplative inclinations and abilities of musicians tend to fall into disuse, even as audiences experience the growing sterility of music.

What was really happening to Hindustānī music in the latter

half of the twentieth century? The tradition – rooted as it was in the feudal-agrarian modes of presentation and in direct interface with audiences – was struggling to remain aesthetically relevant. In this process, it drifted away from the process (contemplative), and focused on the product (expression and communication). The result was interesting.

Hindustānī music lost young concert hall audiences in India, but was retaining the loyalty of the 60+ generation. Simultaneously, the art expanded speedily in the West. There is sufficient evidence to believe that Hindustānī music enthusiasts in the West tend to be, on an average, people of much higher intellect and academic accomplishment than average Indian audiences. Evidently, therefore, the "grey generation" in India and intellectual elites in the West were supporting the contemplative dimension of Hindustānī music, while young Indian audiences were dropping out. But, were they really demanding an abandonment of the contemplative dimension? This question may be tentatively answered later in this paper.

The question before the critic is: is the decay of abstraction/ contemplative process irreversible? The answer depends on whether we regard the cultural process as being linear or cyclical, or entirely open-ended with no pre-determined destination.

Cyclicity

In the last decade, we have seen indications that the contemplative dimension of Hindustānī music is resisting its inundation by adolescent values. The second post-Independence generation of musicians exhibits a considerable involvement with the contemplative dimension and a fresh – though sometimes baffling – approach to it, relatively unfettered by the influence of the pre-Independence generation in music.

A parallel movement has emerged with the aim of reviving the intimate concert *(baiṭhak)* format with small, knowledgeable audiences. This format is gathering momentum with the support of audiences cutting across generations and social class. A minor sub-culture is emerging which even shuns amplification. Simultaneously, it is also bringing young audiences back into the orbit of Hindustānī music.

This is probably to be expected, considering the historical perspectives of the Russian scientist, Nikolai Kondratiev and the Spanish thinker, José Ortega Gasset. This is a vast area. I shall deal with only briefly here, as a more detailed review appears in a later chapter.

Using economic, sociological, political and demographic data from 1790 to 1920, Kondratiev published (1925) a highly respected model of socio-economic cyclicity, which suggests a mega-cycle of 50-60 years in the lives of societies. The Kondratiev cycles consist of 25-30 years of economic expansion and as many years of economic contraction. The expansionary phase has been found to coincide with productivity enhancing technological developments. The comprehensiveness of the model obliges us to regard it as culturally significant.

As an observer of the culture environment, I am inclined to read Kondratiev's work along with Ortega's generational analysis of history and culture.

The Ortega perspective defines 30 years as constituting a "psychological/cultural generation". His theory implies that imperceptible changes are taking place in society constantly because of the interaction between various coexisting generations. Their cumulative effect becomes perceptible as a paradigm shift approximately every 60 years. In simple terms, all the environmental forces acting upon the values of the "grandfather generation" have either faded away or become impotent by the time the "grandchild generation" begins to interact with the world.

The Kondratiev and Ortega models of cyclicity, derived entirely by different logical processes, exhibit a striking similarity of cyclical durations and are therefore even more significant collectively.

The Paradigm Shift

If we regard Independence (1947) as the watershed in India's cultural history, the first post-Independence generation of musicians came on the scene in around 1977 and remained active till 2007 (30 years). It is during this period that Hindustānī music lost audiences in India and gained audiences in the West. It is with the arrival of the second post-Independence generation (born around 1977) and emerging on the stage around 2007, that the abstractionist/contemplative dimension of Hindustānī music appears to be making a come-back.

Music now appears to be making contemporary sense despite a massive churning – or perhaps emerging from it. Established genres of the pre-Independence era are exhibiting signs of aesthetic obsolescence. Their idiomatic boundaries look increasingly blurred. Discontinuities are evident, but continuities have not been jettisoned. At the core of this seeming chaos appears to be an attempt to rediscover the abstract foundations of this music in the *rāga* – the commanding form.

If my reading of the "straws in the wind" of Hindustānī music is valid, we could today be welcoming the dawn of the post-Independence renaissance in Hindustānī music.

8

Shaping a Life in Classical Music

THIS seminar is focused on the pedagogy concerns of the university system. The system represents a massive commitment of public funds. Those directly concerned with the social value of this commitment are best equipped to evolve the processes suited to its objectives. I have neither studied Hindustānī music in the university environment, nor taught in it. I can therefore contribute only tangentially to the theme of today's seminar.

Whatever I say is based on sixty years of research on a perfect sample of one – myself – and my interactions with some of the leading musicians of our times. As I see it, we are talking, essentially, about shaping lives in classical music. And, this will be the focus of my observations.

I have a mildly eccentric view on the serious engagement of individuals with classical music. Most of us in this room consider ourselves "trained musicians" or "trained musicologists". We also gladly admit that we are whatever we are because of our *guru*s/ teachers. In my view, this is a culturally conditioned notion, not entirely supported by the reality. I state this as an academic observation. And, I say this with the benefit of studying with some of the finest *guru*s and without the slightest disrespect to their contribution to my evolution. But, if I, or my *guru*s, try putting our fingers on what precisely was taught, when, and how, we are likely to come up with amusing answers which carry no conviction.

Thousands of people go through degrees in music or personalized *tālīm*, but never emerge as either musicians or

Paper presented at the Seminar on Pedagogy of Performing Arts, hosted by the Lalit Kala Kendra, Gurukul, Pune University, on 6-7 March 2018.

musicologists. It is also possible to prove that many who have devoted their lives to the pursuit of classical music in either role, and even excelled, had no degrees or *tālīm*. So, whether we are talking of the personalized system of art transmission, or of institutionalized teaching, or something entirely different, the key to excellence in classical music lies within the aspirant, far more than in the environment which may claim to shape his/her potential. In addition to their natural endowments of musicality, musicians and musicologists of any significance are born with an obsession with the mysteries of patterned sound, and pursue that obsession irrespective of economic and other consequences.

Allied to this is my view that a life in classical music may flower as a commitment to either performance or scholarship. From my own experience, I can say that when I was only pursuing performance, I was also acquiring a great wealth of musical thought. And, when I began to pursue musicology, the quality of my performance improved steadily and perceptibly. From this, I infer that the same person may pursue different routes simultaneously or at different stages in his life. The two are, indeed, distinct professions, because they are accountable to different audiences and constituencies. But, this does not make theory and performance distinct pedagogical issues – except at an advanced level and except in the department of communication skills. A life in music is a life in music.

This is so because our music is a process, and not a product. It has no existence independently of performance. Without a deep involvement with the process, you qualify neither for musicianship, nor for scholarship. Society changes. The aesthetic assumptions underlying performance change. The music changes. Theory gets rewritten. But, musical thought and performance remain perennially connected.

Having laid out my perspective on a life in music, I shall proceed more systematically to look at the shaping of musicianship, which I possibly understand better than scholarship. I shall deal with the following dimensions of musicianship and consider what each one might signify as a pedagogical issue:

1. The basic equipment of musicianship.
2. The communicative dimension of musicianship.
3. The expressive dimension of musicianship.
4. The meditative dimension of musicianship.

The Basic Equipment

An individual qualifies for a serious involvement in music by having an above-average endowment of two faculties:

1. *Pitch differentiation*: the ability to distinguish sounds as being either higher or lower than others.
2. *Pattern recognition*: the ability to identify sound patterns.

Pitch differentiation is, I suspect, largely a genetically ingrained faculty. An above-average score on this dimension is required for intense involvement with all categories of music. Classical music certainly demands more refined pitch differentiation abilities than other categories of music. I am not aware if research in neuro-acoustics now enables aspirants to improve their scores on this count. My suspicion, however, is that the possibilities for such enhancement would be limited.

Pattern recognition is an entirely different ability of the mind. The word "recognition" provides the clue to its character. We recognize patterns only by relating them to familiar patterns stored in the mind. Some basic patterns may be genetically embedded at birth – I don't know what science has to say about this. But, beyond this, our entire bank of stored patterns is acquired either involuntarily from the environment or by the purposive cultivation of the mind.

Classical music demands a more sophisticated ability of pattern recognition than other categories of music. A person's ability to perceive, store and recall patterns is largely a function of the intelligence and memory. These, too, are grey areas in psychology. There is, to my knowledge, no consensus on the degree to which these are genetically ingrained, or acquired, or to what extent these can be enhanced.

Of immediate concern to us are *rāga* and *tāla* patterns. This sounds easy and manageable. What is "easily" taught, however, is limited by the limitations of the teachers and aspirants. The great musician is known for having explored a canvas of patterns far beyond what can be taught by one *guru* or even multiple *guru*s or at a university. The idea of patterning is not finite. Any cluster of entities which cannot be considered random is a pattern. And, in mathematics, randomness itself is considered only a measure of man's ignorance. So, within what is considered random, many "patterns" may yet be discovered. And, of course, music also has use for obviously random "patterns". So, the pattern recognition/ creation issue is far more complicated than it seems.

Patterning belongs to the territory of "ideation" – abstract thinking – which maestros often develop through a study of abstract subjects like aesthetics, philosophy, psychology, mathematics, metaphysics and even occult sciences like astrology. The personalized mode of art transmission in Hindustānī music adopted the model of mystical apprenticeship, and is known to have encompassed such initiation. Should the pedagogy of institutional art transmission concern itself with this resource of extra-musical ideation? The proposition is worth considering.

The Communicative Dimension

The communicative dimension of classical music relates to the ability of a musician to execute and deliver musical ideas to his/ her listeners. This has two facets. The first is technical command over his instrument/voice. The second is a command over the architecture of the genre in which he/she performs. Casting the *rāga* (a formless form) into communicable form requires the agency of an established genre, each with its distinctive interaction between melody, rhythm and poetry (where relevant), and movements sequenced "logically" for cumulative absorption, retention and response. Ashok Ranade referred to this process as one of "ritualization".

This dimension of classical music is "mechanical" and structural, and possibly the easiest to teach – whether in the personalized model of art transmission or in the university system. It can be imparted through *riyāz* routines and even memorization.

A command over the communicative dimension is, of course, crucial because a musician experiences two kinds of anxiety in performance – execution anxiety and ideation anxiety. A mastery over the communicative dimension relieves the musician of the execution anxiety during performance and frees his musical energies for attending to the ideational content of the music. But, the communicative dimension – no matter how highly developed – has little musical value unless supported by the flowering of musicianship. This flowering relies predominantly on the remaining two dimensions – the expressive and the meditative.

The Expressive Dimension

The expressive dimension in music produces a manner of manifesting the character, quality of feelings, sentiments or intentions of the musician. Expression is primarily a manifestation of the musician's sense of selfhood and an awareness of himself as the generator of aesthetic value. It is this dimension which Ranade once described as "individuation".

As a pedagogical issue, this is perhaps the toughest challenge. How do you generate/inculcate/activate the sense of selfhood in a musician? *Guru*s in the personalized model perhaps did not see this as a significant issue at all. Enlightened present-day *guru*s have, however, often struggled with this issue for decades even with their most talented students.

Eminent *gurus*, with whom I have discussed this issue, have expressed two views. Some believe that such a flowering of the musical personality usually begins between the ages of 40 and 45. Others believe that a growing involvement in the *rāga*-ness results in the musician building a special relationship with *rāgas* and this relationship causes an "individuation" to surface in its rendition.

These two views could well be saying the same thing. Amercian composer, W.A. Mathieu, well-versed in Hindustānī music, articulates this memorably in his work *A Musical Life*. We often speak of a musical performance as a "piece". What is it a "piece" of? It is, indeed, a piece of life itself. Feeling and expressing a *rāga* in an individualistic manner could well require the musician to have started understanding life – a possibility that crystallizes only after 40.

Does this dimension of musicianship deserve pedagogical attention? Is there a way of speeding up the evolution of a musician's special relationship with the *rāga*-ness ahead of his/her emotional maturity as a person? Or is the whole dimension of expression to be left to the natural processes of personality development?

With a musician's involvement in *rāga*-ness being a factor, we are approaching the meditative/contemplative dimension of Hindustānī music.

The Meditative Dimension

The meditative dimension of Hindustānī music – the element of "ideation" – is fundamental because the Hindustānī musician combines in himself the role of the composer and performer, both roles working simultaneously during performance. Performance is nothing but the rendering/translating/interpreting the formless form of the *rāga* in communicable form. Being formless, the *rāga* is pregnant with a virtually infinite number of aesthetically coherent melodic ideas. This is why we need to recognize three levels of access to the *rāga* form.

1. *Gurumukhī Svarūpa*: This is the *rāga* form that a musician imbibes from his *guru*/*gurus*/teachers.
2. *Sarvamānya Svarūpa*: The consensual melodic personality of the *rāga*, as has been explored by all musicians whose music is available – an aggregate of all the melodic ideas hitherto explored – and which listeners recognize as belonging to a *rāga*.
3. *Virāṭa Svarūpa*: This represents all the melodic possibilities of the formless form of the *rāga* – including those yet remaining unexplored. This notion of *rāga-svarūpa* is limited only by the boundaries between the specific *rāga* and other *rāgas*.

Our tradition expects that every musician will aim at penetrating/transcending the *sarvamānya svarūpa* and access the *virāṭa svarūpa* for newer insights into the melodic and emotional possibilities latent in the *rāga*. But, how can he penetrate the *sarvmānya svarūpa* without having first mastered it?

This is a serious pedagogical issue for institutionalized education which, I suspect, remains, largely neglected. Even in my interactions with serious young musicians, I have found the greatest lethargy on this count. A *rāga* belongs to nobody. Every musician participates in its evolution. The musical culture has not been able to come to terms with the reality that a serious study of the tradition is a rent every generation has to pay in order to occupy a place in the tradition. It is clearly absurd to assume or believe that anyone can be an original interpreter of a *rāga* without having taken the trouble of absorbing every facet of it that has already been explored.

The Key to Excellence

This brings me to the argument I suggested in the earlier part of my observations. Hindustānī music cannot produce either a great musician or a significant musicologist without a vast exposure to performed/recorded music. No *guru*, no university, no books can cultivate his musical/critical abilities to a level of excellence without extensive and intensive listening. And, fortunately for today's aspirants, never before in history, has a 100 years of music been available for study, thus permitting a panoramic as well as encyclopaedic understanding of the tradition.

With such exposure, the aspiring musician/scholar has access to all the three dimensions of Hindustānī music – the communicative, the expressive and the meditative. He can absorb the insights according to his innate endowments of musicality. His insights can grow at a pace permitted by his intellect, memory and his exposure to the world beyond music. His individuality can grow as he evolves his "personal musical statement" with the help of all the inputs he has absorbed. There is a pedagogical perspective here.

Of particular pedagogical significance to aspiring performers as well as scholars are (to quote Ustad Ali Akbar Khan) the two processes of listening to learn, and learning to listen. These processes are only partially – though not always systematically – covered by the personalized system of art transmission in Hindustānī music. It seems important that the university system formalize and introduce these processes into its pedagogical philosophy. If we accept that Hindustānī music has no existence except in performance, it follows logically that the analysis of performance needs to form an integral part of formalized music education.

A summary look at the syllabi of the major universities in the US and Europe suggests that "listen to learn" and "learn to listen" is an important aspect of pursuing a life in music. Allied to these is the idea that aspirants must also acquire a comprehensive understanding of historical trends in performance. In the context of Hindustānī music, this is even more crucial because the tradition combines the role of the composer with that of the performer. Our methodologies for this process cannot be the same as those followed in Western classical music. They have to be invented afresh, and standardized across the network of institutions involved with music education.

But, this is possibly less important than my basic argument. A life in classical music is largely a self-driven journey. There is a space in it for mentors, inspirations and even guides. If one tries to define this space, it gets narrowed down to two processes: (1) the cultivation of the communicative dimension of music, and (2) the cultivation of the ability to learn from the study of performed music. There is, in this suggestion, a potential for the university system to achieve superior results, and possibly contribute elements of pedagogy that personalized apprenticeship has not consistently encompassed. To this extent, and with reference to the contemporary environment, the musical culture may be continuing to attach an unwarranted premium to the role of the *guru* (mentor).

If a great musician has spent a total of 10,000 hours receiving *tālīm* from his *guru,* he has almost certainly spent 20,000 hours of life listening to other musicians of stature. If a significant scholar of music has spent 5,000 hours pursuing degrees in music, I am certain that he has spent 10,000 hours studying works unrelated to the syllabus. And, those who match a yardstick of excellence in either department can be expected to have had intensive exposure to other department as much as their own pursuit.

Classical music is a philosophical art. Involvement with it arises from a thirst for unravelling a mysterious territory of human experience. It can be compared, in some ways, to spiritual pursuits with which the more evolved souls are born. Those born to this calling are known to have quenched their thirst, with or without any guidance.

9

Who Is a Maestro in Hindustānī Music?

I GREW up in an era generously populated with Hindustānī music maestros – both vocal and instrumental. Over the years, I sensed a marked shrinkage in the number of musicians I could place in this category. This might have been nothing but the onset of "aesthetic sclerosis". I might well have been applying an obsolete yardstick of musicianship, to which my juniors amongst musicians were not obliged to conform – after all, their music was addressing their generation and not mine!

However, the Hindustānī tradition expects a fundamental continuity in its musical environment, while permitting the peripherals to change over time. This expectation arises from the fact that the "operating system" of Hindustānī music – its total resource of *rāga*s, *tāla*s, genres and *bandiś*es – is fairly stable. The yardstick of musicianship can therefore safely be considered valid for a couple of generations.

This is why I often witness and get drawn into discussions about whether a certain contemporary maestro matches up to a certain departed maestro; or how many real maestros we have today in Hindustānī music, who they are, and what qualifies them for this stature? To discuss this issue intelligently, one must begin with defining a maestro. The issue often gets controversial because even a consensual grading mechanism – such as did exist till the first half of the last century – has faded away without an adequate replacement, and any musician now feels free to anoint himself a "Paṇḍit" or "Ustād".

It is not my purpose here to provide answers to these oft-debated issues. Instead, I intend to test a formulation I stated recently in one such discussion. The proposition was articulated rather casually, then with no purpose beyond delivering a quotable turn of phrase. The proposition is as follows: "A maestro is a musician who is able and willing to perform as long as the audience is willing to listen."

In retrospect, I felt this formulation requires to be tested against a more rigorous definition of a maestro. Hence, this inquiry.

Maestro, Ustād, Paṇḍit : The Definition

The Short Oxford English Dictionary (5th edn) defines a "Maestro" as: (1) An expert in music; a great musical composer, teacher, or conductor; (2) a great performer or leader in any art, profession, etc.

An Urdu word of comparable usage is "Ustād". The *Urdu-Hindi Shabdakosh,* published by UP Government Hindi Department, has the following entry against the word: A teacher of any art, clever/crafty. *The Nalanda Vishal Shabdasagar* (Hindi) defines "Ustād" as: Teacher (especially of courtesans), highly skilled, adept and knowledgeable.

The Hindi/Sanskrit word of similar usage is "Paṇḍit". The Nalanda dictionary defines a Paṇḍit as: Learned man, intellectual, competent, clever, a person with exceptional theoretical knowledge of his subject, a brāhmaṇa.

Collectively, these connotations would qualify an artist for the pinnacle of stature by virtue of:

a. exceptional theoretical knowledge,

b. exceptional capabilities as a composer,

c. exceptional performing competence,

d. tendency towards craftiness/manipulation, and

(e) noteworthy competence as a teacher.

The "brāhmaṇa" connotation of the word *paṇḍit* might seem irrelevant because of its casteist connotation. If contextually interpreted, however, it need not be so. In the original context of division of labour in society and resultant classifications, "Brāhmanism" is viewed as a way of life dedicated exclusively to the acquisition, preservation and dissemination of knowledge, irrespective of economic consequences. This is the context and meaning in which I propose to interpret the lexical intention. The "brāhmaṇa" idea may, therefore, suggest the highest level of sanctity to the relationship between the artist and his art, which values knowledge above all else.

Implications of the Formulation

"A maestro is a musician who is able and willing to perform as long as the audience is willing to listen."

Before I submit the formulation to scrutiny against lexically derived connotations, it helps to verbalize the assumptions and implications of this formulation.

AUDIENCE PROFILE

In this formulation, I have not either specified or qualified the "audience" with any adjectival or adverbial description. This omission obliges us to consider several scenarios. The music of a real maestro delights listeners at the intellectual level and at the emotional level.

The first scenario is that by the time he reaches such stature, a maestro has acquired a well defined "loyal" following. "His" audiences know what to expect from him and he delivers it to them, thus holding them "captive" at an intellectual as well as emotional level as long as he wishes to do so.

The second scenario is of an audience which has a "normal" distribution of highly discerning, moderately discerning and almost undiscerning audiences. In such a scenario, it is fair to assume that the appeal of a maestro's music is not dependent entirely on audience profiles and bypasses their variable levels of discernment. If the real test of music is the delivery of emotional meaning through the *rāga* experience, the relatively more discerning and the less discerning audiences could well be equally receptive to it. By this argument, a maestro can stimulate an insatiable thirst for his music, cutting across all levels of aesthetic discernment. Such a phenomenon can result in a concert which will end only when it will end.

The third scenario to consider is that of an audience which is almost totally uncultivated. In such a scenario, a maestro – if he wishes to win that audience – could avoid taxing them altogether and present music that is wholly undemanding.

CONCERT DURATION

I am more than suggesting that a maestro does not contract a concert of 90 or 120 minutes of music. His contract, as he sees it, is for sending home a group of people filled with joy.

Rarely, if ever, is a concert announced as being of indeterminate duration. This feature takes shape progressively during the concert, as the unstated "standard" duration is ignored by both, the musician and the audience by mutual consent.

The mutual consent inherent in this situation implies that a totally interactive and consultative relationship is established between the musician and the audience. Inevitably, this means that the musician receives requests for repertoire of the audience's choice, and is willing and able to satisfy them without the need to have planned it beforehand.

In this context, the most obvious qualification of a maestro is his extraordinary physical stamina. This implication is certainly obvious, but not the dominant consideration. The more important facet of indeterminate concert duration is a maestro's aesthetic stamina. By aesthetic stamina, I mean the ability to counter the aesthetic fatigue of audiences – listening to the same artist through six, or eight, or ten items, many of which would be of the same genre. Without the aesthetic stamina to sustain interest through a marathon, the musician cannot have audiences asking for more after each item.

These two aspects of a maestro concert define the single most important qualification of a musician so described. A maestro has authoritative command over a vast and diverse repertoire,and can deliver almost any part of that repertoire engagingly without advance planning or preparation. And, to be able do so engagingly over a long duration, possibly cutting across levels of audience discernment, a maestro needs also to command a variety of stylistic resources even within each genre.

THE MAESTRO PERSONALITY

It is obvious that a maestro is a musician of exceptional talent. It is also obvious that he is committed to almost super-human effort towards the perfection of his craft. What, however, does need to be emphasized is that a Hindustānī music maestro is obsessively in search of wider knowledge and skills in terms of repertoire and stylistic resources. In this search, he draws constantly upon external and internal resources. He has neither time, nor energy, nor fondness for any activity other than the cultivation of his musical personality. Even his ability to charm audiences is only a result of what he is, and not of what he attempts to do or does. A real maestro is a musician, nothing else.

Testing the Formulation

In the above implications and connotations of my formulation, I appear to have adequately conveyed the notions of expertise, composing brilliance and performing competence. The contextual "Brāhmanism" of the maestro is also adequately reflected. Three aspects of probable mismatch require to be reconsidered. The first is the relevance of audience profiles to the appeal of a maestro's music. The second is that of cleverness or craftiness. The third is that of competence as a *guru*/teacher.

With respect to audience profiles, we have considered three scenarios above. Under the third scenario – an audience which is almost totally uncultivated – the formulation being tested exposes its limitations. Faced with such a situation as described, a maestro cannot hold audience interest for long and cannot perform music worthy of a maestro. The possibility of such a situation may seem negligible. But, the music world is known to have placed the greatest of musicians in the most unenviable positions, with varying results.

The clever/crafty connotation hints towards a flaw of character. It may appear irrelevant here, but need not be summarily dismissed in the present context. There is an element of artifice in art which cannot be denied. Besides being contemplative and expressive, Hindustānī music is – like all music – also a communicative art, and involves the deployment of devices designed specifically to elicit certain qualities of response.

When a musical performance makes you cry, the musician is not actually unhappy. He has artfully communicated to you the idea of sorrow. In turn, you too are not unhappy when you cry in response to music. You cry in appreciation of the cleverness with which the musician communicates to you the idea of sorrow without actually being unhappy himself. Your experience of sorrow in this context is actually a pleasant experience because it has made you aware of your heightened emotionality. By the same logic, the communication of more unpleasant emotions such as violence, hatred and disgust can also deliver a pleasant experience – because of the artifice that lies in art.

Therefore, a maestro who can hold audiences in voluntary surrender over a concert of indeterminate duration must be accepted as "crafty" because he has a command over a massive range of musical devices appropriate for eliciting the desired emotional responses.

The *guru* connotation of a maestro/Ustād/Paṇḍit does not fall – whether explicitly or implicitly – within the scope of this formulation. The omission is substantive and represents an infirmity.

Obliquely, the *guru* connotation is related to the Brāhmanical value, which enjoins upon a maestro the additional role of knowledge acquirer, preserver and disseminator. In acknowledgement of this supposedly non-remunerative responsibility, Indian society has traditionally devised various ways to keep maestros materially comfortable. One such device is remunerating them for transmitting knowledge. However, quite independently of this, perpetuation of the tradition is seen as a part of a maestro's social responsibility. So, a maestro who does not teach – for whatever reason – falls short of the Brāhmanical tenet related to his profession.

Does a performing maestro with an insignificant presence as a teacher, then, weaken or forfeit maestro status? In Hindustānī music, the verdict of recent history is unclear. Yes, indeed, several maestros have groomed brilliant disciples. On the other hand, several acknowledged performing maestros have been reluctant or ineffective teachers. Several maestros who did not impart systematic personalized training became immensely influential models of music making through their recordings. And, history is replete with near-legendary teachers who never attained the performing competence, characteristic of maestros.

Despite this lack of clarity on the connection between the roles of a performer and teacher, every maestro insists that a serious musician must teach and that teaching is as beneficial to his own growth as a musician, as to his disciples, and to the tradition. How this happens would be beyond the scope of this essay. Suffice it here to observe that process of imparting knowledge and skills of music requires a maestro to force upon himself a clarity of musical thought, ideation and aesthetic intent, which he may otherwise practise only by rote, imitation or intuition. His teaching experience may therefore be considered contributory and germane to his excellence as a performing maestro.

In the contemporary scenario, performing excellence is rewarded by the music community, irrespective of what goes into the making of a musician. It may therefore be fair to presume that such excellence will generally be associated with a musician who has all the qualifications of an effective teacher, but may not actually be active as one.

In conclusion, the above formulation may be considered broadly defensible in the contemporary environment, though limited by its focus on performing excellence and partially by an extreme assumption relating to audience profiles.

10

The Critical Environment and the Musical Culture

THE invitation to participate in this seminar is an opportunity for conceptualizing what I have been doing for almost half of my working life and interpreting the environment in which I have worked. My familiarity with the critical environment is limited to Hindustānī music. Hence all my observations may be considered to pertain only to this tradition.

Over the last two decades, I have worked in all the media that service the discernment needs of connoisseurs and scholars of Hindustānī music – traditional periodicals and books, commercial media and also modern online media. Another half of my professional life has been spent as a media analyst and journalist. Now, I can tie up all the loose ends for my own benefit, while also sharing the experience.

Defining Musical Criticism

Encyclopaedia Britannica defines musical criticism as:

> Musical criticism is a branch of philosophical aesthetics concerned with making judgements about composition, or performance, or both. There is really no organized body of knowledge called "musical criticism". The entire history of musical criticism represents a struggle to emerge as a suitable tool for coming to terms with the art of music.

This paper was presented at a seminar on the theme: "The Absence of Critical Attention and Analysis" at the Indian Institute of Advanced Study, Shimla, 4-6 September 2017.

When any activity has to struggle to validate itself, it is obviously functioning in an environment which is ambivalent towards its usefulness. The uniqueness of music, as an art, is responsible for this ambivalence. This uniqueness is well understood and not necessary to enumerate here. The ambivalence of the music world towards music criticism will probably remain and so will music criticism as an activity, because society needs an independent assessment of any art.

The Function of Art Criticism

David Levi Strauss, an eminent art critic says:

> Art needs something outside of itself as a place of reflection, discernment, and connection with the larger world. ... If you want to engage, if you want discourse, you need criticism. ... Criticism involves making finer and finer distinctions amongst like things. If criticism is devalued, artists and curators have no other choice in the current crisis of relative values but to heed the market's siren song.

The critic assesses art by artistic yardsticks, and protects it from being buffeted by the forces of the market. To this extent, he also influences the market rating of individual artists and individual works of art. It is perfectly understandable, therefore, that a majority of artists should view criticism as a regulatory force. Without doubt, artists have always tolerated, rather than loved, art critics. David Levi Strauss, once again, describes this phenomenon succinctly:

> I used to think that the plight of criticism was to always be the lover, and never the beloved. Criticism needs the art object; but the object doesn't need criticism. Now, I agree with Baudelaire: "It is from the womb of art that criticism was born. Artists who disparage criticism are attacking their own progeny, and future."

Music criticism has remained relevant because it has taken a realistic view of the larger reality of art criticism along with the unique features of classical music (more appropriately described as "art music") as an artistic endeavour. This view is best expressed by Harold Schoenberg, who served the *New York Times* from 1960 to 1980, and was the first music critic ever to be awarded a Pulitzer Prize for journalism:

> I write for myself – not necessarily for readers, not for musicians. I'd be dead if I tried to please a particular audience. Criticism is only informed opinion. I write a piece that is personal reaction based on a lot of years of study, background, scholarship, and whatever intuition I have. It is not a critic's job to be right or wrong. It's his job to express an opinion in readable English.

The Critic and the Music World

Music criticism originated in the seventeenth and eighteenth centuries, along with the arrival of newspapers and periodicals. Interestingly, a journal named *Critica Musica* (founded by Johann Mattheson) devoted exclusively to classical music appeared as early as 1722.

With a history of almost three centuries behind him, the critical commentator on music is now accepted as an integral part of the music ecosystem. He can be seen as a part of the quality-control mechanism that is intended to support the maintenance and enhancement of the artistic standards of the music in circulation. In the performance of his function, he can legitimately hold the other major participants in the ecosystem accountable – the musicians, their intermediaries (e.g. impresarios/recording companies/TV channels, etc.) and their audiences/patrons. However, he is, in turn, accountable to them for performing his role with competence and fairness. He cannot also escape the critical evaluation of his own work by his peers in the profession.

In the contemporary environment, critical endeavours manifest themselves in a wide range of media activity ranging from simple concert reviews to serious musicological discourse, crossing into several allied disciplines such as cultural anthropology, neuro-acoustics, organology, linguistics and cognitive science.

Generators of Critical Output

Content of critical value (or critical intent, including critical pretence) can be generated by any/all of the following categories of persons:

a. newspaper reporters/editorial staff,
b. columnists – press/other media,
c. scholars of music/allied disciplines,
d. performing musicians – active/retired,
e. connoisseurs,
f. filmmakers, and
g. lay audiences.

Categories of Critical Endeavour

For the purposes of this paper, I am treating the music ecosystem as analogous to a "market" consisting of service providers (musicians), trade channels (impresarios and distribution channels for recorded music) and consumers (audiences).

I am inclined to view critical endeavour as being broadly of four kinds:

a. *Personality oriented*: In this category, I include all possibilities of coverage of individual musicians – from the strictly personal/biographical to astute stylistic analysis.
b. *Event oriented*: In this category, I include all categories of events such individual performances, individual recordings, specific events such as music festivals, or even seminars and conferences related to music.
c. *Trend oriented*: In this category, I include the analysis of

Table 10.1: Ecosystem/Orientation Grid

Musicians	*Intermediaries*	*Audiences*
Personality Oriented	Personality Oriented	Personality Oriented
Event Oriented	Event Oriented	Event Oriented
Treands Oriented	Treands Oriented	Treands Oriented
Ideas Oriented	Ideas Oriented	Ideas Oriented

all linear/cyclical trends, ranging from short term to long term.

d. *Ideas oriented*: In this category, I include endeavours which seek to validate, refine or redefine existing ideas, or explore new ideas pertaining to any part of the music ecosystem.

This classification of critical content can be understood better in a tabular form (Table 10.1).

In relation to the grid presented here, it is tempting to think of "critical" content as being predominantly "trend oriented" or "ideas oriented". But, this would be only moderately valid.

Personalities and events can equally effectively be submitted to critical evaluation as epicentres/protagonists/initiators/ representatives of trends and ideas. Any of these orientations can be the primary focus of critical assessment, with the others being secondary (Table 10.2).

Even with respect to categories of media, a simplistic

Table 10.2: Primary and Secondary Orientations

Personality	*Event*	*Trend*	*Ideas*
Event	Personality	Personality	Personality
Trend	Trend	Event	Event
Ideas	Ideas	Ideas	Ideas

pairing of content categories and media cannot be made. The traditional model was of academic journals being quarterlies or even annuals, special interest (connoisseurs) magazines being monthlies and event-oriented coverage being typical of dailies and weeklies. This pattern has become obsolete with the growth of online social media, which have made the periodicity of publication irrelevant to the nature of the content.

Material of considerable critical and analytical value is now available in the online media through non-text content – recorded seminars, lectures and interviews. The engaging potential of non-text content could, in the years to come, make the online media progressively more valuable to the serious scholar/critic, as the economics of publishing drive the print media out of niche market coverage.

Any category of critical content, focused on any of the segments of the classical music ecosystem, can now be encountered in any of the media. It is obvious, of course, that some media may be preferred for carrying certain categories of ecosystem focus and critical orientation. In a limited manner, I will consider this issue later in this paper.

The Volume and Quality of Critical Content

The above ecosystem/orientation grids were drawn to examine whether the Indian environment justified a degree of satisfaction with respect to critical endeavour in any of the segments identified.

It is possible, but not necessary, to survey each medium separately to establish the self-evident and well accepted position – that the critical landscape of Hindustānī music is barren. In this paper, therefore, I propose to present an overview of the musical culture which might begin to explain the barrenness of the landscape. My listing is not, by any means, exhaustive. It merely highlights the factors with which I have been confronted.

The Critic as a Service Provider

My professional training is that of an economist. Hence, I will look at the art music universe as a "market" or an "ecosystem". Just as the musician is a service provider, the critic may also be viewed as a service provider to other members of the ecosystem. He exists and functions only as effectively as other members of the ecosystem require and enable him to do. In short, the volume and quality of critical content generated will depend on the demand for it. Whether the demand for a critic's services is supported by remuneration, or not, is not germane to this argument. The demand needs to exist in order to create a supply – whether paid or honorary.

My view is that in the last fifty years, the demand for critical content within India has shrunk. The demand has shrunk because the demand for classical music itself has shrunk – in absolute terms and perhaps also as a percentage of the population. This connection is obvious because the demand for discernment is a subset of the demand for its enjoyment.

While this is true, a contrarian argument would be equally valid – that the providers of critical content failed the music community. The crucial distinction between classical music and other categories of music is that its enjoyment grows hand-in-hand with the knowledge of its aesthetic assumptions and of the process of music making. To this extent, the providers of critical and analytical commentary on the music ecosystem can be held answerable for the shrinkage of the market for music, along with (and in response to) the shrinkage and deterioration in the quality of critical output.

Whether viewed from the demand end or the supply end, the picture is uninspiring and suggests a serious infirmity in our musical culture.

Social and Economic Change

Hindustānī music, as we know it today, is a legacy of the feudal-agrarian society, patronized largely by the aristocracy. After Independence, recording technologies and public broadcasting shifted this music to the urban–industrial–commercial centres of India. Nehruvian India placed a high premium on technological and scientific activity. Post-Nehru liberalization unleashed a powerful commercialism into India's culture. As a result, the humanities and the arts have been progressively pushed into a small corner of the nation's agenda.

A neo-Marxian interpretation of this transition would also be in order. The technologies of income generation determine culture. The growing importance of manufacturing and commerce as the predominant sources of livelihood in urban India created a large bourgeois class. The emergence of this class substantially influenced society's relationship with music and, hence, also its musical tastes and preferences. The emerging India created a strong bias in favour of the enjoyment of music in preference to, and even to the exclusion of, discernment. The distinction between the demand for discernment and the demand for enjoyment of music is fundamental to my argument.

In a democratic society, it was also natural that public policy would be broadly populist, though not necessarily anti-culture. This is reflected in the steady fading away of public broadcasting as a purveyor of classical music and the gross neglect of publicly funded academic institutions engaged in imparting musical knowledge and skills.

The Failure of Public Broadcasting

The share of Hindustānī classical music in the total broadcasting time on the northern, western and eastern stations of AIR (All India Radio) has shrunk steadily over the last 50 years. A query under the RTI (Right to Information Act) , if honestly replied, would validate this statement. State support of the film industry (never too obvious to the general public) and the emergence of the gramophone record unleashed a massive amount of capital in support of the popular music industry. The medium wave (local) channels of All India Radio, which were the primary protection of classical music against the onslaught of popular (film) music, gradually forsook the protectorate.

No wilful neglect can be alleged as the forces of democracy were at play. We are witnessing merely the ignorance among our rulers of the social value of classical music, how it remains alive and how an involvement in art music is cultivated and sustained.

A familiarity with classical music is acquired through a largely involuntary and mysterious process involving involuntary exposure, imitation and intuition. Musically-sensitive people learn classical music merely by living in an environment of ample availability. This process is akin to learning a language. A familiarity, once acquired, can grow into connoisseurship, scholarship or musicianship.

The hardcore classical music audiences of today are predominantly above 60. They were cultivated largely by the ample availability of classical music on All India Radio in their childhood and youth. Based on my observation and exploratory research, I venture to suggest that Hindustānī music failed to involve perhaps an entire generation of urban Indians. Admittedly, several other forces are at play in this regard. But, public broadcasting cannot escape a substantial part of the responsibility.

AIR virtually abandoned the nursery which nurtured the classical music community and allowed Hindustānī art music – and indeed several other categories of Indian music – to be swamped by the tidal wave of popular music.

With specific reference to critical content, a far less pardonable neglect is visible in the academic system, which is explicitly paid for generating the demand as well as supply of critical material focused on Hindustānī classical music.

Failure of the Academic System

The academic system consists primarily of universities which grant degrees in classical music. The need for a comprehensive review of this system has been discussed at several seminars on music education. An important reality of this system – among several others – is that it does not recognize scholarship as an independent pursuit (independently of performance), except perhaps at the doctoral level.

Our universities employ a large number of scholars, from whom they can demand high quality of critical output to qualify for employment or promotion. These scholars guide a large number of doctoral aspirants, on whom demanding standards of scholarship are supposedly imposed for the grant of a degree. There is scant evidence to suggest that either of these mandates is being fulfilled.

Outside the universities, the Indian academic system consists of distance learning and examining bodies like the Gandharva Mahavidyalaya and the Prayag Sangeet Sabha. Their certifications are considered on par with those of Indian universities. The demand for their qualifications, though numerically large, appears focused on bachelor-parity certifications. These non-government institutions neither aim to groom scholars, nor appear to produce them in significant numbers.

It stands, however, to the credit of the academic system that its syllabus-based examination process has created a decent supply of textbooks which provide a panoramic view of the Hindustānī music tradition. These textbooks are published in several languages and make basic knowledge available to a large number of examination candidates. It is, of course, debatable, whether these textbooks would qualify as "critical" literature in the strictest sense of the term.

This large and qualified human resource associated with the universities as faculty and degree aspirants has a poor record of creating either the volume or the quality of scholarly output commensurate with the resources that society has invested in them.

When a serious researcher on Hindustānī music – whether Indian or foreign – starts looking for significant Indian material, he ends up relying largely on scholars who neither had qualifications in musicology, nor teaching jobs in academia to support their pursuit of musicology. Their specific names are not important; the pattern is well known and sufficiently eloquent.

The Size and Nature of the Classical Music Community

According to recording industry sources, Hindustānī classical music accounted for about 1 per cent of the total recorded music market about twenty years ago. It is obvious that only a small proportion of buyers of recordings would welcome access to critical content aiding their discernment of aesthetic values. On reasonable reckoning, we could well be looking at as little as 1 per cent of the recordings market. This is an indication of the considerations that drive the traditional print media, which relies on numbers for economic viability.

The viability issue is aggravated by the fact that this microscopic audience for critical content is now scattered all over the world and represents a diverse linguistic profile. Even within India, a special-interest magazine for Hindustānī music connoisseurs cannot be economically viable in Hindi or English. To appeal to a majority of its potential readers, it would need to be published in at least four languages – English, Hindi, Bengali and Marathi. The economics of such an enterprise can be absurd.

Similar constraints militate against the viability of book publishing for the classical music connoisseur or scholar. Book publishing, however, remains reasonably active in the field of musicology and is able to circumvent the limitations of scale through appropriate cost management and pricing strategies.

Commercial Pressures on the Periodicals Media

Historically, the major periodical publishing houses have played an important role in servicing the classical music ecosystem. These publishing houses once had a diversified portfolio of dailies, weeklies and monthlies in several languages. Over the last two decades, they have been subjected to several pressures which make the coverage of classical music unattractive and uneconomical. As a result, their presence in the music criticism space is drifting towards insignificance.

First, the periodicals publishing business is far more dependent on advertising revenue than subscription revenue. Classical music coverage itself does not either encourage subscriber loyalty or attract advertising revenue. Classical music competes for space against advertising, and non-cultural editorial content with broad-spectrum public appeal. Its appearance in the newspaper columns is either an act of compassion or subversion or, worse, a random occurrence.

Second, the dependence on advertising revenue makes publishers/editors vulnerable to pressures which can compromise the integrity of their coverage of the arts. Publishers and editors can easily take the view that they do not need such pressures just to service a microscopic reader segment, which also does not attract additional advertising revenue.

Till recently, a few diversified periodicals publishing houses – such as *Times of India*, *The Hindu*, *The Hindustan Times*, *The Ananda Bazar Patrika* and *The Deccan Herald* – whose owners have some commitment to culture, had retained a significant presence in the discerning coverage of classical music. Some had full-time Arts Editors of considerable scholarly credentials. However, diversified publishing houses are fewer and fewer, as weeklies and fortnightlies started winding up with television robbing them of their advertising support. These once-diversified publishers are increasingly dependent on their dailies for their profitability.

In their very nature, dailies are limited in terms of what kind of coverage they can meaningfully offer of the performing arts. Their ability to secure reader involvement is now seriously threatened by the online social media with their immediacy of coverage, along with the irrelevance of periodicity.

The Online/Social Media

The online/social media potentially offer solutions to most of the limitations of the traditional print media we have considered above. Their most important strength is that they have turned the traditional logic of the media upside down. In the traditional media, the message went looking for its audience. In the online space, it is the audience that is looking for the message.

Irrespective of the ecosystem focus and depth of coverage that a Hindustānī music critic/scholar offers, there will be somebody somewhere in the world looking for it. True to its potential, the Internet is now flooded with scores of platforms for access to information and knowledge on Hindustānī music. Almost all provide free access and are produced and edited through voluntary efforts. In this sense, the Internet permits any music enthusiast to engage with the music world in any manner he wishes and find a receptive audience.

The biggest casualty of this abundance is the professional critic, who was once paid by print media publishers to service the classical music community with competence and impartiality. The implications of this phenomenon are obvious. Online content is uploaded largely by people with the most to gain from its publication. In the online media, a perennial question mark hangs over the impartiality of the critic's function, the reliability of the information purveyed and the soundness of the assessment proffered.

The Consequences

Serious Indian musicologists are obliged to rely on the critical output of scholars groomed in the Western academic tradition. The Western tradition is to be respected for its academic rigour. But there is a worrisome implication to a total reliance on it for the study of Hindustānī music.

To paraphrase the eminent musicologist, Ashok Ranade, music supports three categories of literature – (1) writing "about" music, (2) writing "related to" music, and (3) writing "on" music. This third category demands "getting into" the music, before it can be critically tackled. It is, therefore, this third category, "writing on music" for which the Indian connoisseur/critic/scholar is uniquely qualified and the Western scholar singularly handicapped.

Hindustānī music is unlike Western music because it has no existence as music, except in performance. Hindustānī music is unique in being meditative, expressive and communicative at the same time. The concepts and methods of Western scholarship are not designed to handle the complex simultaneity of composition and performance. Western scholarship is also ill-equipped to interpret the dimension of "cultural meaning" that lies beyond musical meaning.

It is also significant that in the US/European tradition, musicology is treated as an independent branch of knowledge and academic pursuit. As a profession unto itself, it can set academic goals entirely unrelated to the dynamics of the performing tradition. By an excessive reliance on Western scholarship, the critical examination of issues in Hindustānī music risks a disconnect between itself and the performing tradition.

Critical endeavours in Hindustānī music need to account for the uniquely Indian relationship between the musician and his art, between the musician and his audiences, and between the aesthetic assumptions of the art and the larger traditions of Indian thought.

Academic traditions are not culture-neutral, nor are their research methodologies. Their yardsticks of excellence differ; consequently, their methods of evaluation also differ. To state this differently, a microscope is not the most useful observation device, when you need a telescope – or vice versa.

Critical output emerging in an environment dominated by Western scholarship may win academic laurels and acquire an international following amongst Hindustānī music enthusiasts. But, if Indian scholarship cannot establish a meaningful dialogue with the performing tradition, both the traditions will soon be heading for sterility.

11

The Idea of Rāga Grammar

The idea of grammar belongs to the discipline of linguistics. Musicological research is increasingly applying the analytical tools of linguistic analysis to the understanding of the melodic identities of *rāga*s. Admittedly, a perfect correspondence between the grammatical concepts of language and those of *rāga*s is not to be found. An attempt may, however, be made to test the value of traditional notions of linguistic grammar to *rāga* grammar as documented in the twentieth century. This is a tentative formulation, published in full awareness that it is conceptually obsolete, when considered against the present-day sophistication of linguistic analysis.

For several centuries, the Western idea of grammar was synonymous with the study of Greek and Latin. Their grammatical structures were considered the standard by which all other languages were judged. Only in the seventeenth century did the structure of English become a subject of serious study, leading to the maturation of linguistics in the nineteenth and twentieth centuries.

Interestingly, an influential nineteenth century grammarian, Samuel Kirkham, defined grammar as "the art of speaking and writing the English language with propriety". The key ideas in this definition are "art" and "propriety". Grammar was once seen as a system of aesthetically pleasing communication and as a component of social etiquette. The notion emphasized the expressive and communicative facets of a language – the two dimensions we also associate with music. Its structural aspects were either ignored or taken for granted.

Modern linguistics, however, looks at grammar very differently. First, grammar can signify the internal, and largely unconscious, system that we use to combine sounds into words, and words into larger meaningful units. Native speakers of any language learn this system intuitively as children without explicit training. A codification of this process explains how language is generated and hence is useful as a pedagogical device, and also a yardstick for the assessment of communicative efficiency.

The rules of grammar are, to an extent, similar to the laws of cause–effect in the natural sciences. The rules are hypotheses about the way a language works. They make assumptions/ predictions about consequent events, which can be tested. As in the natural sciences, any hypothesis that does not work has to be revised or rejected. Some rules are periodically revised and some are abandoned or replaced with others, because languages change. And grammarians, as custodians of the linguistic process, are vitally interested in tracking these changes.

Language and Grammar

For the following discussion on grammar and grammatical coordinates, I propose to follow the *Merriam Webster Dictionary.* For conceptual consistency, it is proper to preface this discussion with the Webster definition of "language".

DEFINITION OF LANGUAGE

As relevant to our context, Webster defines language as:

a. the words, their pronunciation and the methods of combining them used and understood by a community,
b. audible, articulate, meaningful sound as produced by the action of the vocal organs,
c. a systematic means of communicating ideas or feelings by the use of conventionalized signs, sounds, gestures or marks having understood meanings,

d. suggestions by objects, actions or conditions of associated ideas or feelings,
e. the means by which animals communicate,
f. a formal systems of signs and symbols including rules for the formation and transformation of admissible expressions, and
g. the vocabulary and phraseology belonging to an art or a department of knowledge.

THE DEFINITION OF GRAMMAR

In the present context, the *Merriam Webster Dictionary* defines "grammar" as follows:

1. (a) The study of the classes of words, their inflections, and their functions and rela+tions in a sentence.
   (b) A study of what is to be preferred and what avoided in inflection and syntax.
2. (a) The characteristic system of inflections and syntax of a language.
   (b) A system of rules that defines the grammatical structure of a language.
3. The principles or rules of an art, science or technique.

The primary focus of grammar is the "propriety" of a sentence. In the present context, the *Merriam Webster Dictionary* defines a sentence as follows:

> A word, clause, or phrase, or a group of clauses or phrases, forming a syntactic unit which expresses an assertion, a question, a command, a wish, an exclamation, or the performance of an action, that in writing usually begins with a capital letter and concludes with the appropriate end punctuation, and that in speaking, is distinguished by characteristic patterns of stress, pitch and pauses.

This definition provides the grammatical framework for the discussion of *rāga*-music as a language, and an individual *rāga* as a "linguistic" statement/sentence.

THE ESSENTIAL CHARACTER OF GRAMMAR

From this set of definitions, we derive the essential character of grammar:

1. Grammar is a set of rules governing spoken/written communication.
2. Grammar is descriptive as well as prescriptive.
3. Compliance with the rules anticipates a desired response.
4. The rules collectively constitute a yardstick of propriety.
5. Grammar treats the word as its basic unit of meaning and the sentence as the consummation of the meaning-delivery process.
6. Grammar codifies the harmonious arrangement of the linguistic elements (words, clauses, phrases).
7. Grammar codifies the role of punctuation in highlighting the grammatical function of elements.
8. The notion of grammar is applicable also to the arts and sciences.

An attempt is made, in this essay, to apply the principles of grammar to outline the attributes by which each *rāga* stands uniquely differentiated from all others and, therefore, becomes a carrier of unique meaning.

Grammar and the Rāga

The selection, sequencing, and treatment of *svara*s (relative to the tonic) constitute the definition of its melodic form. The broadest outline of the *rāga* form, but by no means insignificant, is provided by its *āroha–avaroha* (ascending and descending motions).

ĀROHA–AVAROHA

The *āroha* and *avaroha* of a *rāga* are a pair of ascending and descending strings of *svaras*, generally covering one octave, but sometimes up to one and a half octaves. The *āroha–avaroha* pair of *svara*-strings performs several grammatical functions.

They define the primary melodic region in which the *rāgas* melodic personality is most effectively expressed. In many cases, they may define a notional scale-base for the middle octave, which is different from *sā* (the tonic) in the middle octave. Some examples of this dichotomy are discussed in the next chapter. These prescriptions are often crucial for distinguishing these *rāgas* from their melodic neighbours.

These strings conform to the rules of exclusion and inclusion of *svaras* prescribed in ascending and descending melodic movements. Thus, they define the permitted pattern of phrasing. As a result of these patterns, *rāgas* acquire either smooth or zigzag phrasing patterns. Bilāskhānī Toḍī is an interesting example. In ascending motion, the *rāga* omits *mā* (4th) and *ni* (7th) degrees. In descending motion, the *rāga* omits the higher octave tonic (*sā*) and *pā* (5th). The application of these rules gives the *rāga* its zigzag phrasing pattern, which distinguishes it from Bhairavī, its closest melodic neighbour. This feature refers to the *chalan* (skeletal phraseology) aspect of *rāga* grammar discussed later in this chapter.

The *āroha–avaroha* pair becomes even more significant as an outline of the *rāga*'s melodic personality in the case of compound *rāgas*, formed by a purposive and systematic dovetailing two or more *rāgas*. There are three different conventions for the fusing of *rāgas* into compounds:

i. *Āroha* of one *rāga* dovetailed with the *avaroha* of another *rāga*,

ii. *pūrvāṅga* (lower tetrachord) of one *rāga* fused with the *uttarāṅga* (upper tetrachord) of the other *rāga*, and

iii. a compound *rāga* configured as a collage of alternating phrases from the two or more component *rāga*s.

Musicians have considerable freedom in deploying these dovetailing conventions. The process of blending two or more *rāga*s can even introduce into the compound some non-descript phrases, which belong to neither of the two components of the compound. Compound *rāga*s are discussed in greater detail in a later chapter.

Some authorities have even argued that documenting the grammar of compound *rāga*s is futile. Despite this reservation, many compound *rāga*s have been documented, though variously. In such situations, the *āroha–avaroha* of compound *rāga*s can be the primary statement of the creator's intent.

By treating the individual *svara* as a meaningful sound capable of being configured into a *rāga*-specific and more meaningful phrase, we have bypassed the notion of the "word" as the basic unit of meaning, as viewed by linguistics. This leap is defensible.

PHONEMES/ALPHABET CHARACTERS

Linguistics theory commences with the proposition that alphabet characters or their corresponding sounds are devoid of meaning and need to be configured into familiarly sequenced clusters (words) in order to express meaning. The sounds associated with the alphabets "A", "B" and "C" do not, for instance, deliver any meaning to the listener or reader. They require to be meaningfully sequenced in a word, such as "CAB", in order to become carriers of meaning. *Rāga* theory is at variance to this proposition.

In linguistics, a phoneme is defined as any abstract units of the phonetic system that correspond to a similar set of speech sounds, which are perceived to be a single distinctive sound (*Merriam Webster Dictionary*).

Superficially, this definition may appear to correspond to the definition of a *śruti/svara* in the theory of Indian classical music. The two are, however, not comparable. A *śruti* is a pitch (relative to the scale-base/tonic), differentiated as higher or lower than all others constituting the scale, while there is no such scalar/hierarchical perception available to a phoneme.

As the following discussion argues, *śruti*s/*svara*s are intrinsically rich in meaning and do not require to be combined with other sounds to form words to become pregnant with meaning – as in the case of the basic units of meaning in a language. The *śruti/svara* in Hindustānī music, in fact, fulfils the definition of a "word" as "a speech sound or a series of speech sounds that symbolizes and communicates a meaning without being divisible into smaller units capable of independent use" (*Merriam Webster Dictionary*).

ŚRUTI/SVARA AS INTRINSICALLY MEANINGFUL

Classical texts have defined *svara* as derived from *sva* = the self + *ra* = illumination. This derivation permits several interpretations:

a. A sound that is illuminated by its own light.

b. A sound through which the self shines forth.

c. An utterance which leads to enlightenment (self-illumination).

This etymology has two clear implications – a *śruti/svara* is meaningful without requiring the company of other *śruti*s/*svara*s, and that its meaningfulness arises from the relationship of the musician/listener with that particular sound, and not from any extraneous criterion of meaningfulness.

This proposition needs to be understood in overall context of the Indian musical tradition. Indian music, across all categories – classical, popular, folk, tribal, devotional, martial – is tonal, monophonic music. This is made amply clear by the very name of the tonic/scale-base: The scale-base/tonic called *sā* is an abbreviation for *ṣaḍja*, which means "the carrier or repository of six". "Six" here refers to the remaining basic *svara*s of the scale, which, according to this nomenclature, acquire their meaning only in relation to the scale-base.

The Indian musical culture is so deeply rooted in tonality that it is impossible for the Indian mind to perceive any sound – musical or otherwise – without reference to a scale-base, irrespective of whether it is explicitly present in the environment or not. At a slightly esoteric level, one can argue that each individual – not just a musician – has a "reference pitch" embedded in his neuro-acoustic apparatus, to which he relates all sounds for access to their meaning. We may speculate that this "reference pitch" may either be genetically programmed or culturally acquired, or perhaps conditioned by the habitual intonations of an individual as manifested in the spoken word.

This speculation finds some support in the fact that, in the Hindustānī tradition, the musician is totally free to adopt a scale-base of his choice for his musical endeavours. His choice does not have to conform to any acoustic measure or yardstick and is, thus, entirely subjective. It represents – in a very real sense – the frequency with reference to which his "self shines forth". In a metaphysical sense, it is the frequency at which his being establishes a meaningful relationship with the unheard sound of the planets in their heavenly orbits.

It may thus be argued that every *śruti*/*svara* in Hindustānī music is rich in personal meaning, melodic meaning and philosophical/mystical meaning. In addition to these dimensions of meaning, classical literature has built an elaborate system of imagery around each *svara*, which imparts a degree of sanctity to the *svara*s of the scale.

In classical literature, each of the *svara*s is found to have been assigned "compatible/comparable" bird or animal sounds, social castes, emotional ideas, presiding deities and patron saints. They have even been attributed a complexion, locations in the human body, zodiac signs and constellations. This complex framework of imagery – inexplicable to the modern mind – places each *svara* in the totality of the culture, thereby highlighting its autonomous status as a repository/ communicator of meaning. In *rāga* music, therefore, meaning begins with the *svara*. The *śruti/svara* is the grammatical idea in Hindustānī music corresponding to the "word" in linguistics.

We have argued that "meaning" in a *rāga* is intrinsic to the *svara*. By implication, each *svara* contributes to the meaning-delivery process of the sentence/statement, i.e. the *rāga*. This contribution is partly made through the grammatical notion of "inflections".

INFLECTIONS

Inflections in grammar are defined as:

1. The act or result of curving or bending.
2. The change in the pitch or loudness of voice.
3. The change of form that words undergo to mark such distinctions as those of case, gender, number, tense, person, mood or voice.
4. A form, suffix, of involved in such variations.
5. A change in curvature of an arc or curve from concave to convex or conversely (*Merriam Webster Dictionary*).

The linguistic notion of "inflection" will cover most of the prescriptions of *rāga* grammar pertaining to the "treatment" of *svara*s.

a. Some *rāga*s utilize suppressed or enhanced frequencies (*śruti*s) of one or more of the tweleve standard *svara*s of the scale.
b. In many *rāgas*, *svara*s are prescribed either abbreviated or elongated intonation. This refers to the *alpatva–bahutva*

prescription discussed later in the book.

c. In many *rāgas*, specific *svaras* are prescribed for fractional intonation, thus imposing the function of a suffix. The position of *re* and *dh* in Bihāg conforms to this requirement.

d. Some *rāgas* acquire their uniqueness by some *svaras* exhibiting a near-imperceptible/subliminal presence in a *rāga*.

e. In many *rāgas*, *svaras* are prescribed for oscillated treatment. An example would be the treatment of *gā* and *dh* in Rāga Darbārī.

f. Some *rāgas* express their melodic uniqueness by being approached in a continuous melodic flow from another *svaras*, defining a curvilinear path (*mīṇḍ*).

g. Some *rāgas* are characterized by phrases involving jerky melodic contours (*murkī* and *khaṭkā*).

h. Some *rāgas* are prescribed for predominantly staccato treatment of *svaras*, and the shaping of stark/bold melodic contours.

These dimensions of treatment are as important in determining the uniqueness of a *rāga*'s melodic personality as are the selection and sequencing of *svaras*. These prescribed/characteristic inflections are intimately related to the other grammatical elements in the *rāga* as a complete meaning-delivery system.

A crucial role in the meaning-delivery system of a *rāga* is played by two *svaras* (words) described in modern *rāga* grammar as *vādī* and *saṁvādī*.

Vādī Svara as the Verb

A verb is defined as:

> A word that characteristically is the grammatical centre of a predicate and expresses an act, occurrence, or mode

> of being, that in various languages is inflected agreement with the subject, for tense, for voice, for mood, or for aspect, and that typically has rather full descriptive meaning and characterizing quality, but is sometimes nearly devoid of these especially when used as an auxiliary or a linking verb.
>
> – *Merriam Webster Dictionary*

This definition of a verb comes closer to describing the concept of *aṁśa svara* found in classical literature and discussed later in the book. Its modern variant is the *vādī svara* in *rāga* grammar.

The *vādī svara* in *rāga* conforms to the verb in its centrality to expressing the "mode of being" suggested by the *rāga* and is hence frequently subjected to characteristic "inflections" in order to express its "full descriptive meaning and characterizing quality".

Admittedly, the *vādī* in *rāga* grammar does not represent the active element of the statement in the same sense that it does in a spoken/written language. However, the *vādī* is called the *prāṇa svara* (the melodic soul) of the *rāga* and is often the sole discriminator of a *rāga* from its melodic neighbours or twins. In any case, the *vādī* is the predominant focal point of melodic activity in a *rāga*. To this extent, its dominance of the *rāga* is comparable to that of the verb in the grammar of a language.

SAṀVĀDĪ SVARA AS AN ADVERB

In modern *rāga* grammar, the *saṁvādī svara* is prescribed as having a special/complementary relationship with the *vādī svara*. Some authorities also insist that the two pivotal *svara*s need to be in 1st - 5th (or 1st - 4th) acoustic correspondence with each other. Though this requirement of consonance is not uniformly fulfilled, it remains a grammatical ideal in the prescribed hierarchy of *svara*s (words). Because of this prescription, the grammatical function of the *saṁvādī svara* may be considered analogous to an "adverb" in linguistic grammar.

An "adverb" is defined as:

> A word belonging to one of the major form classes in any of numerous languages, typically serving as a modifier of a verb, an adjective, another adverb, a preposition, a phrase, a clause or a sentence, expressing some relation to the manner or quality, place, time, degree, number, cause, opposition, affirmation or denial, and in English also serving to connect, and to express comment on clause content.
>
> – Merriam Webster Dictionary

The *saṁvādī svara* qualifies for such consideration because

1. it modifies/qualifies/supplements the communicative intent of the *vādī*/verb,
2. it expresses some relation to the manner and quality of the *vādī*, and
3. it connects or expresses comment on the content of the statement/sentence, i.e. the *rāga*.

ANUVĀDĪ SVARAS

Modern *rāga* grammar defines all *svara*s other than the *vādī* and *saṁvādī* as *anuvādī svara*s. The word *anuvādī* derives from the Sanskrit *anuvāda* = translation or interpretation. This etymology would support the view that the grammatical function of the remaining *svara*s is that of interpreting or translating the meaning of the dominant/pivotal *svara*s, the *vādī* and the *saṁvādī*. This process takes place through the practice of phrasing.

To the extent that *rāga*s can be considered to be "partially composed melodies", we are obliged to consider word-clusters that populate the *rāga*. The word "phrase" is commonly – and perhaps justifiably – used to describe clusters of *svara*s characteristic of a *rāga*.

Melodic Phrasing and Rāga Grammar

A "phrase" is defined as:

> (a) A group of two or more words that expresses a single idea, but do not usually form a complete sentence, (b) a brief

> expression that is commonly used, (c) a short musical thought typically two to four measures long, closing with a cadence, (d) a word or group of words forming a syntactic constituent with a single grammatical function.
>
> – *Merriam Webster Dictionary*

The linguistic definition of "clauses" does not find a corresponding notion in *rāga* music. Considering the suitability of "phrase" for describing *svara*-clusters in a *rāga*, the distinction between a phrase and a clause need not be pursued here.

There exists – in documented *rāga* grammar as well as in the pedagogical tradition – the notion of a "skeletal phraseology", called *chalan*, for each *rāga*. The constituent phrases of a *chalan* are, indeed, brief expressions, comprising usually a minimum of three intonations (but sometimes even just two), in appropriate sequence. In conjunction with the appropriate punctuation (pauses), they can suggest a cadence.

The crucial grammatical function of the *chalan* phrases is to identify the permissible opening and terminal points for phrasing. Conceptually, this function corresponds to the notions of *graha*, *nyāsa* and *apanyāsa svaras* encountered in classical literature, but, neglected in current grammatical discourse which treats the hierarchy of *svaras* as being of prime significance.

The *chalan* is a group of generally seven to eight phrases, together covering at least one complete octave. In some *rāgas*, their number can be as small as four or five. Just as *rāga* grammar functions within a hierarchy of *svaras* (words), the multiplicity of phrases in a *chalan* may also be viewed as constituting a hierarchy. In this context, the hierarchical notion of "clauses" in linguistic grammar can be considered relevant.

Pakaḍ and the Hierarchy of Phrases

The hierarchy of clauses in linguistic grammar provides for a primary and subordinate clauses. Similarly one of the *chalan* phrases, called the *pakaḍ* (catch phrase), is assigned the status of a "primary phrase" because it constitutes the unique signature of the *rāga*. The *pakaḍ* phrase will, in almost all cases, include or terminate on the *vādī svara* of the *rāga*. The *pakaḍ* phrase distinguishes a *rāga* from its melodic neighbours or near-identical twins, and identifies it beyond reasonable doubt.

Other than the *pakaḍ*, all other phrases in the *chalan* may be considered "subordinate" or "dependent" phrases, because they only assist/supplement the *pakaḍ* in outlining the melodic form.

The *pakaḍ*, along with other phrases lower in the hierarchy, performs another important grammatical function. This function refers to the *aṅga prādhānya* dimension of *rāga* grammar.

Aṅga Prādhānya

Each *rāga* is characterized by the relative emphasis on a different limb (*aṅga*) of the melodic canvas, normally treated as being of two octaves. The lower half is called the *pūrvāṅga* while the upper half is called *uttarāṅga*. *Rāga*s are classified as either *pūrvāṅga-pradhān* (biased towards the lower half) or *uttarāṅga-pradhān* (biased towards the upper half).

Some *rāga*s centred categorically in the mid-octave region of the middle octave are described as *madhyāṅga-pradhān* (focused on the middle of the melodic canvas). And it is, indeed, the inclination of some scholars to view the octave as consisting of three overlapping tetrachords, rather than two discrete tetrachords. This idea is explored in a later chapter.

*Pūrvāṅga-pradhān rāga*s will tend to have their *vādī svara* as well as its *pakaḍ* phrase located in the lower half. The remaining phrases of the *chalan* may also tend to exhibit a concentration in the relevant region. Likewise, *uttarāṅga-pradhān* and *madhyāṅga-pradhān rāga*s will exhibit a similar bias in their respective regions of the melodic canvas.

Because of its multi-dimensional coverage of features unique to a *rāga*, some influential segments of the music establishment regard the *pakaḍ* and *chalan* phrases as a more useful guide to composition, performance and pedagogy than the hierarchy of *svaras* (words).

The notions that integrate all these grammatical functions into a completeness of communicative intent are syntax and punctuation.

Syntax and Punctuation

Syntax is defined as:

> (a) The way in which linguistic elements such as words are put together to form constituents such as clauses or phrases, (b) a connected orderly system; the harmonious arrangement of parts or elements, (c) the formal properties of a language.
>
> – *Merriam Webster Dictionary*

Punctuation is defined as:

> (a) The act or practice of inserting standardized marks or signs in written matter to clarify the meaning and to separate structural units, (b) something that contrasts or accentuates.
>
> – *Merriam Webster Dictionary*

The syntax of a *rāga* has to be viewed at two levels.

First, the overall syntactical framework provided by the *āroha–avaroha,* which defines which *svara* can be permitted to succeed any particular *svara* in ascending and descending motions.

Second, and partially guided by the first, there is an internal syntax of each phrase which may feature either only ascending motion, only descending motion, or a combination of ascending and descending motions.

Punctuation, likewise, requires attention in two respects. First, the pauses required between phrases to allow them to be received as distinct grammatical entities. Second, the internal punctuations within each phrase implicit in the prescribed inflections (treatment) of each *svara* included.

Issues of syntax and punctuation become doubly significant and complex in the case of compound *rāga*s, wherein two or more *rāga*s may be configured by different musicians in different ways, using different conventions for dovetailing the component *rāga*s.

In essence, then, the *rāga*-specific uniqueness of each phrase, as perceptibly distanced from others, gives the musician the freedom to configure the *rāga* (the sentence) in a variety of ways.

In strictly grammatical terms, and as the basis for identification, therefore, it is reasonable to view the *rāga* as "partially composed melody" or a "melodic matrix".

12

Rāga Clusters in Hindustānī Music

I HAVE chosen to share with you my understanding of *rāga* clusters, formed by *rāga* transformations and compound *rāga*s, as practised in Hindustānī music. I chose this subject on the advice of knowledgeable friends in Chennai. They thought this phenomenon was largely unfamiliar to those cultivated in the Carnatic tradition. As audiences in the south get progressively exposed to Hindustānī music, a discussion could aid a better appreciation.

The Perspective

As a melodic entity, a *rāga* is a set of rules governing the (a) selection, (b) sequencing, and (c) treatment of *svara*s.

This definition has two perspectives – one is the scale (selection of *svara*s) and the other is the melodic personality (sequencing and treatment). The scale is the skeleton of a *rāga,* while the sequencing and treatment are the flesh and blood. The melodic personality subsumes the scale and is therefore a larger perspective and closer to the notion of *rasa,* which is fundamental to *rāga*-based music.

Hindustānī music devotes a lot of attention to the melodic personality as a guide to the performing tradition. Based on this focus, it classifies a large number of *rāga*s into clusters which share the same melodic personality. In Hindustānī music, these clusters have been variously called *rāgā aṅga rāga*s or *rāga prakār*s.

Lecture demonstration at The Music Academy, Madras, 18 December 2011.

I shall avoid using the term *ragāṅga rāgas* because of the possibility of stepping into the medieval classification of *rāgas* into *ragāṅga, bhāṣāṅga* and *kriyāṅga rāgas*, which I do not understand.

I am also avoiding the colloquial notion of *rāga* families; and for a good reason. There exists an ancient classification of *rāgas* into

1. six primary *rāgas*,
2. thirty *rāginīs*/wives,
3. *napuṅsaka rāgas*,
4. *putra rāgas* / sons, and
5. *putra-vadhu rāgas*/daughters-in-law.

This is an area I have not studied and do not understand. I will therefore continue with the caveat that there is no reference here to this ancient classification either.

I shall stick to the nomenclature of *rāga* clusters. In music theory, I am relying on a concept that is primarily twentieth century (post-Bhatkhande) and using a term (cluster) derived from modern social sciences research, which suggests a synchronicity and commonality without necessarily implying any causality between members.

How the Clusters Are Conceived

Clusters are formed around the major/popular melodic personalities encountered in Hindustānī *rāgas* – treated as the "reference/base" *rāgas*. All *rāgas* do not necessarily belong to particular clusters. But, many do.

Examples of base/reference *ragas* which serve as the nucleus for *rāga* clusters are:

1. Bhairav (reference *rāga*: Bhairav),
2. Bilāwal (reference *rāga*: Bilāwal),

3. Toḍī (reference *rāga*: Miyā kī Toḍī),
4. Sāraṅg (reference *rāga*: Vṛndāvanī Sāraṅg (?),
5. Kānaḍā (reference *rāga*: Darbārī Kānaḍā),
6. Malhār (reference *rāga*: Miyā kī Malhār),
7. Bahār (reference *rāga*: Bahār), and
8. Kauṅs (reference *rāga*: Mālkauṅs).

[*Note*: This list is not exhaustive, as several other reference *rāgas* / *rāga* clusters have been proposed by different musicians / scholars.]

Membership of the *rāga* clusters is defined broadly by two types of transformations with the reference *rāga* as the focal point.

a. A change in the scale or phrasing in the reference *rāga*, which is so minor that, although it creates a different *rāga*, it does so without permitting the shadow *(chhāyā)* of another major *rāga* from falling upon the transformation. I have chosen to call this category a "*rāga* transformation".

   Historically, these transformations need not necessarily have been derived from the "reference *rāga*". But, it is possible that many of them are derived. Śahānā Kānaḍā of the Kānaḍā cluster (bearing no similarity to the Carnatic *rāga*, Śahānā), for instance, probably precedes the emergence of Darbārī Kānaḍā. Ahīr Bhairav of the Bhairav cluster is, however, considered a derivation from Bhairav.

b. A purposive and deliberate combination of two or more *rāgas*, in which both/all the component *rāgas* are visibly present, but one of them dominates the totality of the musical experience. Although this process of combining *rāgas* can take several forms, they can be clubbed together in the category of "compound *rāgas*". In modern musicological literature, they are also occasionally referred to as *saṅkirṇa rāgas*.

The Logic

Why is it important to practise a notion of *rāga* clusters based on the melodic personality?

The aesthetic purpose of *rāga* transformations and compound *rāgas* is to establish or create relatively unfamiliar melodic entities within, or from, relatively familiar melodic material. In these transformations/compound *rāgas*, the familiar boundaries of the reference *rāga* are "breached". But, the resultant melodic entity does not lose its anchoring in the melodic personality governing the *rāga* cluster.

To achieve this result, the scale is clearly insufficient because in Hindustānī music, the same scale can deliver a multiplicity of *rāgas*, each governed by a different melodic personality.

Many instances of this phenomenon can be cited. I will limit my observations to just two. Take for instance, the scale of Rāga Madhyamavatī in Carnatic music. The same scale delivers two *rāgas* in Hindustānī music – one is Rāga Megh, performed as a member of the Malhār cluster, and the other is Madhyamādi Sāraṅg, performed as a member of the Sāraṅg cluster. Consider another example – the Bhūp (Mohanam in Carnatic) scale of Hindustānī music delivers three different Hindustānī *rāgas* – Bhūp/Bhūpālī, Deśkār and Jait. The scale is identical, but the sequencing and treatment of *svaras* is distinct.

The second issue is the importance of improvisation in the totality of the music-making process. I am not competent to compare this facet of Hindustānī music with Carnatic music. Within Hindustānī music, however, the post-*dhrupad* era has seen Hindustānī music progressively become a highly individualistic, improvisation-dominant art. It has steadily shrunk the role of the pre-composed element and progressively enlarged the role of the musician as a composer. As it has expanded the role of improvisatory process, musicians – and their audiences – have sought a more categorical anchoring in the melodic personality within which the *rāga* functions. Originality and creativity have flowered because of the ability of the musical experience to remain anchored in the familiar.

The Essence of the Cluster Phenomenon

Rāga transformations and compound *rāga*s both constitute deviations from the established grammar of the reference *rāga* considered in isolation. In effect, they enable the musician to enlarge his role as a composer beyond the boundaries of familiar *rāga* grammar. Although the deviations do follow certain conventions, all musicians may not interpret the conventions in an identical manner. To this, extent, within limits, the musician actually writes the grammar of these melodic entities. As a result, *rāga* variants, bearing the same name, may differ in their detailing of the transformed/compound melodic entity.

Broadly, however, certain statements can be made on this subject:

a. *Rāga transformations* do, by and large, exhibit a standardized *rāga* grammar. For instance the Rāga Śahānā Kānaḍā is performed as a variant of Rāga Darbārī Kānaḍā, the reference *rāga* of the Kānaḍā cluster. To my knowledge, Śahānā Kānaḍā is encountered in three variants, each very close to the other. All the variants identify themselves as Śahānā Kānaḍā instantly.

b. *Compound rāga*s can often exhibit what looks like "non-standard" *rāga* grammar because *rāga*s can be dovetailed/combined in a variety of ways. Even within the same dovetailing convention, the same compound *rāga* performed by one musician may sound slightly different from the same *rāga* performed by another musician. For instance, the Rāga Kauṅsī Kānaḍā (a combination of Mālkauṅs/Hindolam and Darbārī Kānaḍā) sung by different musicians may sound marginally different, depending on the musicians' interpretation of the combination. And, yet, the compound will identify itself instantly as Kauṅsī Kānaḍā, and as a member of the Kānaḍā cluster.

It would be incorrect to see this phenomenon in Hindustānī music as a region of grammatical laxity. Its logic is well documented in the scholarly tradition and the major variants of each cluster are documented in terms of rāga grammar. But, a musician is not entirely bound by the documented versions. The critical viewpoint subjects the performance of these *rāga*s to a different yardstick of validation – the emphasis here is on aesthetic coherence, handling of the deviations from the reference *rāga* (in the case of *rāga* transformations), the dovetailing of the component *rāga*s (in the case of compound *rāga*s) and the element of novelty/surprise.

Patterns in Rāga Transformations

1. The dominant and identifying melodic features of the base/reference *rāga* are kept intact.
2. With no change in scale, only some *svara saṅgati*s or phrasing patterns may be changed.
3. Or: Some *svara*s may be altered from *śuddha* to *komal/tīvra* or the other way around.
4. Or: Some *svara*s of the reference/base *rāga* may be omitted in the ascent or descent or both.

TRANSFORMATION

Example 1

Rāga Khem Kalyāṇ belongs to the Kalyāṇ cluster.

Reference rāga: Yaman Kalyāṇ.

Features: The scale is identical to Yaman Kalyāṇ. But *re, mā* and *dh* are omitted in the *āroha* and (*tīvra*) *mā* is used subliminally in the *avaroha*.

Demo: Yaman Kalyāṇ by Shujaat Khan; Khem Kalyāṇ by Purnima Sen.

Example 2

Rāga Śukla Bilāval belongs to the Bilāval cluster.

Reference rāga: Bilāval.

Features: One signatory phrase (SGRGM) is added to Bilāval to create Śukla Bilāval.

Demo: Bilāval: Abdul Kareem Khan; Śukla Bilawal by Kalyāṇ Mukherjea.

Example 3

Rāga Gauḍ Malhār belongs to the Malhār cluster.

Reference rāga: Miyā kī Malhār.

Features: (the most common version) *Komal gā* of Miyā kī Malhār is replaced with Śuddha *gā*.

Demo: Miyā kī Malhār by Ameer Khan; Gauḍ Malhār by Vilayat Khan.

Conventions for Forging Compound Rāgas

The forging of *rāga*s into compounds follows two classical conventions:

1. *Rāga*s are classified as either *āroha pradhān* (ascent dominant) or *avaroha pradhān* (descent dominant). The compound is forged by dovetailing the *āroha* of the *āroha pradhān rāga* with the *avaroha* of the *avaroha pradhān rāga.*
2. *Rāga*s are also alternatively classified as *pūrvāṅga pradhān* (centred in the lower tetrachord) or *uttarāṅga pradhān* (centred in the upper tetrachord). A compound can be forged by fusing the *pūrvāṅga* of a *pūrvāṅga pradhān rāga* with the *uttarāṅga* of an *uttarāṅga pradhān rāga*. *Uttarāṅga*

pradhān rāgas are (as Bhatkhande observes) also frequently *avaroha pradhān rāgas*. Therefore, the dovetailing may not always seem clinically rigorous.

In a compound *rāga*, there is no distinction between "native" and "alien" melodic features. Both are explicitly present in a predetermined relationship, though one of the components tends to dominate the musical experience. The conventions for forging compounds work efficiently under most conditions. However, in extraordinary conditions, Hindustānī music resorts to the third category of binding/dovetailing.

Extraordinary Conditions

What does a musician do if he wishes to fuse one *āraoha pradhān rāga* with another *āroha pradhān rāga*? Or, one *uttarāṅga pradhān rāga* with another *uttarāṅga pradhān rāga*? And, what will he do if he wishes to blend more than two *rāgas*? The classical conventions for fusing *rāgas* will not work.

In recent history, musicians have attempted to perform fusions of up to ten *rāgas*. Pandit Omkarnath Thakur, for instance, frequently sang Rāga Paṭmañjarī, a combination of five *rāgas*. Kesarbai Kerkar often sang Rāga Khaṭ (Ṣaṭh), which is a combination of six *rāgas*. The Gwalior tradition has documented a Rāga Sāgar, which is a combination of ten *rāgas*. One may question the aesthetic purpose of fusing more than three *rāgas*. But, this has been attempted, and its melodic logic can be deciphered.

In such *rāgas*, typical individual phrases from the component (primary) *rāgas* are fused together in alternating sequence in order to forge a novel melodic entity. As a result, in every melodic line (or at least in the entirety of the composition), you would experience the features of three or more different *rāgas* in interesting juxtaposition.

As may be expected, such multiple *rāga* combinations belong to a territory beyond grammar as applied to a single *rāga* or even to compounds of two *rāga*s. Their "grammar" lies in their ability to distinctly express the different melodic identities they incorporate, the coherence of the resulting melodic entity and the handling of the transitions between the different *rāga*s as it takes place in the fused melodic entity.

COMPOUND RĀGA

Example 1

Rāga Basant Bahār belongs to the Bahār cluster.

Reference rāga: Bahār.

Features: Bahār in *āroha* and Basant in *avaroha.*

Demo: Hirabai Barodekar.

Example 2

Rāga Kauṅsī Kānaḍā belongs to the Kānaḍā cluster.

Reference rāga: Darbārī Kānaḍā.

Features: Mālkauṅs in *āroha* and Darbārī in *avaroha.*

Demo: Vilayat Hussain Khan. Malkauṅs in *āroha* and Aḍānā (a Darbari variant) in *avaroha*.

Example 3

Rāga Jog Kauṅs is a member of the Kauṅs cluster.

Reference rāga: Mālkauṅs.

Features: Jog in the *pūrvāṅga* and Mālkauṅs in the *uttarāṅga.*

Demo: Vilayat Khan.

COMPLEX COMPOUND (MORE THAN TWO RĀGAS)

Rāga Sampūrṇa Mālkauṅs

This is not a *rāga*, but a *rāga* enhancement concept, providing a variety of options. Mālkauṅs (SgMdn) is an *auḍava jāti* (pentatonic) *rāga*. It can be made *sampūrṇa* (heptatonic) by adding *re* and *pā*. This can be done in a variety of ways.

One approach: Practised in Jaipur-Atrauli Gharānā of *khyāl* vocalism. A dovetailing of Mālkauṅs, Kāfī and Bāgeśrī.

Demo: Dhondutai Kulkarni.

Reconsidering the Term "Saṅkīrṇa"

I do not claim scholarship in Sanskrit. But, in addition to the connotation of (from *saṅkramaṇa*= transit) "compounds" of different elements, the dictionary also suggests the connotations of "narrow" and "inferior". On the evidence of the quality of music that has been delivered in the *saṅkīrṇa* category in recent times, the derogatory suggestion warrants a second thought. It is plausible that *saṅkīrṇa rāga*s provide limited freedom for improvisation, compared to the major *rāga*s, which function as their reference *rāga*s. But, in a different sort of way, they provide a wider canvas for individual creativity.

To some extent, they liberate the reference *rāga* from its established grammar. And, it is this liberating effect that places them in the region of literature. But, it is not as if they are liberated from all forms of discipline that governs *rāga*-based classical music. They have their own guiding principles. They constitute only a partial leap into unfamiliar melodic territory. They are governed by a more amorphous – but equally meaningful – entity I have chosen to describe as a *rāga svarūpa* (melodic personality). Music performed within such a framework is a creative challenge to musicians and an intellectual challenge to *rasika*s.

It challenges the musician to create something new from familiar melodic material while abandoning the safety of well-established grammatical rules. He has to achieve this result within the overall melodic personality governing the transformation or compound.

It is an equally great challenge to *rasika*s. They are shaken out of the comfort of the entirely familiar melodic experience and obliged to listen more attentively to the music being performed. Mature *rasika*s can not only enjoy the novelty of the experience but also the nuances and subtleties of its melodic engineering. Understandably, *rāga* transformations and compound *rāga*s are performed mainly by musicians of some stature. And, of course, they are performed selectively, for audiences of high aesthetic cultivation.

In the early half of the twentieth century, it was a common practice for the leading musicians to start performing any *rāga* without announcing it. The musician often tried cleverly to disguise the melodic logic of his *rāga* and the *rasika*s managed to astutely decipher it.

Obviously, we are talking about a bygone era. Barring a few *rāga* transformations which have become quite popular and are easily recognized (e.g. Ahīr Bhairav of the Bhairav cluster or Śahānā Kānaḍā of the Kānaḍā cluster), the performance of such *rāga*s is now rare. Fewer and fewer musicians can handle such *rāga*s. And, fewer and fewer audiences can appreciate them.

Although today I am addressing a predominantly Carnatic-oriented audience, it seems to me that contemporary Hindustānī audiences also need to be re-educated on this enchanting region of Hindustānī music.

13

Wherein Resides the Rāga

IN MY writings on Hindustānī music, I have described *rāgas* as having their "melodic/aesthetic home" in one of three overlapping regions of the scale – *pūrvāṅga* (lower tetrachord), *madhyāṅga* (a mid-octave region) and *uttarāṅga* (upper tetrachord). This perspective, occasionally charged with revisionism, is a musician's interpretation of *rāga* grammar as a codification of aesthetic intent.

This perspective has great value for performance because it focuses the musician's attention upon the "aesthetic grammar" of a *rāga* – as distinct from its "melodic grammar", which merely identifies the *rāga* beyond reasonable doubt. The three-way overlapping partitioning of the octave implies that each *rāga* resides in a specific region of the melodic canvas. It also warns against an indiscriminate distribution of melodic activity in performance, which can have the effect of diluting the aesthetic intent of a *ŗaga*.

The Vādī and Its Location

Amongst the grammatical concepts emerging from the work of Bhatkhande in the second quarter of the twentieth century, the most widely used is the concept of the *vādī svara*, pivotal to the melodic personality of the *rāga*. Following the Western notion of tetrachords, Bhatkhande attributes significance to the location of the *vādī* in either *pūrvāṅga* (lower tetrachord) or *uttarāṅga* (upper tetrachord). This partition is mentioned as analogous to a division of the 24-hour day into two equal parts and the tendency of the *vādī svaras* (the dominant *svara*, explained later) of *rāgas* to be located in different regions of the scale corresponding to their prescribed time of performance.

Bhatkhande presents the relationship between the two ideas as being synchronous, without any suggestion of causality. The location of the *vādī svara* is a "given" facet of the manner in which *rāga*s have evolved organically and are performed. It is an acoustic–aesthetic reality. On the other hand, the two-part division of the 24-hour day and the prescribed time of performance for *rāga*s are both theoretical constructs superimposed on the "given" reality as additional layers of cultural meaning. These need not concern us here.

The real value of this proposition lies in attaching significance to the location of the *vādī svara* and its role in defining a *rāga*'s "melodic/aesthetic home".

Bhatkhande on the "Vādī"

Bhatkhande deals with this subject in the early pages of volume 1 of his epic work – *Hindustani Sangeet Paddhati*. The *vādī*, according to him, is the *svara* which identifies/personifies a *rāga*. In classical literature, it has been referred to as the *aṁśa svara*. The musical importance of the *aṁśa/vādī* is highlighted by musicians using a variety of musical devices. The pivotal *svara* therefore tends to be intoned repeatedly during the course of a rendition. A musician who does not know how to highlight the significance of the *vādī* cannot express the aesthetic intent of a *rāga*.

The implication here is that a *vādī* does not perform its function in isolation. It does so through its repetitive deployment in a variety of phrasing devices configured in its vicinity. The *vādī* is, therefore, the focal point of melodic action identifying/highlighting the unique melodic personality of a *rāga*.

The "Aṁśa" Svara

The *aṁśa svara*, as defined in Bharata's *Nāṭyaśāstra* (28.72-74) is freely translated from the Sanskrit verse as follows:

> The *svara*, which embodies the *rāga*-ness of the *rāga*; that *svara* that is crucial to the generation of the *rasa* of the *rāga*, or itself immersed in it; that which is at least five *svaras* away from the lower octave and of the higher octave; that *svara* which is surrounded by a plethora of phrasing patterns, i.e. that which is never isolated; that which has strong *svaras* in correspondence with itself; that which always remains in focus, even when *svaras* of lower hierarchical status in the *rāga* are being intoned; such a *svara* is best qualified for the status of the *aṁśa* as an expression of a *rāga*'s personality.

The implication here is that the melodic personality of a *rāga* is articulated effectively by a concentration of melodic activity in a specific region of the melodic canvas, within which the *aṁśa svara* has the status of being the "spokesperson" or "representative" of the *rāga*.

Classical literature identifies an additional and allied *rāga* attribute of *taratva-mandratva*. Premlata Sharma (1989) has dealt with this in her paper "Raga Lakshana". She explains that the aesthetic value of the same *svara* varies depending on the particular octave in which it is intoned – *mandra* (lower), *madhya* (middle) or *tāra* (higher) octaves. Hence, the location of a *svara* on the three-octave melodic canvas is an important vehicle of its expressiveness and plays an important role in the expression of a *rāga*'s melodic personality.

These grammatical notions are to be viewed along with the guidelines that Bhatkhande and other significant authorities have listed for performance (and composition) to support the aesthetic intent of *rāgas*. These guidelines go beyond the "melodic grammar" of *rāga* identification and may be considered a part of the "aesthetic grammar" of Hindustānī music. Some examples are cited below.

Guidelines for Performance

With respect to Purīyā and Sohanī, Bhatkhande says that the two *rāgas* feature identical *svaras*; but are residents of different regions of the melodic canvas. Purīyā (*vādī* = *gā*) expresses its aesthetic intent best in lower-octave and mid-octave melodic action, while Sohanī (*vādī* = *dh*) does so in the upper registers, with a special emphasis on the higher-octave *sā*. Manikbuwa Thakurdas (*Raga Darshan*, vols I-IV), another respected scholar, advises minimal *uttarāṅga* melodic activity for Purīyā, lest its melodic form get confused with that of Sohanī.

Bhatkhande isolates at least four other *rāgas* for similar attention. According to him, Miyā ki Malhār (*vādī* = *mā*), Maluhā Kedār (*vādī* = unidentified), Gārā (*vādī* = *gā*) and Sindh Bhairavī (*vādī* = *dh*) are all residents of the lower registers and the exploration of their melodic personalities should be focused in the lower and middle octaves. The implication here is that their aesthetic intent would be compromised to the extent that their exploration crosses into the upper half of the three-octave melodic canvas.

In this group, Gārā is a special case, which Subba Rao (*Raga Nidhi*, vols I-IV) describes as *pañchamantya* – a *rāga* whose melodic span terminates at the *pā* of the middle octave. Thus, implicit in several discussions on *rāga*-grammar is a "notional octave" which may differ from the "normal octave" spanning the eight *svaras*/seven intervals of the middle octave. This notional octave may begin deep in the lower octave as in Gārā (lower *pā* to middle *pā*) or shift upwards, as suggested for Sohanī (middle *gā* to higher-octave *gā*).

This idea is interesting because, the notional octave does not render the "normal" tonic redundant. On the contrary, its aesthetic value depends precisely on its tonality with respect to the middle-octave tonic. So, the aesthetic value of the relevant *rāgas* relies on two tonics, one notional and the other normal.

These guidelines suggest a broader principle – that the psycho-acoustic character of a *rāga* may be changed by shifting its *vādī* to a different octave. For instance, Rāga Mārwā (*vādī* = *dh*) was commonly performed as a strident ascent-dominant *rāga* until the 1950s. Ameer Khan merely shifted the *vādī* from the middle octave to the lower octave and performed it as a sombre descent-dominant *rāga*. Likewise, *rāga*s with the *vādī* located in the lower tetrachord can shift the *vādī* to the higher octave, causing a marked change in their aesthetic appeal. This is seen to happen to several *rāga*s as performed by vocalists of the Gwalior tradition, which has a marked fondness for the upper registers.

The meticulous attention given in these guidelines suggests the intention to insulate these *rāga*s categorically from the aesthetics of mid-octave region. This is a significant indicator of the mid-octave region as an independent psycho-acoustic territory for the aesthetic value of specified *rāga*s.

This issue surfaces in bold relief in the guidelines for Purīyā Kalyāṇ (*vādī* = *gā*) documented by Manikbuwa Thakurdas (*Raga Darshan*, vol. II). Purīyā Kalyāṇ is a compound *rāga*, which combines the melodic personality of Purīyā in the lower half with Kalyāṇ (Yaman) in the upper half of the scale. The *rāga* exhibits the two faces of its components effortlessly at the two ends; but it can express its composite uniqueness only in the mid-octave region, where the component *rāga*s are dovetailed. Thakurdas argues in favour of a mid-octave focus for the melodic exploration of the *rāga* to ensure that the uniqueness of its compound character is not swamped by the melodic features of its components.

There are, indeed, other methods of configuring compound *rāga*s – besides a dovetailing at the scalar midpoint. But, as a general perspective, we may recognize that a compound *rāga* – a substantial category in terms of frequency of performance – makes abnormal demands on the notion of a regional focus. This focus enables the expression of a compound *rāga*'s melodic uniqueness and balances the presence of its component *rāga*s.

Wherein Resides the Rāga

Grammatical concepts considered above indicate that, in addition to having dominant focal points for melodic action and also by virtue thereof, *rāga*s are "residents" of specific regions of the melodic canvas. In this perspective, *svara*-level, phrase-level, and octave-level specifications are all collectively significant for the expression of a *rāga*'s aesthetic intent. The interesting issue to consider is how best the melodic canvas can be partitioned in order to be musically useful, while also being true to the essential character of Hindustānī music.

At the macro scale/octave level, the human neuro-acoustic system has already provided three octaves as a natural and universal melodic canvas. It is at the micro-level, within an octave, that we need to determine a suitable partitioning.

Mutually Exclusive vs Overlapping Regions

By Bhatkhande's own admission, his notion of a two-part division of the scale into mutually exclusive regions draws upon the Western notion of lower and upper tetrachords in an octave. This approach overlooks the fundamental difference between the musical ideologies of Western and Indian music.

Western music defines the scale as an "octave", a cluster of eight tonal points, while Hindustānī music defines the scale as a *saptak*, a continuum of seven intervals. In line with this difference, Western music functions with a bias in favour of absolute pitch values and largely staccato intonation, while Hindustānī music functions with pitches relative to a tonic and a fluid – rather than static – approach to intervallic transitions. Classical literature provides detailed descriptions of the various intervallic transitions in use.

A notion of overlapping divisions of the scale therefore appears to be truer to the reality of Hindustānī music than a mutually exclusive partitioning. This view is supported by the manner in which Bhatkhande and his predecessors have viewed the function of the *vādī svara,* along with allied notions of regional bias as an important facet of a *rāga*'s melodic/emotional personality.

The Mid-Octave Region

By Bhatkhande's own computations of pitch values, *pā* is an acoustically imprecise bifurcation point because it does not define acoustically equal halves. *Pā* is the 5th degree to base *sā* with a pitch ratio of 1:1.5, while the higher octave *sā* is the 4th degree from *pā* with a pitch ratio of 1:1.33.

If we apply the lower tetrachord (*sā-pā*) ratio of 1:1.5 to the upper tetrachord, the matching acoustic distance would be *mā-sā'* and not *pā-sā'*. If we apply the upper tetrachord acoustic distance of 1.33 to the lower tetrachord, you get *sā-mā* as the acoustic space, not *sā-pā*. The notion of an acoustic mid-point for a two-part division must therefore reckon with both *mā* and *pā*.

With two acoustic midpoints, we are obliged to acknowledge overlapping, rather than mutually exclusive partitions of the octave. But, a mid-octave region consisting of two *svara*s is not musically useful. Melodic phrasing requires a minimum of three *svara*s in order to shape a distinct contour. But, the classical definition of the *aṁśa svara* also says that it should be surrounded by phrases which incorporate *svara*s in acoustic correspondence. Fulfilling this requirement demands a minimum of four *svara*s to constitute a notional "mid-octave region". The two mid-octave points (*śuddha mā* and *pā*) therefore require at least one *svara* to be added on each side to constitute a notional "mid-octave region" (*madhyāṅga*).

This argument would suggest that *gā-mā-pā-dh* would be an appropriate definition of a mid-octave region. This, however, creates a different problem. *Śuddha gā* and *śuddha dh* are not in either first-fourth (1:1.33) or first-fifth (1:1.50) correspondence, and would hence create a *madhyāṅga* acoustically incongruent to the acoustic regions defined at the two extremities of the octave.

The requirement of correspondence within a phrase incorporating or surrounding the *aṁśa svara* is fulfilled only by enlarging the space of acoustic midpoints (*śuddha mā* and *pā*) to include *śuddha gā* below and *dh* as well as *komal nī* above. Each of the overlapping segments so defined would then be mutually congruent with a pitch-ratio of 1:1.33 from the first included *svara* to the last.

On the face of it, this proposition looks clumsy because it adds one *svara* below and more than one *svara* above to the acoustic midpoints (*śuddha mā* and *pā*). Theoretically, however, this is the soundest way of defining the mid-octave region. For ease of communication, the proposition can be compromised as follows.

The totality of *rāga* grammar in Hindustānī music appears to notionally – though not explicitly – divide the octave into three overlapping regions of the octave for defining the regional bias of a *rāga* – *pūrvāṅga* (lower tetrachord), *madhyāṅga* (mid-octave region) and *uttarāṅga* (upper tetrachord). The *pūrvāṅga* consists of *S-R-G-M*. The *uttarāṅga* consists of *P-D-N-S'*. The *madhyāṅga* consists of *G-M-P-D*. Despite its compromise with acoustic precision, this division is musically useful because each overlapping division has four natural *svara*s, and the mid-octave region (*madhyāṅga*) overlaps two *svara*s of the (*pūrvāṅga*) lower tetrachord and two of the upper (*uttarāṅga*).

At the *rāga*-specific level, it is argued here that an isolation of the mid-octave region as the melodic centre of gravity is musically useful. It is also necessary to examine whether this refinement substantially alters our perception of the *rāga* universe as the larger reality that governs the melodic personalities of individual *rāga*s.

Survey of the Rāga Universe

For this survey, I rely on an analysis of three major authorities, who have documented *rāga* grammar on a substantial scale:

1. V.N. Bhatkhande, *Kramik Pustak Malika* (vols I-VI).
2. Vinayak Rao Patwardhan, *Raga Vigyan* (vols I-VII).
3. B. Subba Rao, *Raga Nidhi* (vols I-IV).

It is accepted that the identification of *vādī svara*s by each of these authorities will not be identical. It is also accepted that each of these authorities could have considered a different set of *rāga*s for the categorical identification of the *vādī svaras*. Despite this limitation, their respective perceptions of the universe of *rāga*s can offer valuable insights into the grammatical and aesthetic value of the *madhyāṅga* as a distinct melodic centre of gravity in a *rāga* (see Table 13.1).

Bhatkhande identifies *vādī svara*s for 127 *rāga*s, of which 71 per cent fall in the *madhyāṅga* region. Patwardhan identifies *vādī svara*s for 188 *rāga*s, of which 68 per cent fall within the *madhyānga* region. Subba Rao, whose work documents the largest number of *rāga*s from a large variety of textual sources, identifies *vādī svara*s for 283 Hindustānī *rāga*s, of which 73 per cent fall in the *madhyāṅga* region.

Table 13.1: Sectoral Dispersion of the Rāga Universe

Source	*Pūrvāṅga Number*	*Uttarāṅga Number*	*Total Number*	*Madhyāṅga Number*	*Madhyāṅga (% of total)*
Bhatkhande *Kramik Pustak Malika* (I-VI)	90	37	127	90	70.9
Patwardhan *Raga Vigyan* (I-VII)	115	73	188	127	67.6
Subba Rao *Raga Nidhi* (I-IV)	190	93	283	206	72.8

These orders of magnitude suggest that the *madhyāṅga* is a distinct centre of melodic gravity which cannot be ignored. A simplistic partitioning of the octave into lower and upper tetrachords can lead to the melodic neglect of a musically important region of the scale. In an improvisation-dominant art form, such as Hindustānī music, the "aesthetic grammar" of a *rāga* is as important as the "melodic grammar". If this is not correctly understood, composers and performers are exposed to the risk of over-emphasizing those scalar regions which are inconsistent with – and perhaps even disruptive of – the aesthetic intent of the chosen *rāga*.

14

The Emerging Generation of Khyāl Vocalists

WE ARE looking at Hindustānī *khyāl* vocalism at a very interesting stage in its evolutionary history.

In the social sciences, a period of thirty years is widely accepted as representing a generation. Change is happening constantly, but remains imperceptible on a day-to-day basis. Every thirty years, however, we can expect to observe significant changes in all segments of human activity. This will logically include literature, arts and culture generally.

With specific reference to Hindustānī music, I have found it useful and convenient to regard Independence as the watershed event from which trends can be plotted. The first thirty years (1947-77) were ruled by maestros of the pre-Independence generation. In the second thirty years (1977–2007) we experienced the music of the first post-Independence generation. And, now, starting 2007, we are witnessing the emergence of the second post-Independence generation of musicians. And, it is useful to track what the music of each of the post-Independence generations appears to represent.

At a function to release CDs recorded by two young vocalists in Bengaluru, I was requested to make a few observations. These observations formed the hypothesis which was subjected to empirical validation. The results of the validation study are reported in the six-part series on "Aesthetic Obsolescence and Paradigm Shifts in Hindustani Vocalism" which follows (chaps 15-20).

The First Post-Independent Generation

It is my observation that *khyāl* vocalism of the first post-Independence generation evolved largely under the shadows of the pre-Independence generation. This is neither good nor bad; it is just the way it happened. Thus, we saw the emergence of Kishori Amonkar Xerox no. 4382; Bhimsen Joshi Xerox no. 2597; Ameer Khan, Xerox no. 1573 and Kumar Gandharva Xerox no. 845.

During this period, it was evident that Hindustānī music – vocal music perhaps more than instrumental music – experienced a thinning of concert audiences. I have seen brilliant 40-year old vocalists performing for audiences primarily above 65. And, it occurred to me that this music would very soon have to address empty seats.

Two things probably happened which might explain this phenomenon. The corresponding generation of audiences could not relate to their music because it was out of sync with the aesthetic values of that generation. And, the senior generation of audiences (pre-Independence generation) saw no great value in it because it was largely a poor xerox of the music of the pre-Independence generation which was available in its original on concert length recordings.

I believe something different is happening now.

The Second Post-Independence Generation

I observe that, with the emergence of the second post-Independence generation (+/– 30 age group today) of musicians – particularly vocalists – younger audiences are returning to the concert halls. Recording companies confirm that there is now a healthy demand of fresh young talent and a shrinking demand for recordings of the pre-Independence masters. It appears that an entirely new audience has emerged for Hindustānī vocalism and the corresponding generation of vocalists is able to relate meaningfully to it. The reasons for this are many and complex. But, in strictly musical terms, one can hypothesize what might be happening.

The *gharānā* model of grooming has largely faded away. The *guru–śiṣya paramparā* is gasping for breath. Aspirants to a life in music are now drawing their musical ideas from a variety of sources. The vibrant media environment enables the most promising among them to address substantial audiences much earlier in their performing careers than the earlier generations could do. In their search for their personal musical statement, and their need to present coherent music, they are forced to draw upon the source of music within themselves much earlier than their senior generations needed to do.

The result is an engaging freshness and originality in their approach to music, and in their expression which their preceding generation did not have till much later – if at all. As their music matures – around the age of 40 – it promises to be considerably different from that of the earlier generation at that stage. It is obvious that they have studied the music of the pre-Independence maestros perhaps as textbooks; but their music is no longer being created under the shadow of pre-Independence musical values. They are authentic products of their generation and appear to be making sense to their own generations of listeners.

Managing the Dissonance

To their senior generations of listeners, their music can easily seem enigmatic and even bewildering. The uncharitable – and those suffering from aesthetic sclerosis – may even dismiss it as confused, or lost, or worse, "wrong". The truth, however, is that change is inevitable and even desirable so that music remains aesthetically relevant. The eminent musicologist, Ashok Ranade, has enunciated the idea that just as every society has economic and political needs which are changing all the time, it also has musical needs which are dynamic in nature. Music remains relevant by changing in order to address these changing needs.

Foreign scholars with deep involvement in Hindustānī music have often envied our musical tradition for its ability to balance continuity with change, tradition with modernity and conformism with originality.

It is in this spirit that the custodians of the musical culture – now consisting primarily of the first post-Independence generation – must learn to viw the music of the next generation. As Shivkumar Sharma wrote in the Foreword to my first book *Hindustani Music: A Tradition in Transition*, "The only thing constant in music is change". What remains relevant for all times, he added, is the "musician's truth", the sanctity of the musician's relationship with his art.

15

Aesthetic Obsolescence and Paradigm Shifts in Hindustānī Vocalism: I

AT AN event in December 2014 to release the CDs of two young Hindustānī musicians in Bengaluru, I had observed as follows:

> A period of thirty years appears appropriate as defining a generation with respect to our musical culture. The first post-Independence generation of Hindustānī vocalists, which appeared on the stage in the mid-1970s was performing music largely under the shadow of the pre-Independence generation. This could explain why Hindustānī music experienced shrinkage of audiences during the last quarter of the twentieth century. The second post-Independence generation emerging on the concert platform now (2010-15), is exhibiting a perceptible freedom from the shadow of the pre-Independence generation. They appear to be addressing their own generation of listeners more effectively, and drawing young audiences back into the concert halls.

After I finished my speech, several young musicians approached me to say that they did not fully understand my argument. I promised to explain myself in greater detail at a later stage. This study is intended to fulfil the promise made to my young friends that evening. But, it is also an opportunity for me to submit my public statements to scrutiny.

I wish to relate this issue to the observations I have made on an allied subject in my first book – *Hindustānī Music: A Tradition in Transition*. I summarize them here:

ONE: The Hindustānī music tradition is so designed that, knowingly or unknowingly, every significant musician is a product of his generation, speaks on behalf of his generation and addresses primarily his own generation of listeners. Implicitly, therefore, every musician's music "shuts out" – to some extent – audiences belonging to the generations behind him and the generations ahead of him.

TWO: Despite the apparent stability of the "operating system" governing Hindustānī music, there is no such thing as "timeless music". On the contrary, there is evidence to establish aesthetic obsolescence as a phenomenon which pushes the music of a certain past generation out of circulation and allows more recent music to reach music lovers. The departed generation eased out of the market, however, may retain a marginal presence in the market as academic reference material – perhaps as a virtual *guru*.

THREE: Running counter to aesthetic obsolescence, there exists a phenomenon of "aesthetic sclerosis" among Hindustānī music audiences, which makes listeners above a certain age (I suggested 50/55) unable to accept the musical values of the emerging generation of musicians (+/– 30). I have also observed that elderly audiences retain lifelong loyalty to the musical values to which they were exposed between the ages of 20 and 50. And, as Indians are increasingly living longer, it is this phenomenon that sustains the market for recordings of vintage/archival music.

I attempt a scrutiny of these observations by drawing upon profound anthropological and historical thought, and also on relevant macro-economic research.

The Method of Generations in History

Jose Ortegay Gasset is regarded as one of the most influential European philosophers of the twentieth century. I draw upon his landmark work *Man and Crisis* (1959) for his perspective on history as a product of intergenerational interactions.

EXTRACTS FROM "MAN AND CRISIS"

> Community of date and space are the primary attributes of a generation. Together, they signify the sharing of an essential destiny. The keyboard of environment on which coevals play the *Sonata Apassionata* of their lives is in its fundamental structure one and the same. This identity of destiny produces in coevals certain secondary coincidences which are summed up in the unity of their style. A generation is an integrated manner of existence or, if you prefer, a fashion of living, which fixes itself indelibly on the individual. …
>
> In the "today", in every "today", various generations co-exist and the relations which are established between them according to the different conditions of their ages, represent the dynamic system of attractions and repulsions, of agreement and controversy, which at any given moment makes up the reality of historic life. The concept of generations, converted into a method of historic investigation consists in nothing more than projecting the structure upon the past.
>
> A generation is the aggregate of men who are the same age. … The concept of age is not (however) the stuff of mathematics, but of life. Age, then, is not a date but a zone of dates.

For understanding the historical process as an interaction between various coexisting generations, he proposes the following analysis of generations:

ONE: Lives can be divided into five phases of approximately fifteen years each. (1) Childhood: 0-15, (2) Youth: 15-30, (3) Initiation: 30-45, (4) Dominance: 45-60, and (5) Old age: 60+. In some ways, Ortega suggests, the face of the world changes every fifteen years. However, he classifies the third and fourth stages, representing the thirty-year period from age 30 to 60 as the historically significant phases of an individual's/generation's life.

TWO: In his 30s man acquaints himself with the world into which he has fallen, and in which he must live. Between 30 and 45, he begins to react on his own account against the world that he has encountered, starts to reshape his world and learns to defend it against the generations that rule it. Between 45 and 60, he devotes himself fully to the development of the inspirations he has received between 30 and 45. The period of 30-45 is his period of gestation, creation and conflict, while the period between 45 and 60 is his stage for achieving dominance and command over his world.

The Ortega perspective implies that, after accounting for imperceptible changes that are taking place constantly because of the interaction between various coexisting generations, a perceptible change, a paradigm shift, can be expected to surface every sixty years. This is because all the forces acting upon the values of the earlier generations have, by now, either faded away or become impotent.

This implication would support my observation that the second post-Independence generation of Hindustānī musicians (emerging 60+ years after Independence) is charting a new path, which may create some dissonance among their senior generations of listeners.

Ortega describes the 30-45 stage as representing strategy development and the 45-60 phase as that for strategy implementation. This description matches the widely held belief about the evolution of Hindustānī musicianship. It is well articulated by the contemporary maestro, Ulhas Kashalkar, in the Foreword to my book – *Khyāl Vocalism: Continuity within Change* – and also his interview carried in the book (page xi):

> Today, a vocalist – if he is good – is exposed to public scrutiny right in the middle of the most vulnerable stage of his evolution – the stage when he is struggling to break out of the shell of his training, and to make his own original statement. ... Even with the best of training, the process of self-discovery in a vocalist matures only around the age of 40.

Briefly, then, we are looking at three periodicities implicit in

Ortega's argument as being relevant for plotting the generational dimension of change in Hindustānī music:

ONE: Human life is most meaningfully divided into five stages of fifteen years each. As a reflection of this, the face of the world changes in some way every fifteen years.

TWO: Historic changes can be expected to become evident every 60 years.

THREE: The thirty-year period between the ages of 30 and 60 is the historically most significant period in the life of each generation.

By Ortega's own argument, the clue to these periodicities of perceptible or imperceptible change lies in the "keyboard of environment on which coevals play the *Sonata Apassionata* of their lives [which] is in its fundamental structure one and the same".

The Keyboard of the Environment

It appears fair to argue that culture is substantially a reflection of the economic environment in which each generation seeks to express its unique destiny. In the light of this proposition, it seems appropriate to examine empirical evidence and theoretical constructs related to the patterns of economic activity. Specifically, we should be looking for evidence of periodicities of fifteen, thirty and sixty years postulated by Ortega in patterns of economic change. The various theories of business cycles are relevant from this perspective.

Business cycle or economic cycles are waves formed by the expansion and contraction of economic activity. Our argument can be that the cultural manifestations of buoyant economic activity would be substantially different of depressed economic activity. As an extension of this argument, we may also argue that each phase of expansion and contraction will leave behind some cultural residues, which carry forward into the next upswing/downswing. But when a society has seen the complete long wave of contraction and expansion, it will emerge from the experience with a changed perception of itself and its arts will exhibit signs of a paradigm shift.

THEORY AND EVIDENCE OF ECONOMIC CYCLES

ONE: In the nineteenth century, Clement Juglar first identified a cycle of seven–eleven years signified by accelerated or retarded societal investments in fixed assets. Juglar did not, however, claim any regularity for these waves.

TWO: In the twentieth century, Simon Kuznets identified a cycle of fifteen-twenty-five years, signified by the expansion and contraction of societal investments in infrastructure (also called the "building cycle").

THREE: In 1947, Edward Dewey and Edwin Dakin identified a fifty-four year cycle, based on a statistical analysis of wholesale prices in the US.

FOUR: In 1925, Nikolai Kondratieff estimated a long business cycle of fifty–sixty years, based on a study of trends in commodity prices, interest rates, wages, production, coal consumption, private savings, gold production, as well as political trends from 1790 to 1920. Kondratieff's work also established that each expansion of economic activity is associated with the emergence of productivity enhancing technological innovations. Because of the comprehensiveness of the phenomena considered, Kondratieff's work is also the most significant cyclical formulation from the cultural perspective.

The Kondratieff model has been confirmed by rigorous statistical testing, using spectral analysis. These procedures also suggest that each Kondratieff wave subsumes three sub-cycles of seventeen years each, partially supporting the Kuznets suggestion of shorter cycles of fifteen–twenty-five years.

The implications of this refresher course in macro-economics for our subject of enquiries are as follows:

ONE: Ortega's suggestion of sixty years as the fulfilment of a generation's historic mission would result in the appearance of a paradigm shift every sixty years. This finds support in the fifty–sixty year cycle of economic activity observed by Kondratieff, Dewey and Dakin.

TWO: The shorter seventeen-year subcycles within the Kondratieff long wave support Ortega's observation that our world is changing in some ways every fifteen years because the stages of human life are most meaningfully seen as periods of fifteen years each.

THREE: That the Kondratieff long cycle is fifty–sixty years will tend to represent twenty-five-thirty years of contraction and twenty-five–thirty years of expansion in economic activity. This would support Ortega's view of the thirty-year period (age 30-60) as being the historically most significant period in the life of each generation.

While viewing these indications of periodicity, it is important to recall Ortega's own observation: "The concept of age is not (however) the stuff of mathematics, but of life. Age, then, is not a date but a zone of dates."

Corroborating this perspective, economists studying economic cycles have not been able to assess the occurrence of peaks and troughs with astronomical precision. Keeping this in mind, an attempt may be made to represent this concept graphically.

A Conceptual-Graphic Model of Generational Shifts

The model is not intended to either prove or establish any theory pertaining to the periodicity of perceptible changes in musical values. It attempts merely to demonstrate the interactions between the various significant participants, creating an interplay of continuity and change.

Five historically significant roles are considered in this model:

1. The performer generation,

2. the *guru* generation to the performer which is thirty years senior to him,

3. the traditional benchmark of musicianship which may be the *guru*'s *guru* or other influential musicians – sixty years senior to the performer,

4. rival to the performing generation which is partly his own generation and partly his senior generation, and

5. the audience of the performing musician which we assume to be the same as the performing generation.

Following a combination of Ortega and Kondratieff arguments, the model divides the timescale into distinct fifteen-year periods, with two of these consecutive periods constituting a significant thirty-year generation with respect to all participants in the musical culture (Table 15.1). The point to

Table 15.1 : Generational Shifts Relevant to Musical Values Conceptual-Graphic Model

	1880-1895	1895-1910	1910-1925	1925-1940	1940-1955	1955-1970	1970-1985	1985-2000	2000-2015	2015-2030
Performer							GEN-1			
Guru										
Benchmark										
Rival										
Audience										
Performer								GEN-2		
Guru										
Benchmark										
Rival										
Audience										
Performer									GEN-3	
Guru										
Benchmark										
Rival										
Audience										
Performer										GEN-4
Guru										
Benchmark										
Rival										
Audience										
Performer			GEN-5							
Guru										
Benchmark										
Rival										
Audience										
Performer				GEN-6						
Guru										
Benchmark										
Rival										
Audience										

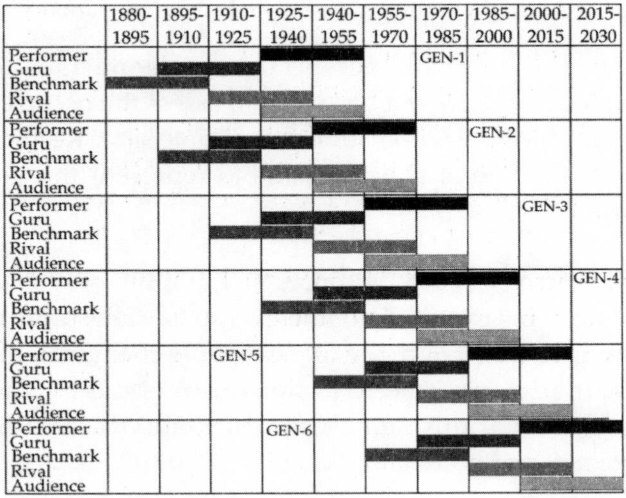

remember here is we are not talking of a generation as a birth-to-death duration, but a thirty-year time span which is historically the most significant for the performance of each generation. Each generation has been given a number for ease of comprehension.

THE PATTERN EXPLAINED

G-1, the performing generation of 1925-55, begins to perform the *guru* role for G-2 and continues to do so for G-3 and G-4, and thereafter becomes the benchmark generation, with decreasing influence till G-5. By G-6, it has fallen totally off the radar of the musical culture.

The *guru* generation of G-1 (1895–1925) retains part of its influence as a *guru* for G-2, and then drifts into the benchmark area through G-2- and G-3, drifting into insignificance thereafter.

The benchmark generation of G-1 (1880-95) remains partly relevant as a benchmark for G-2 and fades into history thereafter.

The rival generation of G-1 (1910-40) becomes a part of the *guru* generation in G-2 and thereafter remains relevant, with diminishing influence, till G-4 as a benchmark generation.

The audience generation of G-1 (1925-55) remains an influential force for G-2 and thereafter gives way to younger audiences.

By the time we come to the performing generation G-6 (2015-30), none of the generations of participants of G-1, G-2, G-3, G-4 and G-5 has any historically significant influence. The world has changed far too much between 1955 and 2015 for the musical values of G-1 to either to exist or to deserve an audience. A paradigm shift is to be expected.

The structuring of this conceptual-graphic model merely happens to deliver a paradigm shift expectation in approximately sixty years. It could have been fifty, seventy or even eighty years. The exact periodicity is not as important as is the demonstration of the generational interactions through which aesthetic obsolescence and periodic paradigm shifts appear to take place.

16

Aesthetic Obsolescence and Paradigm Shifts in Hindustānī Vocalism: II

In the previous chapter, I have suggested (1) that aesthetic obsolescence is a reality in classical music, and (2) that a paradigm shift in aesthetic values can be expected at intervals of fifty–sixty years. Those propositions were based on anthropological and macro-economic constructs evolved in the American/European/global context. Despite their intuitive appeal, they are not sufficient to support a definitive view with respect to Hindustānī music. Indian evidence with respect to such phenomena needs to be considered.

The Hindustānī music audience accesses and consumes music through an increasing variety of sources, and their mix itself is changing constantly. Many of these sources are either informal, or generate quantitative information on consumption patterns, which is available only to its providers. The Hindustānī music market is just not large enough to spawn independent sources of reliable quantitative information. The glimmer of hope in this regard comes from YouTube, which now features a substantial and increasing volume of Hindustānī music, and is emerging as a valuable depository of archival music for music lovers.

YouTube as Data Source

Every video recording featured on YouTube now provides information on the date of uploading, and the number of views against each recording. By dividing the total viewership of a recording by the number of months/weeks since the date of uploading, it is possible to get a measure (views per month/ week) which enables a comparison of individual recordings and musicians on the level of audience of involvement and interest logged up to a given date. This simple measure can be submitted to systematic segmental analysis for extracting valuable insights.

YouTube is, admittedly, not a perfect solution to our problem. Even amongst Internet-based music repositories, it is one of the many, though perhaps the largest and the most popular. Net-based repositories are themselves one of the many media through which Hindustānī music is being accessed. It is impossible to account for the various determinants of availability of any recording on YouTube or alternative Internet music portals/archives. It is also impossible – without access to YouTube's internal analytics – to appreciate how YouTube defines viewership, thus making a comparison between recordings and musicians an uncertain exercise.

Another major issue concerns YouTube itself. The portal itself is growing constantly in terms of content diversity, content volume and usership base. Inevitably then, its global audience profile is also changing constantly. So, it becomes conceptually tricky to compare, say, fifty views per month for a recording of Fayyaz Khan in 2010 with fifty views per month of the same recording in 2014. Do the two represent the same level of public interest and involvement?

The methodological issues raised by this data source are innumerable. With all its limitations, however, YouTube is the most substantial repository of Hindustānī music, which also reports quantitative information on the level of audience interest and involvement in archival music starting from the early years of the twentieth century. It therefore makes sense to examine YouTube data for possible indications of aesthetic obsolescence and paradigm shifts with respect to Hindustānī music.

Research Design

This study is based on recordings of deceased *khyāl* vocalists because, in Hindustānī music, only the *khyāl* genre enjoys considerable structural stability across the century we are looking at and features a continuous flow of significant musicians to monitor. Admittedly, several *khyāl* vocalists have achieved additional popularity and stature because of their non-*khyāl* repertoire such as *bhajans*, *ṭhumrīs* and *ṭappās*. There is clearly no way of isolating the effect of this facet of their musical personality on their mainstream persona. To keep all musicians and recordings comparable, the study chose to ignore the non-*khyāl* recordings of the considered musicians available on YouTube.

The selection of significant musicians to monitor was based on the author's knowledge of *khyāl* vocalism, sometimes constrained by the availability of sample data. An attempt was made to ensure that significant vocalists from every major *gharānā* of *khyāl* vocalism were included in the study. Even an otherwise significant musician was not considered if his/her YouTube presence did not cross five different *rāgas*. This gave a total listing of twenty-one vocalists, whose YouTube presence was even indicatively measurable.

For every significant musician considered, at least one recording of every *rāga* available on YouTube was included. Wherever more than one recording of the same *rāga*, or even the same performance was available, all were considered. Because of the varying pattern of availability, it could not be helped that, the study considers as many as fifty-eight recordings of one musician at the upper end, and as few as six of another at the lower end.

In a vast majority of the cases, the considered recordings had been uploaded between 2010 and 2015. In very few cases, upload dates go back into 2008 or 2009. The number of months for which each recording had been available was computed using 1 May 2015 as the cut-off date. The data was recorded between 2 May and 4 May.

Table 16.1 shows the computations of audience involvement/ interest/viewership of the considered musicians. The graph below presents average viewers per month of the musicians

Table 16.1: Viewership up to 1 May 2015 by Birth Year of Vocalist

Name	*Birth Year*	*Videos*	*Total Exposures Months*	*Total Views*	*Average Views/ Month*
Ramkrishna Vaze	1871	9	270	9,981	37
Abdul Kareem Khan	1872	18	610	2,49,904	410
Sawai Gandharva	1886	6	291	26,568	91
Faiyaz Khan	1886	51	485	53,249	110
Kesarbai Kerkar	1890	47	1,544	1,53,319	99
Vilayat Hussain Khan	1895	15	790	21,421	27
Omkarnath Thakur	1897	22	397	50,336	127
Bade Gulam Ali Khan	1903	57	1,734	5,21,933	301
Mogubai Kurdikar	1904	7	191	9,961	52
Hirabai Barodekar	1905	10	316	34,665	110
Mallikarjun Mansur	1910	35	715	1,48,893	208
Nivruttibua Sarnaik	1912	11	60	1,133	19
Ameer Khan	1912	58	1,002	4,86,749	486
Gangubai Hangal	1913	30	1,181	1,31,642	111
Roshanara Begum	1917	39	677	70,234	104
Latafat Hussain Khan	1920	9	423	15,141	36
D.V. Paluskar	1921	29	1,011	2,45,538	243
Bhimsen Joshi	1922	35	823	5,36,198	652
Kumar Gandharva	1924	33	927	1,36,940	148
Yashvant Bua Joshi	1927	18	337	16,305	48
Sharafat Hussain Khan	1930	13	678	16,829	25

plotted against their year of birth. Admittedly, the year of birth is not the ideal landmark for comparability because different musicians have acquired stature and influence at different stages in their lives. No stage-of-life-cycle alternative would have been satisfactory because that would have left out a musician like D.V. Paluskar, who achieved considerable stature in his short life of 34 years.

Indications

The graphic representation of the analysis should be considered first for its conceptual and theoretical implications (*fig*. 16.1).

Fig. 16.1 supports the proposition that aesthetic obsolescence is a reality in Hindustānī music. It exhibits a trend of viewership favouring musicians born more recently as against musicians born in earlier years. A long-term trend-line would suggest that, on an average, a musician born in 1930 would have five more YouTube viewers per month than a musician born sixty years ago, in 1870.

In addition to a secular trend, the graph also exhibits a cyclical trend. Every once in a while there appears to emerge a breakthrough vocalist whose music achieves a higher level of audience involvement than expected. And, this booster evidently provides the momentum for the subsequent breakthrough to seek an even higher intensity of audience involvement. Here,

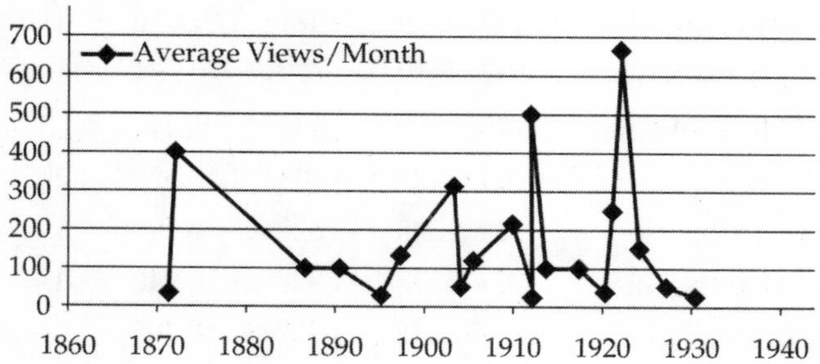

fig. 16.1: Average views per month

of course, we do not know how much of this booster effect is attributable to the music and how much to the dynamism of the media environment – most notably YouTube itself. But, then, media grow on the strength of their content. Therefore, which is the cause and which the effect is an intractable issue.

This three-wave pattern has a defensible generational interpretation. From this, it would appear that currently, there are a three – probably four – sets of musical values which command the involvement of YouTube audiences. The first wave, represented by Abdul Kareem Khan, the second by Bade Ghulam Ali Khan, the third by Mallikarjun Mansur, and the fourth by Bhimsen Joshi, Kumar Gandharva and D.V. Paluskar. This would suggest that three – perhaps four – distinct generations of listeners are currently involved in the recorded *khyāl* music of the twentieth century.

In the history we have plotted, Abdul Kareem Khan (b. 1872) appears as the first breakthrough *khyāl* vocalist. After him, Bade Gulam Ali Khan (b. 1903) represents the next peak. Ameer Khan (b. 1912) defines the following peak. The last peak covered by this study is defined by Bhimsen Joshi (b. 1922). It will be noticed that the time gaps between the successive peaks are not even approximately similar. This is not surprising because art is not obliged to provide the econometrician with convenient solutions to his problems.

The peaks are, undoubtedly, defined by those we consider "landmark" musicians. But, do we have any indications here of a paradigm shift or a long cycle of fifty–sixty years? Possibly, we do. On the graph presented here, we are looking at three smaller waves with the chronological distance between the first and the fourth peak being exactly fifty years. We could well be looking at an Indian version of a large Kondratieff wave of fifty–sixty years, which subsumes three shorter Kuznets waves, as described in my earlier paper (Chap.16) on this subject. If this speculation has any merit, Hindustānī music could today be on

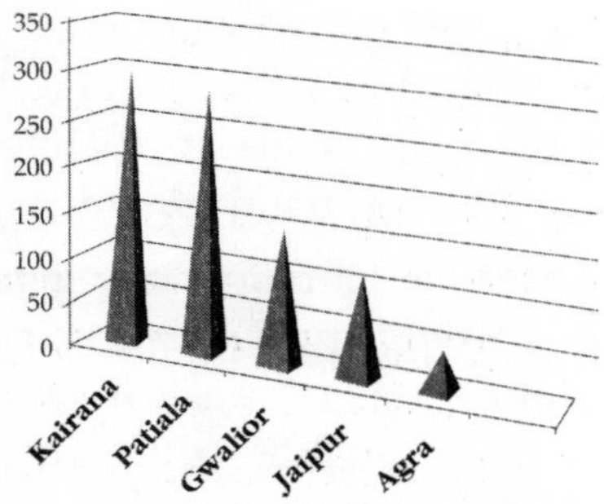

fig. 16.2: Gharānā viewership

the threshold of a paradigm shift – this being the hypothesis I have articulated during my speech in Bengaluru in December 2014, which triggered off this inquiry.

Of course, we need to be circumspect about such speculation because this study does not permit a view on this aspect of the obsolescence theory. This is so mainly because the data source itself is constrained by the history of electronic amplification and recording technologies. It is known that developments in recording and storage-media technologies made a significant contribution to making Abdul Kareem Khan, Bade Gulam Ali Khan, Ameer Khan and Bhimsen Joshi "landmark" musicians. By the same logic, the recordings of "landmark" musicians from the early days of sound engineering – such as Kesarbai Kerkar and Fayyaz Khan – could have suffered truncated aesthetic lives on account of a comparatively primitive acoustic environment.

With the recording industry itself being less than 120 years old, it would be impossible to observe even two full long-cycles of fifty–sixty years, even if they existed, because reliable quantitative data to support such a theory would be impossible to compile. Therefore, the notions of paradigm shifts or long cycles will perhaps remain in the region of scholarly opinion and public debate.

Gharānā Perspectives

While the individual viewership ratings of the various musicians are of wider popular interest, the *gharānā* affiliations and stylistic legacies reflected in this study are of greater importance in understanding the cultural process. The groupings, as attempted, reflect my understanding of stylistic tendencies.

Those who described the demise of Bhimsen Joshi as the "end of an era" were probably more prophetic than they realized. If there is a fifty-year cycle culminating with the musicianship of Bhimsen Joshi, the event might have been acceptably described as the "end of the Kairana era", which began with Abdul Kareem Khan, born exactly fifty years before Bhimsen Joshi, and spawned a veritable galaxy in between.

It is easy to see the Kairana group heading the list with an average of 313 viewers per month. It does so, on the strength of Bhimsen Joshi (652), Ameer Khan (486) and Abdul Kareem Khan (410). Patiala stands tall alongside (301) with just one vocalist, Bade Gulam Ali Khan holding the fort.

The Gwalior group (156) stands almost on par with the Jaipur-Atrauli group (125). But, they present a picture in contrast. With the exception of D.V. Paluskar, the Gwalior group claims its share-of-mind entirely on the strength of highly original, individualistic, or reformist musicians – starting from Ramakrishna Vaze and ending with Yashwant Buwa Joshi. In sharp contrast, the Jaipur-Atrauli group consists entirely of orthodox vocalists, trained by the founding family.

This confirms the view of Bonnie Wade (1984) that in the second quarter of the twentieth century, the Gwalior Gharānā suffered a loss of identity and was obliged to reinvent itself. This crisis resulted in several Gwalior-trained vocalists drifting towards the dominant style such as Agra (e.g. *Yashwant Bua Joshi),* the ascendant style such as Jaipur-Atrauli (Mallikarjun Mansur), or to emerge as highly individualistic originals (e.g.

Omkarnath Thakur and Kumar Gandharva).

This contrasts apparently with Jaipur-Atrauli, which holds its share-of-mind alongside Gwalior so far on the strength of its orthodox musicianship. It is not, however, insignificant, that the *gharānā* group rating is being held up substantially by Mallikarjun Mansur, who performed orthodox Jaipur-Atrauli music, but was in fact a mature migrant from Gwalior. It is also debatable whether Mansur's music ever lost traces of Gwalior vocalism. Also, what is not reflected in this study is the immense influence of Kishori Amonkar of the same lineage, starting from the mid-1970s, which has left the orthodox stream of Jaipur-Atrauli gasping for breath.

Therefore, in the Gwalior group as well as the Jaipur-Atrauli group, we are looking at a reformist phase struggling against the forces of aesthetic obsolescence.

The Agra group (45), headed by Fayyaz Khan (110) is pulled down to the fifth position by his successors.

Individual Highlights

In the Kairana group, Roshanara Begum (104) is a surprise with a viewership rating on par with Kesarbai Kerkar (99) and Fayyaz Khan (110). This is all the more interesting since she migrated to Pakistan at the time of Independence, and visited India only rarely thereafter. She is not known to have performed in India after 1947. Her recordings have been her sole contact with Indian audiences. Merely by belonging to the next generation, and by virtue of her musicianship, she stands today on par with titans of just a generation before her.

The Gwalior group (156) is held up in the third position by D.V. Paluskar (243) who died in 1955 at the age of 34. His present-day rating is almost twice that of Omkarnath Thakur (127) who acquired immense stature and popularity a generation before him. In addition to the perennial youthfulness of his musical legacy, Paluskar enjoyed the advantages of a buoyant recording industry and media environment just a quarter of a century after Omkarnath Thakur.

The Jaipur-Atrauli group (125) is currently placed in the fourth position by Mallikarjun Mansur (208) much more than by Kesarbai Kerkar (99), the empress of the concert platform a generation before him. In this, we once again observe the effect of a generational shift in musical values, supported by the dynamism of the electronic media.

Conclusion

Despite the limitations of the data source, this study broadly supports the notion of aesthetic obsolescence as a reality in Hindustānī music. This constitutes valuable confirmation of reports to the same effect received from significant players in the commercial recording industry as well as the barter market for archival recordings.

This study does not provide clear support to the supposition of a paradigm shift in musical values which, I have observed, is currently taking place. However, considering that the study shows wave patterns resembling three short components of the Kondratieff wave of fifty years, the possibility of an imminent paradigm shift cannot be ruled out either. The argument in favour of such a possibility is that if musical values are changing constantly, the change cannot remain imperceptible indefinitely. At some stage, the accumulation of imperceptible changes will become perceptible in the form of a paradigm shift. Whether such a watershed can be expected every fifty–sixty years, or at shorter or longer intervals – or even at irregular intervals – in the context of Hindustānī music is, as yet, inestimable.

At this point, one may devote a thought to how the accumulation of imperceptible changes over a period becomes perceptible as a watershed or a paradigm shift. When a musical value, considered fundamental to the acceptability of sound music, is abandoned by a majority of performing musicians – without necessarily identifying an emergent alternative – a paradigm shift can be said to have taken place. If such a shift is impending at this juncture, I expect much will be written on this subject in the next few years by astute observers of the Hindustānī music culture.

There is, of course, no reason why the change and periodicity patterns evident in Hindustānī music should fit neatly into anthropological or econometric models developed in Europe. We need, therefore, to be cautious in drawing upon such theoretical constructs for interpreting the Indian reality, with all its probable uniqueness.

However, with sufficient indications favouring the essence of our argument, there could be justification in pursuing an examination of social and economic forces that might help refine our understanding of the musical culture.

17

Aesthetic Obsolescence and Paradigm Shifts in Hindustānī Vocalism: III

The Non-Khyāl Repertoire of Khyāl Vocalists

IN Chapter 16 an attempt was made to ascertain the patterns of aesthetic obsolescence in *khyāl* vocalism across the last century over the period 2010-15. Appropriately for the focus of the earlier study, the non-*khyāl* repertoire of the considered vocalists was left out of the measurement. However, as a parallel reality and as a component of the share-of-mind a musician enjoys with audiences of his own and future generations, it cannot be ignored.

Unlike practitioners of the medieval *dhrupad-dhamār* genre, *khyāl* vocalists have, for long, retained an involvement with the semi-classical genres. This facet of Hindustānī vocalism acquires greater importance because of the major changes that have taken place in the music-scape, particularly after Independence. The specialist singers of the semi-classical *ṭhumrī* and its allied genres have virtually disappeared from the scene. Simultaneously, vocalists trained in the *khyāl* genre have adopted these genres in performance and also added the *bhajan* to their musical persona. Several leading *khyāl* vocalists of the twentieth century are acknowledged to have contributed significantly to the evolution of these two genres.

It is neither possible, nor necessary, for us to ascertain whether their non-*khyāl* repertoire has contributed to their share-of-mind as Hindustānī vocalists or the other way round.

There exists a synchronous relationship between them, which needs to be examined from the point of aesthetic obsolescence. This chapter attempts to explore this relationship.

Research Design

The research design is identical to the design of the study of aesthetic obsolescence of *khyāl* repertoire. The sample consists of the same vocalists, truncated by the non-availability of data for some of the vocalists. Of the twenty-first vocalists considered in the earlier study, eight had to be dropped on account of inadequate or missing data. Expectedly, the number of non-*khyāl* recordings available for logging was consistently much smaller than *khyāl* recordings. The minimum readings considered acceptable for considering any vocalist were three and the maximum readings available for any musician was thirty-four. Average views per month of exposure were computed precisely in the same manner for comparability of results.

The repertoire considered in this study covers *ṭhumrī, ṭappā, dādrā, ghazal, nāṭya saṅgīt, bhajan*s, patriotic songs, regional devotional music and songs performed in Hindi or regional films.

Indications

Table 17.1 and *fig*. 17.1 plot average views per month of recording availability against the year of birth of the musician. The picture differs substantially from the pattern seen in the earlier study of *khyāl* recordings. While the *khyāl* viewership graph showed a long-term linear trend accompanied by a series of wave patterns, this graph is predominantly an exponential graph, with the hint of a wave within it. This means that the more recent the musician, the more disproportionately he gains viewership amongst present-day audiences for his non-*khyāl* repertoire. Worded differently, non-*khyāl* repertoire music tends to become obsolete faster, and with greater certainty, than *khyāl* music.

The two-wave pattern evident in *fig*. 17.1 also has a defensible

Table 17.1: Non-khyāl Views up to 1 May 2015 by Birth Year of Vocalist

Name	*Birth Year*	*Videos*	*Total Exposure Months*	*Total Views*	*Average Views/ Month*
Abdul Kareem Khan	1872	18	620	1,12,561	182
Faiyaz Khan	1886	7	118	14,441	122
Kesarbai Kerkar	1890	8	380	69,785	184
Omkarnath Thakur	1897	14	408	1,02,929	252
Bade Gulam Ali Khan	1903	26	1,309	14,36,252	1,097
Hirabai Barodekar	1905	11	183	4,491	25
Mallikarjun Mansur	1910	12	300	42,826	143
Ameer Khan	1912	14	528	92,170	175
Gangubai Hangal	1913	3	117	11,708	100
Roshanara Begum	1917	27	1,068	1,02,250	96
D.V. Paluskar	1921	23	644	3,45,304	536
Bhimsen Joshi	1922	34	1,871	42,32,639	2,262
Kumar Gandharva	1924	30	1,467	16,69,620	1,138

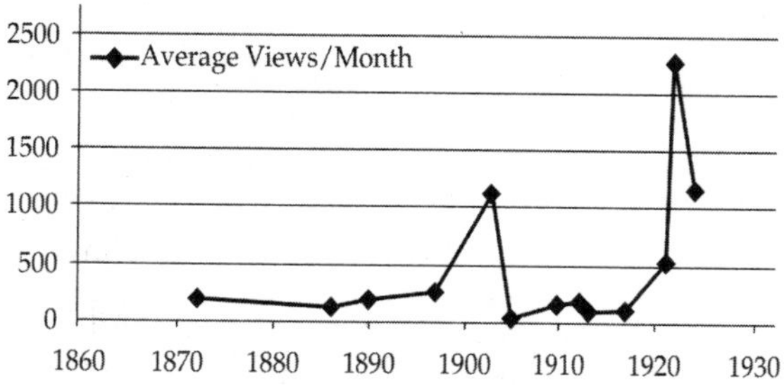

fig. **17.1: Average views per month**

generational interpretation. It would suggest that, currently, the non-*khyāl* musical values of two distinct generations of musicians engage the attention of YouTube listeners. The first is represented by the musical values of Bade Gulam Ali Khan and the second predominantly by Bhimsen Joshi, but also Kumar Gandharva and D.V. Paluskar. It is interesting that the same set of musicians showed a three-wave pattern with four peaks for *khyāl* music. This further establishes the difference between *khyāl* music and the non-*khyāl* repertoire of the same musicians. Their *khyāl* repertoire has an audience of three or four generations, while their non-*khyāl* repertoire commands the attention of only two.

These patterns support what is known about the semi-classical and allied genres of vocal music. Relative to *khyāl* vocalism, they are designed to appeal to a much larger audience, which is more likely to respond to ephemeral musical values than the more durable musical values.

There are no significant cycles apparent in this graph and the possibility of a paradigm shift does not appear to emerge from available data.

Fig. 17.2 provides further insights. On an average, vocalists considered here have logged almost double the viewership for non-*khyāl* recordings compared to his/her *khyāl* repertoire. Even within the overall pattern of faster obsolescence of non-

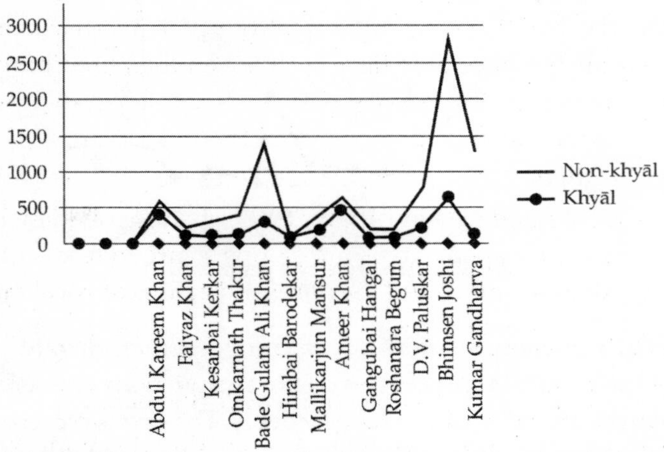

fig. 17.2: Comparative plot for *khyāl* and non *khyāl* recordings

khyāl recordings, the absolute level of durability of appeal is substantially higher for non-*khyāl* music than *khyāl* music. But, the pattern deserves a closer look.

D.V. Paluskar's non-*khyāl* repertoire logs twice the rating of his *khyāl* repertoire. After him, the multiplier shows a smart rise. Bhimsen Joshi's non-*khyāl* repertoire is almost four times more popular than his *khyāl* repertoire. And, finally, with Kumar Gandharva, the non-*khyāl* repertoire almost touches eight times the *khyāl* level in terms of audience involvement. The sharpness of this trend would suggest a backdrop of fairly radical changes in the social and economic environment of which musicians and their audiences are concurrent products.

It appears that the non-*khyāl* repertoire, which has a faster rate of obsolescence, is claiming a progressively higher share-of-mind among audiences. This has several implications for the musical culture, all of which are already on the horizon.

Implications of the Patterns

The inflow of fresh talent into classical vocalism could shrink, with more and more trained singers opting for a career in the non-*khyāl* genres. Because of this, the non-*khyāl* genres could witness the emergence of high-quality specialist performers. *Khyāl* vocalists – once they have established their credibility as trained classical singers – will be drawn towards increasing their involvement with non-*khyāl* repertoire to protect their share-of-mind and share-of-market.

The most significant implication of the patterns evident here is that the *khyāl* appears to be a receding genre in terms of the society's share-of-mind and the non-*khyāl* genres of vocal music appear to be the ascendant genres. This indication may require further evidence to be stated with greater certainty. But, it is not insignificant even with the evidence available here.

The eminent musicologist, Ashok Ranade made some

interesting observations about the behaviour of the dominant genre in times of challenged dominance:

> ... we should look at how any musical form achieves and sustains its dominant position. First, it attracts all kinds of performers towards it. Second, it tries to assimilate the musical tendencies of other forms. Third, it allows individuals enough freedom to express themselves, especially in the initial stages. Fourth, it makes allowances for a distinction between the larger disciplinary model of a *gharānā*, and the style of an individual musician. – Ranade, 1999, "Perspectives on 'Dhrupad' "

This summarizes the history of *khyāl* vocalism fairly accurately. For the present, we may focus sharply at the prospect of the *khyāl* as the threatened genre adopting musical values of its challengers as a protection against its own extinction.

The *khyāl* is a three-dimensional genre – it is a contemplative art, an expressive art and a communicative art. Its contemplative facet involves an improvised exploration of the *rāga*'s melodic and emotional personality. It is this facet that distinguishes it from the non-*khyāl* genres of vocalism. If the *khyāl* is tending towards imitating the non-*khyāl* genres, what it is abandoning is either the *rāga* discipline or the deliberate exploration of the *rāga*'s melodic–emotional personality, or both. It is in this context that the issue of an impending paradigm shift may be relevant.

At this point, we may recall what a paradigm shift means in the present context. When a musical value, considered fundamental for long, is abandoned by a majority of performing musicians – without necessarily identifying an emergent alternative – a paradigm shift can be said to have taken place.

The contemplative facet of *khyāl* vocalism, and the centrality of *rāga* elaboration to it, is a musical value considered fundamental for at least more than a century. It faces the prospect of being abandoned in favour of the more ephemeral musical values of the non-*khyāl* genres. The architecture of *rāga* rendition characteristic of the *khyāl* may remain in circulation even with a shrinking presence. But, its distinguishing feature, as has been understood so far, could be headed for extinction.

This study began with looking at aesthetic obsolescence of the music of eminent *khyāl* vocalists and incidentally of the major *khyāl gharānās*. Now, having considered the divergent patterns in the non-*khyāl* music of the major Hindustānī vocalists, it has raised issues relating to the aesthetic obsolescence of the *khyāl* genre itself. There is insufficient evidence yet to permit a categorical view on this possibility. It may therefore remain, for now, a hypothesis based on astute observation.

18

Aesthetic Obsolescence and Paradigm Shifts in Hindustānī Vocalism: IV

The Music of Non-Khyāl Specialists

In Chapter 17, we found that the non-*khyāl* repertoire of *khyāl* vocalists achieves a much higher level of audience involvement than their *khyāl* repertoire. The musician lives with this reality everyday and responds according to his temperament and inclinations. He does not need to figure out the extent to which this is attributable to his *khyāl*-related status, to the independent appeal of his non-*khyāl* repertoire or to the uniqueness of the combination. But, the researcher does need to resolve this issue.

If we are to judge the strength of the non-*khyāl* segment of the musical culture as a possible challenge/distraction to the fundamental character of the *khyāl* as we know it, we need to isolate the non-*khyāl* segment for measurement. Circumstantial evidence of this can be obtained from the analysis of audience involvement in the music of the specialist performers of the non-*khyāl* genres. In this analysis, the absolute numbers delivered are as important as the trend of obsolescence. This essay attempts to look at these patterns.

Research Design

The methodology followed is identical to the earlier studies conducted on samples of *khyāl* vocalists.

The sample of available YouTube recordings was drawn from the leading specialist performers of non-*khyāl* genres in the segments of the *ṭhumrī* and allied genres, *ghaẓals* and *bhajans*. For want of the author's knowledge, specialist performers of the regional devotional genres were not included. The musicians were chosen for the significance of their presence on the concert platform over a long enough period.

In the *ṭhumrī* segment, Chhannulal Mishra – is still alive and is included. In the *ghaẓal* segment, the sample selection was restricted to the singers of the classical *ghaẓal* – Begum Akhtar and Mehdi Hassan – while the more recent singers of the modern *ghaẓal* have been excluded.

This approach has given us a sample of eleven musicians in whose case, a minimum of fifteen and a maximum of thirty-five recordings were available for the measurement of audience involvement (Table 18.1).

Indications

The following table and graphic plot (*fig.* 18.1) show a long-term growth trend of audience involvement. But, it also exhibits

Name	Birth	Sample Size	Views	Months	Views/ Month
Rasoolan Bai	1902	22	1,61,249	1,054	153
Barkat Ali Khan	1905	29	1,57,828	940	168
Siddheshwari Devi	1908	25	74,059	716	103
Begum Akhtar	1914	34	17,02,977	1,931	882
Shanti Hiranand	1914	19	28,030	579	48
Purshottam Jaloca	1925	15	1,36,962	527	260
Shobha Gurtu	1925	35	6,66,635	1,320	505
Mehdi Hassan	1927	35	57,81,113	1,590	3,636
Nirmala Devi	1927	16	93,007	439	212
Girija Devi	1929	22	3,63,940	914	398
Chhannulal Mishra	1936	27	4,19,325	756	555
Aggregate			95,85,125	10,766	1,027

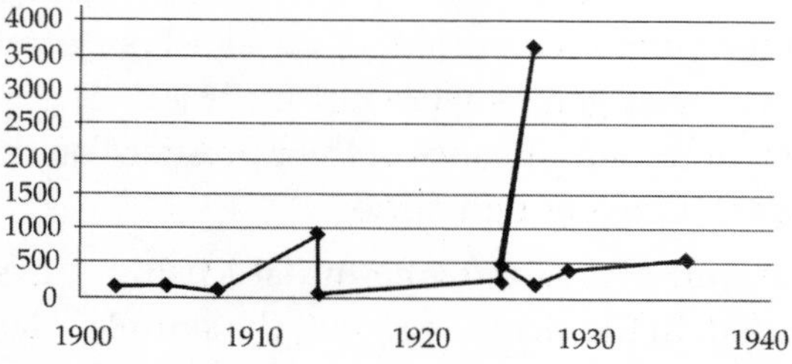

fig. 18.1: YouTube views/month by birth year

two waves within the period considered. The two peaks are represented by Begum Akhtar and Mehdi Hassan. Two waves, within a long-term growth trend, is a pattern very similar to the pattern noticed in the earlier study of the non-Khyāl repertoire of Khyāl vocalists. The generational interpretation of this graph could be similar to that of the graph seen in the earlier study.

It would appear that at this particular juncture in history, two generations of audiences are involved with the music of the specialist performers of the non-*khyāl* genres. However, the two titans who dominate the two visible peaks – Begum Akhtar and Mehdi Hassan – are born at an interval of only thirteen years. This might mean that, in effect, only one generation of musicians appears to dominate the non-*khyāl* music-scape at the moment. This compares with three, perhaps four, generations of audiences involved with the *khyāl* music of the past generations of vocalists.

While we may consider these two giants as representing the same generation and appealing to the same audience generation, a certain obsolescence factor is perhaps evident even in their relative scores. It is probably the younger end of the audience generation which gives Mehdi Hassan a score almost four times the score obtained by Begum Akhtar – ostensibly emanating from the older end of the same generation.

The power of the specialist non-*khyāl* indicator as an influence on *khyāl* music is more sharply reflected in its absolute numbers than in the obsolescence trend. *Fig*. 18..2 tells the story.

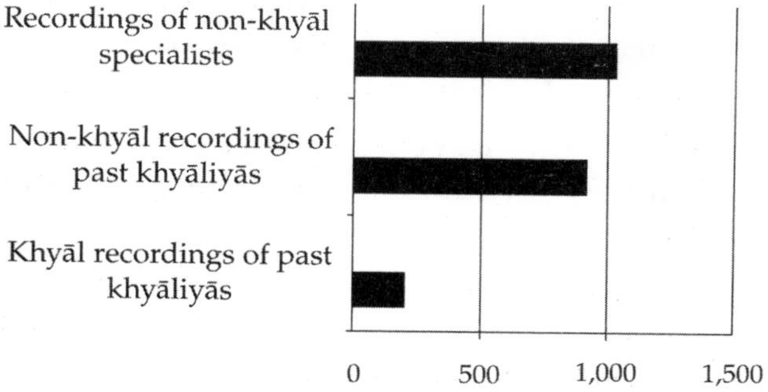

fig. 18.2: Comparative scores for different segments

The *khyāl* music of *khyāl* vocalists begets only 203 viewers per month of recording availability. Compared to this, their own non-*khyāl* music notches up 914 views, and the non-*khyāl* music of the specialist performers of non-*khyāl* music crosses that 1,000 views per month.

Admittedly, this average for specialist performers of the non-*khyāl* genres is greatly bolstered by Begum Akhtar and Mehdi Hassan, and not every musician achieves their level of audience involvement. However, the average of over 1,000 views per month cannot be ignored as a perceptional reality of the musical culture and of relevance to professional musicians.

By pure arithmetical coincidence, if we add the audience involvement ratings for *khyāl* and non-*khyāl* repertoires of *khyāl* vocalists, we get a figure almost exactly equal to the audience involvement rating of the specialist non-*khyāl* performers. We may then surmise that the primary motivation for *khyāl* vocalists to perform non-*khyāl* music is reaching out to a much larger audience.

The Interaction of Genres

With audiences exhibiting a marked preference for non-*khyāl* repertoire, the *khyāl* will tend to shrink in terms of its presence on the concert platform. As this trend gathers momentum, *khyāl* vocalists will begin to lose their aesthetic grip over the *khyāl* as a genre. Their approach to the *khyāl* will increasingly reflect the aesthetic values of the non-*khyāl* repertoire in vogue.

This process may be better understood with a historical analogy from the print medium in the country, which is familiar to most of us.

In the 1950s and 1960s, the mainline dailies published a sports page only twice a week. In those days, several sports magazines (weeklies / fortnightlies / monthlies) showed a healthy growth in sales and revenue. The mainline dailies saw this opportunity for an enlargement of their share-of-mind and share-of-market, and stepped up sports coverage to everyday. By the 1980s all the specialist sports magazines had died for want of readers and advertisers.

The same thing happened to the film-magazine boom of the 1960s and 1970s. By the year 2000, mainline dailies which earlier had only weekly / bi-weekly cinema supplements, began cinema coverage on a daily basis. Almost all film magazines have since been gasping for breath. This history repeated itself with the arrival of specialist society / celebrity magazines in the 1980s. By 2010, society and celebrity coverage has become regular daily material in the mainline dailies. The specialist magazines in this segment of journalism are now extinct.

As a result of these changes, India's mainline English dailies have changed almost beyond recognition in the last thirty years.

In the present context, there is no reason to believe that a transformation of the *khyāl* will drive the *ghaẓal* or *ṭhumrī* totally out of circulation. But, as the *khyāl* starts resembling the relatively *rāga*-neutral genres in some respects, it will shrink the aesthetic space available to them for remaining in independent circulation. And, some would argue that this tendency is visible already.

It has been argued, for instance, that Begum Akhtar and Mehdi Hassan brought so much melodic sophistication to the *ghazal* that they left the original Banaras *ṭhumrī* struggling for survival. It has also been noted that once the *khyāl* genre annexed and enriched the *bandiś-kī-ṭhumrī* as the *chhoṭā khyāl*, the *bandiś-kī-ṭhumrī* lost its footing in the musical culture. Further, it is observed that with the advent of the romanticist brigade in *khyāl* vocalism – Kumar Gandharva, Jasraj and Kishori Amonkar – the *bol-banāv ṭhumrī* and some other semi-classical genres lost a good deal of their aesthetic territory. These are purely aesthetic observations, which are impossible to either prove or disprove. But, they are not rendered invalid by this probable infirmity.

Here we may recall Ranade's argument stated in Chapter 17. The dominant mainstream genre tends to protect its dominance – amongst other tendencies – by adopting the musical features of ascendant rivals. By this reasoning, *khyāl*, the dominant mainstream genre, is likely to respond to the threat/ opportunity presented by the non-*khyāl* genres by adopting their musical values. This possibility does suggest a paradigm shift because the *khyāl* is founded on the durable musical value of *rāga* exploration, while the aesthetic assumptions of the non-*khyāl* genres are fundamentally *rāga*-neutral, even though *rāga*s may in practice inform their melodic content.

Is This Happening Already?

The YouTube data studied so far pertains to vocalists who are either already departed or in their advanced years. We need to examine several additional pieces of contemporary and/or trend-related evidence to support the hypothesis emerging here. These may constitute the objects of continued enquiry.

19

Aesthetic Obsolescence and Paradigm Shifts in Hindustānī Vocalism: V

The Emerging Music-Scape

Chapters 15-18 have looked at this subject from several angles. I now attempt to tie up the various strands of thought by including data on contemporary *khyāl* musicians, using the same measure of audience involvement as in the earlier studies.

Unlike earlier studies, however, I shall not report the audience involvement measures for each musician individually. I avoid this for two reasons: First, such measures are irrelevant to the purpose of this study. Second, there is a danger that individual measures for contemporary musicians might be interpreted in a manner unwarranted by the limitations of the data and the nature of the study.

The contemporary vocalists covered by this study are: Malini Rajurkar, Veena Sahasrabuddhe, Kishori Amonkar, Jasraj, Shruti Sadolikar, Ashwini Bhide-Deshpande, Ulhas Kashalkar, Rajan and Sajan Mishra, Venkatesh Kumar, Ajoy Chakravarty, Gauri Pathare, Arati Anklikar-Tikekar, Manjusha Kulkarni-Patil, Rashid Khan, Kaushiki Chakravarty, Jaiteerth Mevundi, Dhananjay Hegde, Manjiri Asnare-Kelkar and Sanjeev Abhyankar.

With respect to contemporary musicians, a small change had to be made in the selection of sample recordings. For this sub-sample, I have only considered recordings uploaded after

1 January 2010. This is because YouTube viewership data is cumulative from the day of upload of the recordings. This would have made data for the senior and the very young musicians non-comparable. By limiting the duration of the upload dates between January 2010 and 1 May 2015, I have made sure that the data across the contemporary sample remains broadly comparable. This of course assumes that even the youngest of the considered musicians has been on the horizon of significant musicianship for at least five years. This was the only refinement possible to the methodology of a study made using data of known and admittedly limited value.

The Focus

We are now looking at the involvement of the present YouTube

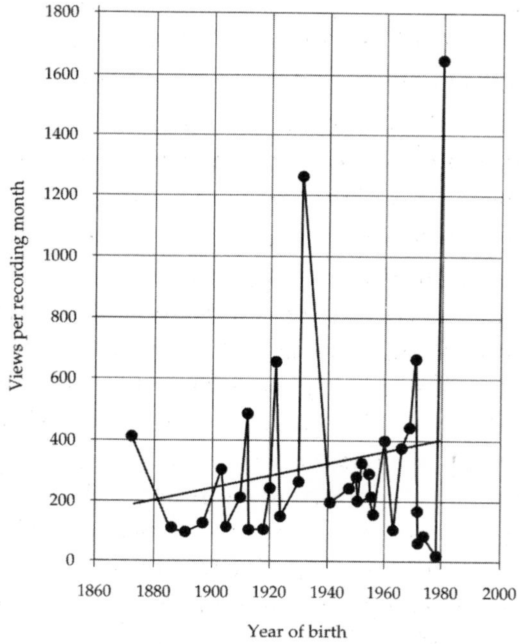

fig. 19.1: Average monthly, YouTube views of thirty-three *khyāl* vocalists

audience in the *khyāl* vocalism specimens of musicians born between 1872 and 1980, a period of 108 years. Assuming that the earliest uploaded recordings were made after the musician had reached at least thirty years of age we are looking at music of the period 1902–2015. At the audience end, we are looking at listeners who are between 30 and 75 years of age in 2015.

By the Jose Ortega generational model of thirty years constituting a distinct cultural generation, we are looking at music made by 3.8 generations of musicians and its hold on the minds of 2.5 generations of audiences. However, Ortega also suggests that the face of the world changes in some ways every fifteen years – which is half a generation. We are therefore probably looking at the music of a period within which the world has changed, in some ways, as many as seven times.

Fig. 19.1 plot the average monthly YouTube views reported for the *khyāl* music of thirty-three *khyāl* vocalists, born between 1872 and 1980. Significant patterns are as follows:

ONE: The long-term trend-line confirms our view that, the older is the music on offer, the less likely it is to be heard by present-day listeners of Hindustānī music. The obsolescence hypothesis is adequately supported.

TWO: The wavelike pattern reflects the simultaneous effect of multiple generations of listeners relating to the same music. In any given population, at any given time, there will be emerging generations, and receding generations of listeners as well as musicians. The musical values and preferences of the two will diverge partially while also being partially convergent. This partial overlap creates a wavelike formation. The graph shows seven or eight waves of varying durations over a period of 105 years of music, perhaps suggesting that the musical culture has thrown up significant representative musicians each time the world has changed a little, i.e. fifteen years.

THREE: The suggestion of a long-wave postulated by the

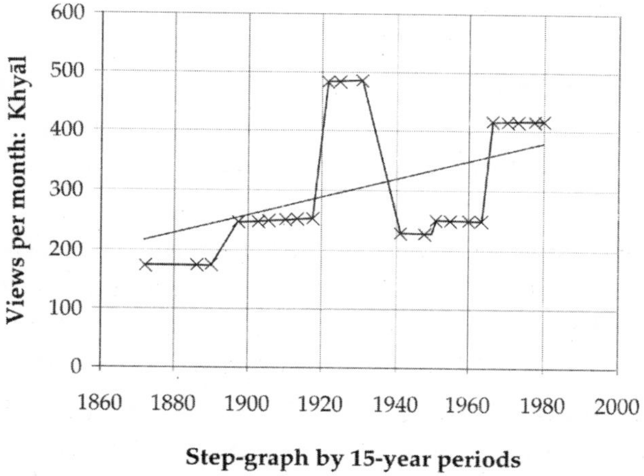

fig. 19.2: YouTube khyāl viewership per month over fifteen-year period (1860-2000)

Kondratieff Model discussed earlier in this series of essays is also evident in this graph. After Abdul Kareem Khan (b.1872), the graph shows the next big upsurge in culturally relevant musical value with Kishori Amonkar (b.1931) – a period of fifty-nine years. Though it may be a bit early to speculate on the emerging scenario, there are signs that the Amonkar peak may be bettered by vocalists born around 1980, i.e. fifty years after her.

FOUR: If the world changes in some ways every fifteen years, it is proper to look at groups of musicians born within the same fifteen-year period (rather than individual musicians) as collectively expressing the "zeitgeist" of the era. The complex pattern of *fig*. 19.1 can be simplified, and made historically more relevant, in *fig*. 19.2, derived from the same set of computations as *fig*. 19.1 .

This graph once again confirms the obsolescence hypothesis and does so perhaps more sharply than the previous one. In addition, it suggests that the world has perhaps changed significantly six times (rather than seven or eight) in the last

105 years. The peak of this step-graph represents the era of D.V. Paluskar, Bhimsen Joshi, Kumar Gandharva, Jasraj and Kishori Amonkar (b.1920-1935).

Two successive half-generations after them do not appear to claim a comparable share-of-mind among audiences. This appears to validate my contention that the first post-Independence generation of Hindustānī vocalists remained under the stylistic shadows of the pre-Independence giants, failed to address their own generation effectively, and thereby caused a substantial loss of audiences to Hindustānī vocalism.

It is with the third half-generation after the peak (b.1965-1980) that audience involvement shows a brisk rise with the possibility of matching – and perhaps surpassing – the highest peak evident so far. If a long wave of fifty-sixty years heralds a paradigm shift, this indication suggests that Hindustānī vocalism could be on the threshold of one.

Non-Khyāl Repertoire

Unlike *dhrupad* vocalists, *khyāl* vocalists have always maintained a non-*khyāl* repertoire as an integral part of their musicianship. In Chapter 17, we have observed that this non-*khyāl* repertoire of departed musicians dominates the interest of contemporary YouTube audiences. This is, of course, a commentary on the musical values of contemporary audiences more than the musical tendencies or temperaments of the musicians of the past.

We may now consider whether the pattern holds true when contemporary musicians are considered along with departed musicians. This relationship is reflected in *fig*. 19.3, which superimposes audience involvement measure with respect to non-*khyāl* repertoire upon the measure for the *khyāl* repertoire. In order to preserve the historical focus of this study, the comparison is, once again, presented by fifteen-year periods, rather than for individual musicians.

The inferences from the emerging pattern are as follows:

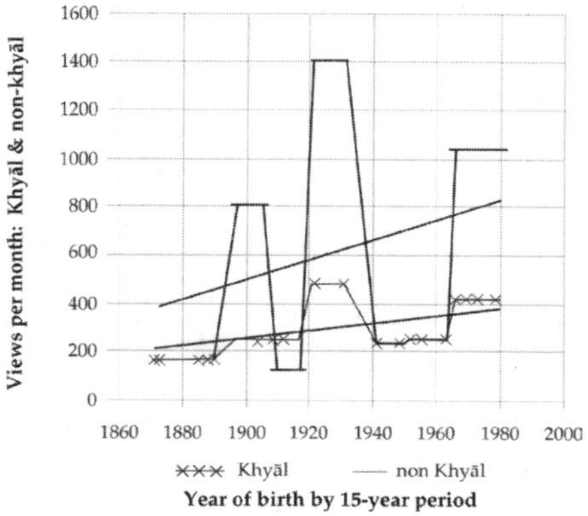

fig. 19.3: Scores for *Khyāl* and non-*Khyāl* recordings – All *Khyāl* vocalists

ONE: The long-term trend-line for non-*khyāl* repertoire exhibits a much sharper obsolescence factor than the trend-line for *khyāl* repertoire. This confirms our earlier observation that non-*khyāl* repertoire responds more efficiently to changing aesthetic values and musical needs of society because of the freedom it enjoys from the relatively more durable musical values characteristic of the *khyāl* genre.

TWO: It is also significant that the upswings in the viewership of *khyāl* recordings have consistently been accompanied by much sharper upswings in the viewership of non-*khyāl* recordings. Likewise, a stagnation or depression in *khyāl* viewership is accompanied by a stagnation or depression in the viewership of non-*khyāl* recordings. This would imply that the appeal of a musician's non-*khyāl* repertoire is more crucial to his/her professional success than that of his/her *khyāl* repertoire.

THREE: The long-term trend-line of the non-*khyāl* repertoire runs at double the audience-involvement level of the *khyāl* repertoire trend-line. This pattern confirms our view that contemporary audiences are far more involved with non-*khyāl* repertoire of any era within their frame of consideration than with the *khyāl* repertoire. This may be interpreted to imply that the *khyāl* genre, as hitherto understood, is fast ceasing to satisfy the musical needs of a vast majority of contemporary audiences.

FOUR: Genres may become obsolete; but musicians do not – because they have to survive. The *khyāl* genre can therefore be expected now to take a back seat in the total musical persona of a classical vocalist, and/or undergo a major recalibration of its aesthetic assumptions in order to remain relevant to contemporary society.

FIVE: From the contemporary perspective, the last paradigm shift in Hindustānī vocalism is traced to the fifteen-year period that felt the impact of D.V. Paluskar, Bhimsen Joshi, Kumar Gandharva, Jasraj and Kishori Amonkar. For that period (see *fig*. 19.3), the audience-involvement for non-*khyāl* music runs at about 900 viewers per month above that for *khyāl* music. For the first time since then, the latest period under review shows a gap of over 600 views per month between the two graphs.

When such a large gap emerges between durable musical values and ephemeral musical values, the community of musicians can be expected to narrow it in the interest of their own economic security. How does this happen? For an answer to this question, we draw again on Ranade's observations on how a mainstream genre builds, maintains and protects its supremacy. Amongst other processes, it does so by (a) adopting the features of the ascendant or rival genres, and (b) by attracting talent from all kinds of sources.

First, the proportion of non-*khyāl* repertoire to a musician's total public presence will shoot up. Instead of being the "dessert" at the end of a meal, it will progressively become the "main course". Second, the stylistic distinction between *khyāl* and non-*khyāl* repertoires will narrow. *Khyāl* renditions will have to start reflecting the musical values of non-*khyāl* genres, if they wish to command an audience at all.

The same process may also be viewed a little differently.

The predominance of non-*khyāl* repertoire as a success factor for professional musicians will tend to attract vocalists who have the training and temperament more suited to non-*khyāl* music than to *khyāl* music. Their presence in the *khyāl* segment – such as they may be able to achieve – will give them the respectability of the "Classical Music" platform, without putting their competence to test. Under such conditions, their *khyāl*s can only remain unconvincing by the traditional yardstick of *khyāl* vocalism. Both these processes would be logical manifestations of a paradigm shift – either imminent or already under way.

What Is Khyāl or Non-Khyāl?

The present author has surveyed the YouTube portfolios of thirty-three departed and contemporary Hindustānī vocalists for this study, recorded over a century. With particular reference to contemporary musicians, he has had to resolve interesting conceptual issues while classifying individual recordings as belonging either to the *khyāl* or non-*khyāl* categories.

The researcher in Hindustānī music today encounters a bewildering variety of "genres", many of which neither have appropriate names, nor a well-defined character. An attempt is made here to list some of the names that have suggested themselves.

Khyāl-ized *ṭhumrī*, ṭhumrī-ized *khyāl*, khyāl-ized *sargam*, sargam-ized *khyāl*, bhajan-ized *ṭhumrī*, bhajan-ized *khyāl*, ṭhumrī-ized *bhajan*, khyāl-ized *bhajan*, kr̥ti-ized *khyāl*, khyāl-ized *kr̥ti*, bhajan-ized scriptures, scripturized *bhajans*, scripturized *khyāl*, khyāl-ized scriptures, vocal–instrumental *jugalbandī*, Hindustānī–Carnatic *jugalbandī*, Hindustānī–Carnatic fusion, Hindustānī–Carnatic–Western Pop/Jazz fusion and Hindustānī–Opera fusion.

All these genres respond to a notion of *rāga*-ness, even if only tangentially or remotely. But, the relationship is incidental more than purposive. Even where the *khyāl* is encountered in its original architecture, the manifestations of *rāga*-ness in the rendition rarely cross a set of identifying phrases.

This suggests that Hindustānī music audiences are now so hungry for novelty that almost any well-trained vocalist can create a niche for himself/herself by creating a new genre, as long as he/she can execute it with competence and confidence. And, if his/her non-*khyāl* repertoire clicks with the audiences, he/she need not fear being astutely evaluated by orthodox audiences for his/her *khyāl* competence.

A great deal of the "bewildering" quality of present-day Hindustānī vocalism reflects the sharp drop in the average age of the Indian population witnessed since Independence. With a median age of 27, India is the youngest country in the world. Projections appear to suggest that a reversal of this trend has already begun, and the median is rising by four years every decade. An entirely new demography is taking shape, whose cultural implications are impossible to anticipate.

A greater number of coexisting generations/half-generations can create a more fragmented aesthetic environment. The emerging pattern need not push the orthodox *khyāl* entirely out of circulation or place it under an immediate threat of extinction. It could still remain (like *dhrupad*) in marginalized circulation for another couple of generations. But, during its residual life, it could change beyond recognition to survive. This is because the very essence of a paradigm shift is that it changes society's perception of itself, never to return to its original state.

20

Aesthetic Obsolescence and Paradigm Shifts in Hindustānī Vocalism: VI

The Limitations of YouTube Data

A GOOD deal of the discussion relating to my recent studies revolved around the reliability and propriety of using YouTube viewership data. The prefatory remarks to my very first essay on the subject (Chapter 15) had admitted that the data source is far from ideal for systematic research and that I was using it in full awareness of its limitations.

This is why I submitted the data to only the most basic level of mathematical analysis. The measure I used was a simple "average views per month of availability" with respect to the aggregate of views over a period. Throughout the reporting of the results, there was only minimal reference to the mathematical ratio. I preferred, instead, to call it an "audience involvement measure". I did not report any of the statistical trend analysis I had done on the data for my own understanding. Even the graphic treatment of my computations was historical and generational rather than musician-specific.

I understand that, despite its known limitations, YouTube viewership data is now being used by researchers even in the more advanced research environments. Presumably because it is better than nothing, its use will not stop, and, because of its known limitations, the controversy over its value, too, will not end.

For those who feel interested in this issue, I decided to write out this report on the subject.

ONE: YouTube reports "views" for each recording. The first question is: what is a view? For a 30-minute video, what minimum duration of viewing qualifies as "view"? Further, is a 10-minute viewing the same viewership value as a full 30-minute viewing? We have no way of knowing this and, therefore, of using the notion of "viewership" more intelligently.

TWO: In the early days of YouTube, there was a duration limit on the uploads. This affected Hindustānī music very significantly, as most performances exceeded the limit, and had to be split into two, three and sometimes four parts for upload. After the duration limit was lifted, mostly complete performances were uploaded. Looking at that data today, can we consider the viewership data for a concert split into three parts comparable with that of a complete performance as a measure of viewership involvement? There is no logical way of building this known discrepancy into our measurement of audience involvement.

THREE: YouTube viewership data is cumulative from the date of uploading. By using that data, I am implicitly accepting one view of 2006 on par with one view in 2015. During this period, YouTube viewership has grown exponentially, and its audience profile for every kind of content has almost certainly changed radically. Intuitively, we know the assumption is flawed. But, we have no way of adjusting for this flaw in our analysis and interpretation of the data.

FOUR: Another problem with cumulative data is that it obliges us, for instance, to equate 20,000 views accumulated over twenty months with 40,000 views accumulated over forty months. Intuitively, this equation does not look reasonable. One of the two has to be more valuable as a measure of audience involvement. If the propensity of a recording to accumulate viewers is important, 40,000 over four years is more valuable. And, if the speed of audience accumulation is considered important, 20,000 over twenty months is more valuable. YouTube data, as available, does not permit us even to ask such a question, leave alone provide its answer.

FIVE: The YouTube audience is global, and so is the audience for Hindustānī music. But, we have no data on the nation-wise mix of viewership for each recording. In our analysis, we are obliged to treat the viewership number as a homogeneous mass – which it certainly is not. By implication, we are assuming that foreign audiences of Hindustānī music – across all nationalities and cultures – have the same relationship with the music, and the same profile, as Indians have. There is enough evidence to show that this is not so. Our analysis and interpretation of the numbers can therefore lead to unjustified and even misleading inferences.

SIX: Although YouTube is a video medium, a large amount of Hindustānī music on it constitutes either only audio content supported by a still visual, or audio supported by a slide show. The nature of the content is itself not uniform. In fact, even the notion of "viewership" may be irrelevant to a lot of the content. Do 100 people listening to an audio recording with just a photograph of the musician on the screen represent the same level of audience involvement as 100 people watching him or another musician in action on film? If not, how do we devise an "equalization factor" between the three formats?

SEVEN: This listing merely covers data source features which impinge directly upon the focus of my studies. Researchers with different perspectives could enumerate a different and perhaps larger set of limitations.

It appears that, with specific reference to Hindustānī music, YouTube neither offers a uniform media experience to its audience, nor publicly provides a rigorous measurement of audience engagement. What, then, is YouTube data good for?

I believe it is better than nothing. It cannot be said to

represent "statistics", but can represent "orders of magnitude". It can be used only as indicative and never as conclusive. Inferences should be drawn most judiciously from its analysis, with every inference reflecting the analyst's awareness of data limitations.

A close scrutiny of YouTube user interface suggests that a lot of very sophisticated analytics are being generated on viewership/audience engagement by its managers for internal consumption. And, these analytics are being used for strengthening the relationship between YouTube and its users and advertisers. It is safe to assume that the viewership information YouTube currently offers publicly is also aimed at strengthening those relationships. It was not intended to be helpful to researchers and may, in fact, have been purposefully kept unusable for such purposes.

As YouTube grows into a major cultural force, it will find it necessary to understand itself better in order to keep growing. For this, it will need to engage constructively with social scientists and media researchers in all the geographies and cultures where it has a significant presence. This could launch an era of greater transparency in YouTube analytics.

Until then, the Indian musicologist should be content with "orders of magnitude" and indicative inferences. Is this better than consulting ten veteran *rasika*s and observers of the music scene? I believe so, because *rasika*s can acquire "personal" preferences (biases, prejudices); impersonally generated numbers cannot.

21

Hindustānī Music in the Baroda State

INDIA has a long tradition of aristocratic patronage of the arts and culture. In addition to the protection and prosperity of subjects, the Indian ideal of kingship has made rulers responsible also for their moral, spiritual and cultural uplift. This tradition could well have decayed during the colonial period, had India's alien rulers demolished the older political structures. The British, instead, found it convenient to retain the traditional structure of Indian society, and allowed the Indian aristocracy to pursue its traditional ideals, while fulfilling their military and financial obligations to the colonial power.

After the First Indian War of Independence in 1857, 562 (569, according to some accounts) princely states came directly under the suzerainty of the British Crown. Of these, a few were granted a special relationship with the sovereign on account of their revenue potential, military prowess and quality of governance. Baroda was amongst these states, along with Kashmir, Patiala, Jaipur, Jodhpur, Gwalior, Indore, Mysore, Travancore and Hyderabad. Under the new dispensation, these states enjoyed special stipends and subsidies, along with greater administrative autonomy and financial freedom. Amongst these jewels of the British crown, the princely state of Baroda, ruled by the Gaekwad dynasty, emerged at the forefront of the renaissance that swept India in the last 100 years of British rule.

This essay was published in the Golden Jubilee Souvenir of Swara Vilas, the premier cultural institution in Baroda. It seeks to document the history of Hindustānī music under the erstwhile Baroda State and the contribution of the Gaekwad dynasty.

Colonial supervision eliminated warfare between neighbouring states, thus bringing peace to the entire sub-continent. With the special status they enjoyed under British rule, the powerful states had the resources and the freedom to become major patrons of sports, literature, architecture and the arts. They patronized scholars, musicians, dancers, poets and sportsmen in large numbers, set up great institutions of learning and built beautiful cities contributing greatly to the quality of life enjoyed by their citizens. In a very real sense, the rulers of these major states became the engineers of a modern Indian identity and precursors to the political leadership that later led India towards independence. Amongst the princely builders of modern India, Maharaja Sayajirao Gaekwad III of Baroda achieved legendary status.

Despite his multi-dimensional contribution to the life of Baroda, Maharaja Sayajirao III is most gratefully remembered for his patronage and encouragement of classical music. The recent history of Hindustānī music cannot be written without referring to musicians and scholars who flourished under his patronage. More than a century after Maharaja Sayajirao established a music school in Baroda (1886), the institution remains the principal provider of music education in the state, with the largest enrollment of students seeking a degree in music, dance and theatre.

Maula Baksh (1833-96)

Maula Baksh was a formidable vocalist, *vīṇā* player and scholar who played a leading role in the establishment of Baroda's musical culture. In that era, he was a rare Hindustānī musician, who had also mastered the Carnatic *vīṇā*. He reportedly learnt Hindustānī music secretly from Ghaseeta Khan, a renowned though inaccessible musician of his era, by overhearing his *guru*'s practice sessions. When the maestro found out, he was impressed enough with Maula Baksh to accept him as a disciple.

Maula Baksh served the royal court of Mysore before he was invited by the Baroda court. In this capacity, he was also given the responsibility for the state music school founded in 1886.

He rendered outstanding services as a musician and as an educationist, authoring several textbooks for music students, and devising perhaps the first comprehensive notation system for Hindustānī music. He introduced several Carnatic *rāga*s to Hindustānī music and pioneered orchestration in Indian classical music. Maula Baksh ran the school for ten years and upon his death in 1896, his son, Murtaza Khan was made principal. In recognition of his contribution, the bust of Maula Baksh now adorns the entrance to the Faculty of Performing Arts of the MS University of Baroda.

Faiz Muhammad Khan (d.1920)

Faiz Mohammad Khan was a contemporary of Maula Baksh and enjoyed virtually parallel status as a musician at the Baroda court. He was a distinguished vocalist of the Gwalior Gharānā. Documented history is unclear about his artistic antecedents. He was reportedly a younger brother of the same Ghaseeta Khan, who was the *guru* of Maula Baksh. According to some accounts, he was a disciple of Natthan Peer Baksh, the founder of the Gwalior Gharānā; but other accounts point out that he was much younger than Haddu Khan and Hassu Khan (the sons of Natthan Peer Baksh) and could have been a disciple of either of them.

There is no doubt, however, that he was a highly influential member of the Gaekwad music establishment. He was assigned the task of prospecting for a young musician who could bring greater glory to the Baroda court, and selected the young Faiyyaz Khan, who later reigned as the uncrowned emperor of the concert platform for almost four decades. Faiz Mohammad also became Faiyyaz Khan's father-in-law.

In addition to his court duties, Faiz Mohammad taught at

the Baroda State Music School and groomed brilliant musicians such as Bhaskar Rao Bakhle.

Vishnu Narayan Bhatkhande (1860–1936)

In the first quarter of the twentieth century, Vishnu Narayan Bhatkhande, a practising advocate from Bombay, took upon himself the task of organizing all available knowledge on the practice and theory of classical music. For this, he travelled across the lengths and breadths of the country unearthing old texts and drawing on the accumulated musical wisdom of as many scholars and musicians as would cooperate. His contribution to Indian musicology is considered on par with that of Śārṅgadeva, who authored the landmark treatise, *Saṅgīta Ratnākara*, in the thirteenth century. Bhatkhande's scholarship and pioneering zeal appealed to Maharaja Sayajirao III, who gave him his wholehearted support.

The first All India Music Conference was organized at Baroda in 1916 under the patronage of Maharaja Sayajirao, with Bhatkhande in the chair. The conference hosted leading scholars and musicians from the Hindustānī as well as Carnatic traditions. It was a landmark event in the history of Indian classical music. Learned papers were read and discussed, and several controversial issues in musicology were settled with the emergence of a consensus.

Maharaja Sayajirao III saw in Bhatkhande's work the possibility of widespread musical literacy and institutionalized music education. Therefore, he enlisted Bhatkhande's guidance for reorganizing the music school. Between 1926 and 1928, Faiyyaz Khan, the pre-eminent musician at the Baroda court served as the principal of the school. When Hirjibhai Doctor was appointed principal (1928), the Bhatkhande methodology was fully integrated into the education system, thus enabling it to evolve into a degree-granting institution.

Vishnu Digambar Paluskar (1872–1931)

A contemporary of Bhatkhande, Vishnu Digambar Paluskar, was the other renaissance man of Hindustānī music in the twentieth century. A product of the influential Gwalior Gharānā and a formidable scholar and musician, he decided to forego success as a performer and devoted his life to music education.

Unlike professional musicians, Paluskar lodged himself unobtrusively in a temple during his visit to Baroda. Devotees at the temple heard him every morning when he practised from 4.00 to 8.00 a.m. Soon the royal household heard of this great musician who was visiting the city incognito. Paluskar was invited to perform at the court. Faiz Muhammad Khan, the influential vocalist at the Baroda court, performed after Paluskar, but failed to make an impression. The Gaekwad court honoured Paluskar with a generous contribution to his missionary work. The Gandharva Mahavidyalaya, founded by Paluskar, remains to this day the leading all-India institution for music education.

Murtaza Khan (1860–??)

Murtaza Khan was a son of Maula Baksh. He grew up in Mysore during his father's tenure at the Mysore court and learnt Kannada and Telugu, besides Urdu, Persian and Arabic. When the family moved to Baroda, he learnt Marathi and Gujarati. He was a child prodigy, who acquired performing competence as a vocalist, *rudra-vīṇā* player and a *sarasvatī-vīṇā* (Carnatic) player while still in his teens. By the age of 12, he was accompanying his father and also performing independently.

On his father's demise in 1896, he was appointed principal of the State Music School. His post was apparently coveted by some other members of the Baroda music establishment. Professional rivalry led to his removal. Despite this, he remained a highly respected musician of the Baroda court, with frequent concert appearances at the palace.

Govind Sharma (1863–1924)

Govind Sharma was the most promising disciple of Maula Baksh. His family hailed from Nizamabad in Andhra Pradesh and moved to Baroda when his grandfather entered the service of the Baroda state as a minor functionary.

He was charmed by the musical prowess of Maula Baksh and served the *ustād* devotedly for many years before he was accepted as a disciple. He was a quick learner and acquired performing competence at a young age. He had a great future as a vocalist, which was cut short by excessive strain on his vocal chords, which cost him his voice. Maula Baksh resurrected his career as a musician by coaching him on the *sitār*. Sharma then served the Baroda state music school as a *sitār* teacher and also authored two valuable books on music. Towards the latter part of his life, he came under the influence of Sant Vaman Buwa, relinquished the world and travelled across the country in the service of his spiritual master.

Bhaskar Rao Bakhle (1869–1922)

Bhaskar Rao Bakhle was born to very poor parents in Kathore village of the Baroda state. His talent was noticed by an influential citizen, Gajanan Bhatavdekar, during a school function. Bhatavdekar sent the prodigy to Maula Baksh to be trained at the state music school. Around that time, the Kirloskar Drama Company was looking for a singer–actor to play female roles, and appointed Bhaskar Rao to the vacancy. When the drama company was visiting Indore, the famous *bīnkār*, Bande Ali Khan adopted him and began to train him. Around the time the drama company left Indore, Bakhle's male voice was emerging, jeopardizing his usefulness.

With no further interest in theatre and passionately committed to a career as a classical vocalist, he returned to Baroda in search of a direction. At this stage, Mr Telang, another senior official of the state, placed him under the tutelage of

Faiz Muhammad Khan, another leading court musician. After several years of Gwalior Gharānā training, Faiz Muhammad sent Bhaskar Rao to study with the Agra Gharānā stalwart, Natthan Khan (1840–1901), then at the Mysore court. Thereafter, Bakhle became a disciple of Alladiya Khan (1855–1946), the fountainhead of the Jaipur-Atrauli Gharānā. With training under three stalwarts of the era, Bhaskar Rao Bakhle emerged as one of the most formidable vocalists of his times. Although never in the service of the Baroda state, he was a product of the rich musical culture that Baroda had established under the patronage of the Gaekwad rulers.

Abdul Kareem Khan (1872–1937)

At the age of 19, Abdul Kareem Khan left his home in Kairana, a village in Shamli district of UP, along with his brother, Abdul Haque, in search of a career. Baroda, a famed centre of music, was an obvious destination. After failing to get an audience at the Gaekwad court, the brothers managed to gatecrash into a court appearance of the famous *dhrupadiyā*s from Jaipur, Allabande and Zakiruddin Dagar. Perchance, the itinerant brothers were also allowed to perform at the soiree. Maula Baksh, the senior court musician, was impressed and advised the *mahārājā* to appoint them in the service of the state. Abdul Kareem Khan served the Baroda court for three years, during which period he successfully wooed Tarabai Mane, the daughter of a nobleman at the Baroda court. Their romance was evidently the trigger for his departure from Baroda. But, their union produced eminently durable results. Their three children – Hirabai Barodekar, Saraswatibai Rane and Suresh Babu Mane – all emerged as formidable torchbearers of the Kairana Gharānā.

Tasadduq Hussain Khan (1876–1946)

Tasadduq Hussain was the son and disciple of Kallan Khan of the Agra lineage. He was also a scholar of Urdu and Persian languages and known for his command over *rāga* grammar.

He was appointed by the Baroda state as a music teacher at one of the state-run high schools, which he served for twenty-two years. He made a contribution to the storehouse of Agra Gharānā compositions under the pen-name "Vinod Piya". In his memoirs, the Agra Gharānā stalwart, Vilayat Hussain Khan named Tasadduq Hussain amongst his several *gurus*.

Faiyyaz Khan (1886–1950)

In the early years of the twentieth century, Maharaja Sayajirao III, asked Faiz Muhammad, a senior court musician, to search the country for a promising musician who could add to the stature of the Baroda court for years to come. In his pan-India search, Faiz Muhammad visited Agra where he encountered Faiyyaz Khan, a scion of the Rangeele Gharānā from his father's side, and the Agra Gharānā from his mother's side. By this time, the young genius had already been honoured by the rulers of Mysore and Hyderabad. On Faiz Mohammad's commendation, Maharaja Sayajirao invited Faiyyaz Khan to perform at the Holī festival at the Baroda court.

At the age of 32, Faiyyaz Khan was appointed to the Baroda court. Over the next four decades, with Baroda as his base, the *ustād* built up a towering all-India presence as the undisputed emperor of the concert platform. V.N. Bhatkhande, the father of Indian musicology, regarded him as the most authentic contemporary exponent of traditional music. The title of "Aftab-e-mausiqui" conferred on him by the Mysore court got permanently attached to his name. And, to this day, he is always spoken of as "Ustad Faiyyaz Khan of Baroda".

In addition to his stature as a musician, Faiyyaz Khan distinguished himself as a *guru*, grooming a small army of great teachers – S.N. Ratanjankar (1900-74), Dilipchandra Vedi (1901-92), Dhruvatara Joshi (1914-92), Latafat Hussain Khan (1921-86), Ghulam Quadir Khan (1917–2002), Sharafat Hussain Khan (1930-85) and Ata Hussain Khan (1903-80). The great *ustād* is also credited with having guided the flowering of the exceptional musicianship of his harmonium accompanist, Ghulam Rasool Khan.

Hazrat Enayet Khan (1882–1927)

Hazrat Enayet Khan was a grandson of Maula Baksh. The "Hazrat" honorific owes to his emergence as an influential sufi mystic on the international scene, along with his stature as a scholar and performer of Indian classical music. He acquired great proficiency in Gujarati, Sanskrit, Urdu, Persian, Arabic and Marathi in his early years and became fluent in English, French and Spanish in his later years. With his multi-lingual facility, Enayet Khan emerged effortlessly as India's first cultural ambassador to the West, a good fifty years before the Dagar Brothers, Ravi Shankar and Ali Akbar Khan placed Hindustānī music on the world's classical music map.

Enayet Khan was a child prodigy, who excelled in academic and musical pursuits from an early age. He was trained as a vocalist and a *vīṇā* player at the Baroda State Music School, and he also showed interest in Western classical music. Impressed by his talent, the Baroda state awarded him a scholarship to go to Europe to study Western music. Gifted with amazing grasping power, Enayet Khan also became an adept at Carnatic music. Using the Maula Baksh system of notation, he authored several valuable texts on music for students and professional musicians.

In 1900, he started travelling all over India and the neighbouring countries with his uncle, Murtaza Khan, performing at several courts, and winning acclaim as a performer of Hindustānī as well as Carnatic music. In 1908-09, he recorded twenty-two discs of classical music for the Victor Recording Company, which provide testimony to his formidable musicianship. He left India in 1910 to spend most of his remaining years in the West, as a missionary of Indian music and sufi doctrine of salvation. In his world view, the two were inextricably linked. The pursuit of classical music was, to him, a systematic cultivation of the human personality and a path to salvation. During his years in the West, he performed and lectured widely on Indian classical music and authored several influential books, which are still held in high esteem for their eloquent exposition of Oriental wisdom.

Hazrat Enayet Khan returned to India in 1926 and died a year later. To this day, his descendants remain active as promoters of his mission committed to the relationship between the classical arts and mysticism.

Bal Gandharva (1888–1967)

Narayan Shripad Rajhans, better known as Bal Gandharva, was one of the greatest Marathi singers and stage actors in the early years of the last century. Maharaja Sayajirao was one of his principal patrons since 1913, and had granted his company an annual retainer. Under the arrangement, Bal Gandharva's company was required to present a new play every year at the Baroda court. The drama company openly acknowledged the patronage of the Baroda state in its advertisements. With the support of Maharaja Sayajirao, Bal Gandharva spearheaded the golden age of Marathi theatre.

Hirjibhai Doctor (1894–??)

Hirjibhai Doctor, a scion of a Parsee family of physicians, was an unlikely eminence to emerge on the musical scene of early twentieth-century Baroda. His ancestors had been personal physicians to four generations of Gaekwad rulers – Maharaja Ganpatrao, Mahraja Khanderao, Maharaja Malhar Rao, and finally, Maharaja Sayajirao III. Hirjibhai, however, showed no interest in medicine. He excelled as a sportsman, pursued music with passion and qualified himself with degrees in the Humanities and Science.

Starting early, he received eight years of training in the violin, and became an adept performer who caught the discerning eye of Maharaja Sayajirao III. He then became a disciple of Jamaluddin Beenkar, and spent many years studying the *dilrubā* and the *vichitra vīṇā* with the *ustād*. Simultaneously, he became an avid follower of the emerging father of modern musicology, Vishnu Narayan Bhatkhande, developed a close association with the scholar and became an expert musicologist. In 1928, Maharaja Sayajirao III appointed Hirjibhai as Director of Amusements and Principal of the Baroda State Music School.

As Director of Amusements, Hirjibhai supervised the activities of all performing musicians in the patronage of the princely state, organized the Baroda state orchestra, and supervised the entertainment of guests at state banquets and other ceremonial events. Alongside these duties, he maintained his presence on the concert platform, performing regularly on the radio and at court appearances. His contribution to Baroda's musical culture was, however, most significant for his work as principal of the music school, which was not doing too well when he took charge.

Hirjibhai overhauled the entire educational system at the music school, introduced a balance between theoretical and practical orientations in the grooming of students utilizing the encyclopaedic work of Bhatkhande as its foundation. Within a few years, the school had become equipped to grant degrees in classical music. His work received meritorious recognition from Maharaja Sayajirao, and continued to receive support from his successor, Maharaja Pratapsingh Rao.

While principal of the music school, Hirjibhai acquired national stature as an educationist and scholar, respected for his lectures and publications on Hindustānī music. By the time the princely state was merged with the Indian Union, the school had a healthy registration of students and was fully equipped to become a department of the newly-formed Maharaja Sayajirao University of Baroda. Hirjibhai continued as the principal of the institution under the university until his retirement.

Gulam Rasool Khan (1897–1986)

Gulam Rasool Khan was amongst the most widely acclaimed harmonium accompanists of the twentieth century. He acquired this status because he was also a trained vocalist of the Agra Gharānā lineage. He received his training from his father Kale Khan, and had earlier served the Lunawada state. When Faiyyaz Khan was appointed as court musician in Baroda, he persuaded Maharaja Sayajirao III to appoint Gulam Rasool (his maternal uncle) to the state payroll as a teacher at the State Music School. Gulam Rasool's musicianship flowered as a permanent accompanist to his brilliant nephew.

Gulam Rasool's son, Shamim Ahmed, studied vocal music with his father and took his diploma in *sitār* from the Baroda Music College in 1955. In the same year, Shamim Ahmed topped the All India Radio national talent search competition as a sitārist and became a disciple of Ravi Shankar. In later years, Shamim Ahmed emerged as a front-ranking sitārist of the Maihar Gharānā, taught at Ravi Shankar's Kinnara School of Music in the US, and achieved national and international stature.

Shrikrishna Ratanjankar (1900-74)

S.N. Ratanjankar was a close associate of V.N. Bhatkhande and first came to Baroda in connection with the First All India Music Conference organized by Bhatkhande under the patronage of Maharaja Sayajirao III. His performance at the conference was greatly appreciated. On Bhatkhande's suggestion, Maharaja Sayajirao appointed him as a teacher at the Baroda State Music School, which he served for five years. During this period, he also became a disciple of Faiyaz Khan and flowered as a composer and performer. He later emerged as a pioneering educationist in his role as principal of the Marris College of Music at Lucknow, now known as the Bhatkhande Music University.

Lakshmibai Jadhav (1901-65)

Lakshmibai Jadhav was an outstanding exponent of the Jaipur-Atrauli Gharānā of *khyāl* vocalism. While her contemporaries in the *gharānā* – Kesarbai Kerkar and Mogubai Kurdikar – had been trained by Alladiya Khan, Lakshmibai was trained by Alladiya Khan's brother, Hyder Khan. Lakshmibai did visit a few other princely states on invitations to perform. But, she was a low-key personality who did not systematically cultivate a concert presence outside her state duties. However, she was no less formidable than the other two as a musician. A substantial archive of her recordings broadcast on All India Radio exists as evidence of her musicianship. She served the Baroda court well into the post-Independence era, and retired in 1952. *(Based on interview with her disciple, Dhondutai Kulkarni, 4 May 2004.)*

Ata Hussain Khan (1903-80)

Ata Hussain Khan was a distinguished vocalist of the Atrauli lineage, an affiliate of Faiyyaz Khan's Agra lineage. He was the son of Mehboob Khan "Daras Piya", one of the greatest composers of the Agra-Atrauli combine. For twenty-five years, he was the closest associate and regular accompanist to Faiyyaz Khan. Simultaneously, he served the Baroda State Music School as a professor. After 1945, he moved to Caclutta under the patronage of Bengal aristocrats.

Nissar Hussain Khan (1909-93)

Nissar Hussain Khan was the son of Fida Hussain Khan of the Rampur-Sahaswan lineage (an offshoot of the Gwalior Gharānā), a vocalist at the Baroda court for over twenty years. In his early years, Nissar Hussain was trained by his grandfather, Haider Khan. Upon the demise of his father, Nissar Hussain was appointed as a court musician at Baroda, where he served till he retired. In his later years, he was persuaded to teach at the Sangeet Research Academy in Calcutta, where he trained his grand-nephew, Rashid Khan, the contemporary maestro, along with several others. The *ustād* enjoyed a long and substantial performing presence all over India, and on the radio.

Madhusudan Joshi (1918–2000)

In 1934, Madhusudan Joshi graduated as the first musician to receive a diploma from the Baroda State Music School. Maharaja Sayajirao convened a special convocation for the grant, to which V.N. Bhatkhande was also invited. In 1936, the *mahārājā* appointed him on the faculty of the Music School, where he also became a disciple of Faiyyaz Khan. Joshi served the institution for forty-two years. Amongst his distinguished students were Shrinivas Khale, Madhukar Pendse and Shubhada Paradkar.

The Śehnāī Tradition in Baroda

The Baroda tradition of *śehnāī* began in the early twentieth century when Ganpatrao Vasaikar (1862–1948) came from Maharashtra to the Baroda court. He moved to Baroda around 1870 from Vasai, near Mumbai. His father was a *śehnāī* player attached to a small temple. He spent his early life playing for marriages and other ceremonies, rendering music of moderate *rāga*-based depth. The temple authorities sensed a spark of genius in him and sent him at their cost to Nazir Khan (details not known) for training in *rāga*-based music. Vasaikar was also a proficient *tablā* player, who had accompanied leading vocalists of his times, including Vishnu Digambar. Once he moved to Baroda, his musical personality flowered.

In addition to performing duties at the court and the palace, Vasaikar groomed several disciples at the state music school, principal among them being Ganpatrao Bidwe, Bhagwantrao Waghmare and Govindrao Shinde. He was also drawn to the scientific approach to music propagated by Maula Baksh within the Baroda music establishment and authored books on the art of the *śehnāī*. He acquired tremendous prestige at the Baroda court, as a musician and teacher, and died at the age of 99.

The Baroda tradition of the *śehnāī* is a *khyāl*-based tradition while the other major *śehnāī* tradition (Benares) is allied to the *ṭhumrī* and the regional and folk genres of eastern UP and Bihar. Maharaja Sayajirao wanted the *śehnāī* players of the state to be thoroughly trained in *rāga*-based music. This could well have been achieved at the Baroda court. But, in his wisdom, the *mahārājā* chose to have Vasaikar trained in Bombay at the state's expense by Aman Ali Khan (1884–1953) of the Bhindi Bazaar Gharānā.

The Baroda *śehnāī* tradition flourished as long as the princely states were under British rule. However, a *śehnāī* player's life was always precarious. The *śehnāī* was a ceremonial instrument. *Śehnāī* players had neither enough performing to do, nor enough students to teach. The state ran an orchestra, which had no use for the *śehnāī*. So, *śehnāī* players trained themselves on at least one more instrument – usually a bow instrument – in order to ensure their usefulness. And, Hirjibhai Doctor, the accomplished violinist and music school principal, took on the task of retraining them. As a result, Baroda also became a significant centre of violin musicianship.

(As narrated by Shri Ramakant Sant (4 April 2004), whose father, Gangadhar Sant, served the princely state of Baroda as a śehnāī player and violinist.)

The Percussionists of Baroda State

Amongst the leading percussionists of the Baroda state, the names of Nasser Khan (1828–1903) and Nanasaheb Gurav Dehukar (1880) are mentioned with special reverence.

Nasser Khan Pakhavaji hailed from Banda in Bundelkhand district of UP. He served the last Nawab of Awadh, Nawab Wajed Ali Shah and migrated to the Rampur court after Wajed Ali was dethroned and exiled by the British in 1857. Maharaja Khanderao

Gaekwad invited him to join the service of the Baroda state, and his successor, Maharaja Sayajirao III continued to hold the *ustād* in great esteem. Nasser Khan travelled extensively in India accompanying leading musicians.

Nanasaheb Gurav was a rare *pakhāvaj* player, who had equal command over the *pakhāvaj* as well as the *tablā*. His family migrated to Baroda from the village of Dehu in Pune district. Gurav's initial training took place under his father, and his advanced training took place in the Nana Panse Gharānā of the *pakhāvaj*. Gurav acquired national stature as an accompanist to Faiyyaz Khan. This stature gave him the opportunity of accompanying most of the leading musicians of his times. In addition, he was a brilliant teacher, who groomed several percussionists at the State Music School. Both his sons later served the Faculty of Performing Arts at the university.

The Bīnkārs of Baroda

The court of Maharaja Sayajirao III was host to a distinguished lineage of *bīnkārs*, known as the Jaipur Beenkar Gharānā. The principal musicians of this lineage were Jamaluddin Beenkar (1859–1919) and his son, Abid Hussain Beenkar.

The *bīnkārs* of Jaipur claim considerable antiquity as a family domiciled in Rajasthan. The recent history of the lineage is traced to one Shahaji Saheb, a late eighteenth-century *bīnkār* who acquired a formidable reputation. Jamaluddin was appointed to the Baroda court at a young age and was highly respected amongst the musicians of his era. He was also the personal music tutor of the then *mahārānī*. Being amongst the leading *bīnkārs* of his generation, he travelled often to other princely states to perform. His son, Abid Hussain Beenkar studied under him, but moved thereafter to the court of the Nawab of Janjira (Maharashtra), where he spent his remaining years.

Another eminent *Bīnkār* at the Baroda court was Ali Hussain Beenkar. He was the younger brother of Enayet Hussain, one of the founders of the Rampur-Sahaswan Gharānā, and a disciple of Bahadur Hussain in the service of the Rampur court. No information is available on his tenure at the Baroda court besides the reports that he trained several students in Baroda in the art of the *vīṇā*.

The early years of the twentieth century saw a speedy decline in the fortunes of the *dhrupad* genre, with which the art of the *vīṇā* was associated. Around this time, the *bīnkār* families were forced to abandon the art and drift towards teaching performers on the emerging modern instruments such as the *sitār* and the *sarod*. As such, most *bīnkār* lineages, including those patronized by the Baroda and Rampur courts, are no longer represented by eminent performing musicians.

The Sitār and the Modern Instruments in Baroda

At the stage when the *dhrupad–vīṇā–pakhāvaj* era was drawing to a close, the Baroda state gave great importance to the cultivation of talent in the modern instruments. Great contributions to this move were made by Allaudin Khan (a son of Maula Baksh) and Bhikhan Khan.

Maula Baksh had two sons who were competent musicians – Murtaza Khan, who served briefly as the principal of the music school after his father, and Allauddin Khan. Like other members of his family, Allauddin Khan too had been trained in the art of the *vīṇā*. He was of a scholarly bent of mind and was fluent in English. At that time, the Baroda court was impressed with the scientific approach of Western classical music and wanted to adopt it for Hindustānī music. Allauddin Khan was chosen by the court to go to England and qualify himself in Western music and bring back its scientific discipline for introduction to Hindustānī music. Allauddin Khan was eminently successful in this endeavour. He won a Gold Medal at the Royal Academy of Music. On his return, he was appointed the first band master of the state band.

Even before the Maula Baksh era, the Baroda state had been host to eminent *sitār* players like Ghaseet Khan, about whom not much is known. Maula Baksh himself took interest in grooming his disciple, Govind Sharma as a sitārist after the latter lost his voice. A major push to post-*dhrupad* instrumental music, however, started with the arrival of two brothers – Bannu Khan and Ammu Kha – both sitārists of the Senīya tradition, from Jaipur. Bannu Khan's son, Bhikhan Khan, was a prodigious vocalist and sitārist, who had to abandon vocalism because of problems with his voice. He was appointed on the state payroll after his father's demise.

As a state musician, Bhikhan Khan also mastered the *dilrubā*, the *vīṇā* and the *jaltaraṅg* and trained several musicians to perform on them. He founded the state orchestra, composed pieces for the orchestra and was given the mandate to perform them in the various gardens and parks that the state maintained for public enjoyment. These public performances took classical music to the general public in an enjoyable and undemanding format and familiarized the lay public with classical melodies. These public performances created a large base of listenership for classical music in an era before the spread of the radio and gramophone records, and well before classical music performances became accessible to the general public. As a result of these efforts, Baroda remains, to this day, a city of cultivated listeners.

Bhikan Khan died in 1943. His sons, Anwar Khan and Sarwar Khan, were also accomplished sitārists and served as the Faculty of Performing Arts of the university till retirement.

Classical Music After Independence

With the merger of the princely state with the Indian Union, a large part of the music establishment of the state was either disbanded or became a part of the Faculty of Performing Arts of the Maharaja Sayajirao University of Baroda. The Gaekwad family, however, continued to retain an active interest in the cultural activities of the city after Independence during the tenure of Fatehsingh Rao and most recently, Ranjit Singh Gaekwad as heads of the Gaekwad family. The moving spirit of this interest was Ranjit Singh, himself an accomplished vocalist and a painter of international repute.

Despite his multifarious interests, including political activity, Ranjit Singh was actively involved with the activities of all the major cultural organizations of the city and also the Department of Music in the Performing Arts Faculty. His was an unobtrusive presence at all significant musical events in the city. He was on the Board of Trustees of several institutions, such as the Maula Baksh Trust and Swara Vilas.

For the first time in history, he opened up the Darbar Hall of the iconic Lakshmi Vilas Palace for holding music concerts for the public. He created a special space for holding cultural events in the premises of the Kirti Mandir, a piece of iconic architecture and the Gaekwad family's memorial to its departed members.

After the demise of this dedicated artist and devotee of classical music in 2012, his widow, Shubhangini Devi – herself brought up in the powerful musical culture of the Gwalior state – continues the family tradition of support to the classical arts as chairperson of the Swara Vilas Trust.

Exemplary Management

In the last 100 years of Gaekwad rule, the Baroda state was perhaps the single largest employer of professional musicians. It also managed to attract and retain some of the most formidable musicians of the era. With this enviable resource, the state ensured the highest quality of music to be performed in the courts and the palaces, developed a quality education system for perpetuating the classical arts and cultivated a substantial base of audiences for classical music.

It is obvious that managing the music establishment was only a small part of the overall task of managing the state. Considering this, the Gaekwad rulers evidently committed a massive amount of managerial energy to conducting such a wide scope of activity with such a large and high-quality human resource. For this, indeed, it maintained an entire department called the Kalawant Karkhana. But, no bureaucracy could have managed artistic activity on such a large scale and with such effectiveness, without the commitment of the Gaekwad rulers in ensuring a rich cultural life for their subjects. It is fair to recognize that, in independent India, no institution – either government or private – has been able to achieve comparable results as a manager of cultural activity.

Acknolwedgements: The author acknowledges the assistance of Prof. Rajesh Kelkar of the Faculty of Performing Arts, Maharaja Sayajirao University of Baroda as a collaborator on this project. The author also gratefully acknowledges the consent of Her Highness Rajmata Shubhangini Devi Gaekwad, President of Swara Vilas, for the reproduction of this essay in this book.

Glossary and Explanatory Notes

Ākāra/Akṛti : *Ākāra* is Sanskrit for "form" as an abstract idea. *Ākṛti* is derived from *ākāra* to signify a definitive, manifestation of form; an artefact.

Ākṛti : See *Ākāra/Ākṛti*.

Ālāp-Joḍ-Jhālā : *Ālāp-joḍ-jhālā* is an entirely improvised prefatory movement characteristic of the idiom of the plucked string instruments in Hindustānī music. The movement is performed without percussion accompaniment. The first tier features free-flowing melody, with no trace of rhythm. The second tier features a simple two-beat pulsation. The third tier suggests a four-beat rhythm. The *Ālāp-joḍ-jhālā* movement is "native" to the *rudra-vīṇā, sitār*, the *sarod*, the Indian slide (Hawaiian) guitar and the *santūr* (the Indian dulcimer). In recent years, performers on the bowed lutes (e.g. violin, *sāraṅgī*) and the wood-wind instruments – particularly the *bāṅsurī* – have enriched their repertoire by its adoption.

Alpatva : See *Alpatva/Bahutva*.

Alpatva/Bahutva : *Alpatva* is an abstract noun (Sanskrit) for the quality of brevity. *Bahutva* is its antonym. The *alpatva/bahutva* parameter in *rāga* grammar deals with the explicitness with which each of the permitted tones/*svaras* of the *rāga* can be intoned, relative to others. Most tones/*svaras* in a *rāga* will receive "normal" weightage. A few may, however, be prescribed either for subliminal or imperceptible intonation, or for prolonged intonation. This is a special and selective dimension of *rāga* grammar, not universally relevant to all *rāgas*.

Aṅga : See *Aṅga Prādhānya*.

Aṅga Prādhānya : The term derives its meaning from Sanskrit *aṅga* = limb/facet + *prādhānya* = dominance. This term refers to classification of *rāga*s on the basis of the region of the melodic canvas in which their centre of gravity falls. In this context, the octave is divided into three overlapping regions (*aṅga*s or limbs). The lower tetrachord (*sā, re, gā, mā*) is called the *pūrvāṅga* (*pūrva* = early + *aṅga* = limb/region). The mid-octave region (*gā, mā, pā, dh*) is called the *madhyāṅga* (*madhya* = middle + *aṅga* = limb/region). The upper tetrachord (*pā, dh, nī, sā*) is called *uttarāṅga* (*uttara* = north = *aṅga* = limb/region).

Aṁśa Svara (with respect to *rāga* grammar) : The *aṁśa* is the conceptual predecessor of the *vādi svara* in modern *rāga* grammar. *Aṁśa* is Sanskrit for fragment. The word is used in ancient literature to describe the pivotal *svara* of a *rāga*, which may be considered most expressive of its aesthetic intent – metaphorically, a fragment of the *rāga*'s melodic personality. Some authorities have also referred to this grammatical entity as a *prāṇa svara* (the soul of the *rāga*).

Anuvādī : In modern *rāga* grammar, all permissible *svara*s excluding the *vādī* and the *saṁvādī* are classified as *anuvādī svara*s. The word *anuvādī* derives from the Sanskrit *anuvāda* = translation or interpretation. Their grammatical function is that of interpreting, enhancing/supporting or translating the meaning of the dominant/pivotal *svara*s, the *vādī* and the *saṁvādī*.

Apanayas : See *Nyāsa, Apanyāsa, Vinyāsa*.

Ārati : The *āratī* is a Hindu religious ritual in which a lamp is rotated before an image of a deity, accompanied by the singing of the relevant prayers, the rhythmic striking of brass bells, and occasionally also drums. The ritual is routinely performed in homes and temples around sunrise and sunset and also at the end of a religious ceremony of any kind at any hour of the day or night. The lamp is a symbol of the sun, the oldest deity of the Hindu tradition. The *āratī* ritual has great cultural significance in the life of Hindu India.

Āroha : Ascending melodic motion.

Āroha Pradhāna : *Rāga*s which express their melodic uniqueness most eloquently in ascending melodic motion.

Arthāśrita : See *Svarāśrita/Padāśrita/Layāśrita/Arthāśrita*.

Auḍava : The word describes pentatonic *rāga*s (those that deploy five tones/*svara*s). The description does not double-count a tone/*svara* if the *rāga* uses the natural as well as its suppressed or enhanced microtones. In this classification, the ascent and the descent are considered together. However, *rāga*s may be described by dual classifications such as *auḍava-sampūrṇa* if, for instance, they are pentatonic in the ascent and heptatonic in the descent. (Also see *Ṣaḍava, Sampūrṇa.*)

Avaroha : Descending melodic motion.

Avaroha Pradhāna : *Rāga*s which express their melodic uniqueness most eloquently in descending melodic motion.

Bahutva : See *Alpatva/Bahutva.*

Baiṭhak : The word *baiṭhak* (Hindi) derives from the verb *baiṭhana* = to sit. In the present context, the word describes an intimate concert format which evolved in the pre-amplification era. It is a format in which the audience, rarely exceeding 100, sits on the floor, around the performers, who may also be seated on the floor – or on a marginally elevated platform. There is no passage separating the performers from the audience. With most of the audience being in eye-contact with the performers, an interactive relationship is established between them, resulting in a more satisfying musical experience.

Bandiś (also called *cīẓ* or *gata*) : The word derives from the Sanskrit verb *bandhana* = to bind. A *bandiś* is that which is bound, encased, pre-composed. The word refers to the pre-composed element in Hindustānī (north Indian) vocal or instrumental music. shell. In art music, a *bandiś* is composed in a specific *rāga*, is set to a specific *tāla*, and conforms to traditional rules of composition. (Also see *Rāga, Tāla.*)

Bandiś-kī-Ṭhumrī : *Bandiś-kī-ṭhumrī* is the older of the two sub-genres of the *ṭhumrī* genre of semi-classical vocal music. The word *bandiś* in this context signifies its reliance on the pre-composed poetic–melodic–rhythmic form. The word *ṭhumrī* signifies its origin as accompaniment to Kathak dance and its continued association with it. The *bandiś-kī-ṭhumrī* exerted considerable influence over the evolution of the idiom of the modern plucked-lute family of musical instruments, principally, the *sitār* and the *sarod*. (Also see *Bandiś, Bol-Banāo-Ṭhumrī, Ṭhumrī.*)

Bhajana : The word derives from the Sanskrit verb *bhaja* = to serve/to worship. A *bhajana* is a song based on devotional poetry. These songs were originally performed in the temples and moved from there into people's homes as solo or choral expressions. They are composed typically in folk tunes or based on a handful of classical *rāgas*. The infusion of classicism into their rendition and their adoption as repertoire for the concert platform are a twentieth-century phenomenon. (Also see *Ṭhumrī, Ṭappā.*)

Bhakti : The word is Sanskrit for devotion/surrender and derives from the verb *bhaja* = to serve/to worship. *Bhakti* is one of the primary *rasa*s (sentiments) of which human beings are capable. Though not restricted to the religious aspirations of man, the sentiment is intimately related to the poetic facet of Hindustānī and Carnatic music.

Bhāva : *Bhāva* is Sanskrit for sentiment/the emotional content of a relationship.

Bol-Banāo-Ṭhumrī : The *bol-banāo-ṭhumrī* is the more recent of the two subgenres of the *ṭhumrī* genre of semi-classical vocal music. The prefix *bol-banāo* describes the leisurely process by which the subgenre uses musical expression to interpret semantic meaning as emotional meaning. The suffix *ṭhumrī* refers to its origins as accompaniment to Kathak dance, and its continued association with it. (Also see *Ṭhumrī, Bandiś-kī-Ṭhumrī.*)

Brahmin/Brāhmaṇa : The adjectival noun derives from Bramhā, the creator and the ultimate source of wisdom in Hindu theology. A brāhmin is one who lives a life dedicated to the acquisition, preservation, interpretation and dissemination of knowledge. The Hindu tradition accords the highest status to the brāhmins in its four-way classification based on the division of labour – the kṣatriyas defend the borders, the vaiśyas create wealth and the śūdras do manual labour.

Carnatic/Hindustānī Music : The word derives from the name of the "Karṇāt" region of India, approximately covering all of peninsular India south of the Vindhyachal range of mountains. Some scholars believe that they are both offshoots of an older, unified tradition. Their bifurcation could have begun in the early part of the second millennium. The north of the country came under increasing Middle Eastern cultural influence consequent to a series of invasions, while south India remained relatively insulated from such influences. This bifurcation was probably magnified by art-music responding more explicitly to the regional musical cultures of the north and the south, and to the differing predilections of its patrons. These forces gave rise to two parallel art music traditions – the north Indian tradition, called Hindustānī music, and the south Indian tradition, called Carnatic music. The two systems have similarities as well as dissimilarities and follow their independent evolutionary paths. However, there is evidence of growing cross-fertilization of musical ideas and practices between the two traditions after Independence (1947).

Chakra (with reference to Viṣṇu) : *Chakra* is Sanskrit for any circular object, specially a wheel. In the Hindu tradition, Lord Viṣṇu is visualized as holding a rotor-blade weapon in one of his four hands. As generally visualized, Viṣṇu's *chakra* is identical to a modern rotary-saw and symbolizes the warrior facet of the deity's archetypal image. The rotor-blade weapon is uniquely associated with Lord Viṣṇu and his most popular incarnation, Lord Kr̥ṣṇa. (Also see Viṣṇu.)

Chalan : The word derives from the Sanskrit *chala* = to move or Hindī *chāla* = gait/demeanour. A *rāga*'s distinctive melodic personality is outlined by a set of characteristic phrases, which incorporate a substantial part of its grammar. This set of phrases, generally not more than eight or ten in number, is collectively called the *chalan* of the *rāga*. (Also see *Rāga.*)

Chhoṭā Khyāl : The word derives from the Hindī *chhoṭā* = minor/small + *khyāl* = vision/imagination. The term denotes the fast-tempo rendition of vocal music in the *khyāl* genre of Hindustānī (north Indian) art music. In such meaning, it encompasses the pre-composed element (the poetic–melodic–rhythmic shell of the rendition) as well as the conventional architecture of the rendition with respect to the improvisatory movements. Compared to the *baḍā khyāl*, the architecture of a *chhoṭā khyāl* presentation is relatively informal. (Also see *Khyāl.*)

Dhrupad (also called *dhrupad-dhamāra*) : The word derives from Sanskrit *dhruva* = fixed/immutable + *pada* = verse. It refers to a genre of *rāga*-based music, which dominated the Hindustānī (north Indian) tradition between the fifteenth and eighteenth centuries. The genre evolved as an art form consequent to the transportation of the devotional music of the Viṣṇu temples to the secular environment of feudal courts. The genre places a high premium on the integrity of its poetic element in rendition and is, therefore, predominantly a genre of vocal music. Its primary instrumental manifestation is the *rudra-vīṇā* (also called *bīn*). (Also see *Rudra-Vīṇā*, *Khyāl*, *Viṣṇu*.)

Dhun Ugam (with reference to *rāgas*) : *Dhun* is a Hindi word (noun) meaning melody, often a well-defined tune. The word also carries connotations of a spontaneous/inspired melodic emanation, accountable neither to a precedent, nor to any rule of composition. It is widely accepted that the *rāgas* of Hindustānī music represent a grammatical formalization of such expressions, derived original from folk and other musical traditions. The suffix *ugam* is an adjective derived from the Hindi verb *uganā* meaning "arising from"/"spawned by". *Dhun ugam rāgas* are melodic matrices of folk/other melodies, grammatically formalized for the first time, by contemporary/modern maestros.

Gadā (with respect to Viṣṇu) : *Gadā* is Sanskrit for a mace, which is the other weapon Lord Viṣṇu holds in his hands. While, the *chakra* (rotor-blade weapon) functions as his remote-controlled "guided missile", the mace represents his mastery over proximity combat. (Also see *Viṣṇu*.)

Gharānā : The word derives its meaning from the Hindī *ghara* (Sanskrit *gṛha* = house). *Gharānā* is a collective noun meaning a group which shares the same homestead. In the era of hereditary musicianship, the term came to represent a lineage, which cultivated a distinctive style of rendering music over successive generations. Once kinship ceased to be the primary criterion for entry into the music profession, the term was redefined to denote a stylistic lineage. As a stylistic lineage, a *gharānā* is characterized by three critical features: (a) a long period of rigorous training and aesthetic indoctrination of each aspirant under an authorized *guru* of the lineage, (b) acquisition of the art through aural transmission, and (c) a loyalty of each member to the music making philosophy and style of his mentor/lineage.

Ghazal : The word is Persian for "addressing a lover in poetic form". Written originally in Persian and later in Urdu, the *ghazal* is a poetry-dominant genre of music. The orthodox mode of recitation involved a simple, repetitive, melodic structure, with no improvisation. In the nineteenth and twentieth centuries, its melodic approach began to drift towards that of the *bol-banāo-ṭhumrī*. The genre, however, continues to accord an autonomous status to the poetic element, far more categorically than the *ṭhumrī* genre does. (Also see *Bol-banāo-ṭhumrī*, *Urdu*.)

Graha (with respect to *svaras*) : *Graha* in Sanskrit means "to get a grip on" or "to be grounded in". Another relevant meaning of the word is "home". In classical texts, this term prescribes the *svara*, from which the *rāga* should commence. This prescription was relevant to the era before the performance of *rāga*s became largely improvised. Its relevance today is limited to phrasing strategies.

Guṇa (with reference to artistic values/motivations) : The Sanskrit word *guṇa* has been translated through its various probable etymologies. The connotations include: elementary property, quality, character, habitual behaviour, invisible essence, attribute, classification, addressing/attitude, enumeration. Collectively, these connotations permit the use of the concept as a classification of personality types, and also to define a person's relationship with a particular facet of his life.

In the present context, both these dimensions of classification are appropriate and intended. Hindu philosophy defines three modes of existence – *sattva, rajas* and *tamas* – which pervade all things and beings in the universe. The balance of the three in each thing or being differs, and it is this balance that determines its behaviour. From these three Sanskrit nouns are derived the three adjectives – *sāttvika, rājasika* and *tāmasika*. (Also see *Sāttvika, Rājasika, Tāmasika.*)

Guru : See *Guru–Śiṣya Parampara*.

Guru–Śiṣya Paramparā : The term derives from Sanskrit *guru* = teacher/mentor/guide + *śiṣya* = disciple/ward/student/aspirant + *paramparā* = tradition. The term refers to the traditional relationship between a teacher and his students, which forms the basis of the transmission of all forms of knowledge, including musical knowledge. The salient features of this relationship are total subordination of the personality of the student to that of his teacher, in return for which the teacher accepts total responsibility for the grooming of the disciple in the chosen field of education. The two-way unconditionality and totality of commitment characteristic of this relationship is critical to its success because of the aural mode of transmission and the personality-transforming goal of education. In this tradition, therefore, the *guru* is accorded a status on par with God. (Also see *Gharānā.*)

Gurumukhī/Sarvamānya/Virāṭa Svarūpa : The involvement of a musician in the exploration of a *rāga* form can be classified into three levels of depth:

1. *Gurumukhī Svarūpa*: This is the *rāga* form that a musician imbibes from his *guru/gurus*/teachers.
2. *Sarvamānya Svarūpa*: The consensual melodic personality of the *rāga*, as has been explored by all musicians whose music is available – an aggregate of all the melodic ideas hitherto explored – and which listeners accept as belonging to a *rāga*.
3. *Virāṭa Svarūpa*: This represents all the melodic possibilities of the formless form of the *rāga* – including those yet remaining unexplored. This notion of *rāga-svarūpa* is limited only by the boundaries between the specific *rāga* and other *rāga*s.

Hindustānī Music : See *Carnatic/Hindustānī Music*.

Iṣṭa : *Iṣṭa* (Sanskrit) has several connotations relevant to the present context. Principal among them are:

1. the one who is sought,
2. the one who is worshipped,
3. the one to whom religious rituals are offered,
4. the presiding deity of the family, and
5. the one who wields authority over the seeker.

The collective significance of these meanings defines a relationship of reverence between the seeker and the sought. This reverence is reflected in the use of *iṣṭa* as a prefix to a *rāga* being performed by a musician.

Jugalabandī : The term derives its meaning from Sanskrit *jugala / yugala* = a couple + *bandī* = linked / tied / locked. The term describes duet performances of music by two lead musicians in collaborative effort. The total ensemble for a *jugalabandī*, including supporting musicians, can go up to six people. Being an improvisation-dominant art form, Hindustānī music is not particularly amenable to collaborative efforts, except under rare conditions conducive to compatibility. *Jugalabandī*s (duets) are, however, a popular format.

Kalāvanta : The word derives from Sanskrit *kalā* = art + *vanta* = owner. Literally, the word denotes the practitioner of any art. In medieval times, the term described a professional singer of the *dhrupad* genre, who belonged to a caste which made a living exclusively as vocalists, eschewing instrumental music. The term later became progressively more accommodative of other musical professions, and has, by now, gone out of circulation. (Also see *Dhrupad*.)

Kārkhānā : *Kārkhānā* is Urdu for a "factory" or a place where paid workers assemble for the purpose of generating products of economic value. The use of this word in the erstwhile Baroda State to describe the administrative department dealing with musicians seems inappropriate. However, it could be a reflection of a sound bureaucratic system installed by the rulers for managing a large-scale patronage of quality musicians.

Kathak : Kathak is the name of the principal genre of classical dance in the north Indian performing arts tradition, closely linked to its musical and poetic traditions. The word derives from Sanskrit *kathā* = story + *kāra* = narrator. Kathak is also the name of an ancient community of storytellers, who specialized in the narration of episodes from the major Hindu epics through mime and vocal–instrumental accompaniment. (Also see *Ṭhumrī.*)

Khyāl : The term derives its meaning from the Perso-Arabic word *khyāl*, meaning idea, imagination, subjectivity, individuality or impression. It represents a confluence of *rūpakālapti*, an ancient genre of Indian art music (eighth/ninth centuries), and Perso-Arabic music. The modern *khyāl* replaced medieval *dhrupad* as the mainstream genre starting in the early nineteenth century. A *khyāl* rendition generally consists of two parts – a slow tempo rendition called the *baḍā* (major) *khyāl* and a medium-to-fast tempo rendition called *chhoṭā* (minor) *khyāl*. (Also see *Dhrupad, Baḍā Khyāl, Chhoṭā Khyāl.*)

Komal (with respect to *svara*/tone) : The word derives from Sanskrit *komal* = soft. The Hindustānī scale consists of seven natural tones, plus mutations representing either suppressed or enhanced frequencies of five of the seven tones. The seven natural tones are called *śuddha*, the suppressed tones are called *komal*, Sanskrit for "soft" while the solitary enhanced tone is called *tīvra*, Sanskrit for "sharp". The Hindustānī scale deploys *komal*/suppressed mutations/frequencies of the 2nd, 3rd, 6th and 7th degrees and a *tīvra*/sharp mutation of the 4th. (Also see *Śuddha.*)

Laya : *Laya*, Sanskrit for tempo, is the time interval between the equidistant beats of a *tāla*, when rendered. It represents a linear calibration of the flow of time, while the *tāla* is a cyclical calibration of it. *Laya* may be expressed as a number of beats per minute, while the *tāla* is defined, amongst other criteria, by the number of beats within a cycle. In performance, a *tāla*, rendered in a particular *laya*, may be defined by number of seconds per cycle. (Also see *Tāla.*)

Layāśrita : See *Svarāśrita / Padāśrita / Layāśrita / Arthāśrita.*

Madhya Saptaka : The term derives from Sanskrit *madhya* = middle + *saptaka* = a group of seven tonal intervals. The term describes the middle octave of the melodic canvas. While the Western tradition considers the scale as consisting of eight points, the Indian system treats the same distance as consisting of seven frequency intervals. Hence the reference to the scale as seven, rather than eight.

Madhyāṅga : See *Aṅga Prādhānya.*

Madhyāṅga Pradhāna : See *Aṅga Prādhānya.*

Mahārājā/Nawāb/Zamīndār : *Mahārājā* (*mahā* = great + *rājā* = king), *nawāb* (feudal lord or nobleman, generally Muslim) and *zamīndār* (*zamīn* = land + *dār* = owner of). These terms denote different levels/ categories of power and influence enjoyed by the aristocracy in feudal-agrarian India. Under colonial rule, the *mahārājā*s, *nawāb*s, *zamīndār*s, were granted autonomy of governance and military protection in return for a share of land revenue. This aristocracy became a significant patron of the fine and performing arts.

Mandra : See *Tāra/Taratva, Mandra/Mandratva* (with respect to *rāga*s).

Mandra Saptaka : The term derives from Sanskrit *mandra* = lower + *saptaka* = a group of seven tones/*svara*s. The term describes the lower octave of the melodic canvas.

Mandratva : See *Tāra/Taratva, Mandra/Mandratva* (with respect to *rāga*s).

Mīṇḍ : *Mīṇḍ* is the primary mode of intervallic transition in Hindustānī music – vocal as well as instrumental. It describes a transition, akin to traction, which literally stretches a tone/*svara* in order to reach another tone/*svara*, defining a curvilinear path. *Mīṇḍ* is the opposite of a staccato transition.

Murkī : The term is colloquial, though probably related to the Hindī verb *maroḍanā* = to twist. The *murkī* is a special type of *mīṇḍ*, where the phrase involves a twisted/wrap-around execution with a jerky motion. This melodic expression is encountered in vocal music as well as instrumental music. (Also see *Mīṇḍ.*)

Napuṁsaka Rāga : *See Rāginī/Putra/Putra-vadhu/Napuṁsaka* (with respect to *rāga*s).

Nāṭya Saṅgīt : The term derives from Sanskrit *nāṭya* = theatre + *saṅgīt* =

music. The term refers to a modern genre of *rāga*-based music from regional theatre, which dominated the entertainment of bourgeois society in the Western state of Maharashtra during the nineteenth and early twentieth centuries.

Nirākāra/Nirguṇa : *Nirākāra* is Sanskrit for "the one devoid of form". *Nirguṇa* is Sanskrit for "the one devoid of attributes". The Hindu tradition acknowledges several varieties of spiritual endeavour and experience, which either transcend or bypass an engagement with personified deities (polytheism). (Also see *Sākāra/Saguṇa.*)

Nirguṇa : See *Nirākāra/Nirguṇa.*

Nyāsa/Apanyāsa/Vinyāsa (with respect to *svaras*) : *Nyāsa* is Sanskrit for "to sit" or "establish". In classical literature, these three categories of *svaras* in a *rāga* (derivations from *nyāsa*) permitted as terminal points of phrasing, followed by varying durations of pause (punctuation), as appropriate to the *rāga*'s grammatical demands. Though these guidelines are still effective in practice, modern *rāga* grammar classifies all these *svaras* as *anuvādī svaras*. (Also see *Anuvādī.*)

Padāśrita : See: *Svarāśrita/Padāśrita/Layāśrita/Arthāśrita.*

Padma (with reference to Viṣṇu) : *Padma* is Sanskrit for the lotus flower. In Hindu iconography, the lotus flower is a symbol of all that is pure, noble, cultured, peaceful and benign in human nature. The lotus is also associated with the iconography of several benign deities, such as Bramhā, Lakṣmī and Sarasvatī. (Also see *Viṣṇu.*)

Pakaḍ : The word is Hindī for "grip". In Hindustānī music, it refers to the signatory phrase or phrases of a *rāga*, which identify it beyond reasonable doubt. (Also see *Chalan, Rāga.*)

Pakhāwaj : The name derives from Sanskrit : *pakṣa* = sides + *vādya* = instrument for sound production. The instrument dates back to the pre-Christian era with its origin shrouded in mythology. The *pakhāwaj*, a horizontal two-faced tapering cylindrical drum, was the principal percussion instrument of the Hindustānī (north Indian) art music tradition, until the advent of the *tablā*. It remains, to this day, the standard rhythmic accompaniment to performances of the *dhrupad / dhamār* genre, but has no presence in the modern genres of art music. Other two-faced barrel drums descended from the *pakhāwaj* are, however, still used in popular and folk music. (Also see *Tablā, Dhrupad.*)

Pañchamantya (with respect to a *rāga*) : *Pañchamantya* in Sanksrit has two components. *Pañcham* = the *svara pā* and the acoustic midpoint of the scale/the 5th degree + *antya* = "that which ends at". *Pañchamantya* is a *rāga* whose melodic region ends at the 5th of the middle octave and, by implication, commences at the 5th of the lower octave. This phenomenon defines a category of *rāgas*, whose melodic action is restricted to the lower half of the three-octave melodic canvas, and transgressions into the upper half are to be kept to the absolute minimum.

Paṇḍit : The word is Sanskrit for a person who commands respect in society by virtue of his knowledge of theory in his chosen field. In the music world, however, the honorific is accorded to any Hindu musician of exceptional attainments as a performer, the knowledge of theory being implicit in his musicianship. A Muslim of comparable attainments is called an *ustād*. No formalized framework exists for conferring such honorifics to musicians. They emerge through an informal process of consensus building within the community of musicians. (Also see *Ustād*.)

Paramparā : See *Guru–Śiṣya Paramparā*.

Prāṇa Svara : See *Aṁśa Svara*.

Pūrvāṅga Pradhāna : See *Aṅga Prādhānya*.

Putra Rāga : See *Rāginī/Putra/Putra-vadhu/Napuṁsaka* (with respect to *rāgas*).

Putra-Vadhu Rāga : See *Rāginī/Putra/Putra-vadhu/Napuṁsaka* (with respect to *rāgas*.)

Rāga : The word, generally encountered as a suffix, is Sanskrit for sentiment/attitude/quality of response/emotional content of a relationship. In music, it has come to denote a melodic idea or a framework associated with a specific quality of emotional response. The notion of *rāga*-ness is, therefore, inseparable from the concept of *rasa* in Indian aesthetics. A *rāga* is a psycho-acoustic hypothesis, which states that melody, created and rendered in accordance with a certain set of rules, has a high probability of eliciting a certain quality of emotional response. The set of rules for the creation and rendition of the melody constitutes the grammar of a *rāga*. An awareness of the target response enables a musician to transcend grammar and enter the realm of literature. (Also see *Rasa/Navarasa*.)

Rāginī : See *Rāginī/Putra/Putra-vadhu/Napuṁsaka.*

Rāginī/Putra/Putra-vadhu/Napuṁsaka (with respect to *rāgas*) : This classification of *rāgas* belongs to an ancient attempt to group the growing corpus of *rāgas* into clusters based on some indicator of melodic affinity and/or approach to performance. *Rāginī* is Sanskrit for a "female *rāga*". *Putra* in Sanskrit is "a son", hence a derived *rāga*. *Putra-vadhu* in Sanskrit is a "daughter-in-law", implying probably a compound *rāga*. *Napuṁsaka* in Sanskrit is "impotent/infertile", hence perhaps a stand-alone *rāga* incapable of spawning derivations. In later years, this classification has been rendered obsolete by several objective or aesthetic classifications.

Rajas : See *Sāttvika/Rājasika/Tāmasika.*

Rājasika : See *Sāttvika/Rājasika/Tāmasika.*

Rasa/Navarasa : The Indian aesthetic tradition views the sensory experience as a pathway to the emotional and the emotional as a pathway to the spiritual. This reflects the fundamental transcendentalism of Hindu thought. All art is, therefore, validated by a single dominant criterion – its ability to elicit an emotional response. This criterion acknowledges that, at its most intense, the experience of beauty evokes a response that transcends its qualitative aspect and acquires a mystical quality. This defines the potential of the artistic endeavour, and its reception, for personality transformation and spiritual evolution. At the intermediate aesthetic level, however, the tradition allows for the classification of works of art on the basis of the quality of the emotional response. The name given to these qualities is *rasa*, a metaphorical expression derived from the Sanskrit *rasa* = extract/essence/juice.

Orthodox aesthetic theory, annunciated in pre-Christian texts, recognizes nine basic emotions/sentiments, called *navarasa*, Sanskrit for *nava* = nine + *rasa* = qualities of sentiment/emotional experience. The nine are:

1. Śṛṅgāra (the romantic sentiment),
2. Karuṇa (the sentiment of pathos),
3. Hāsya (the sentiment of mirth),
4. Raudra (the sentiment of wrath),
5. Vīra (the sentiment of valour),
6. Bhayānaka (the sentiment of fear),

7. Bībhatsa (the sentiment of disgust),
8. Adbhuta (the sentiment of surprise/marvel), and
9. Śānta (the experience of peace).

Over the two millennia since this enumeration, critical literature has added several other sentiments and combinations of orthodox sentiments to the interpretation of the emotional content of artistic endeavours. (Also see *Rāga.*)

Rasika : The word is a common noun derived from the Sanskrit *rasa* = the target emotional response of a work/piece of art. The word is loosely translated as "connoisseur" but is unique in its cultural meaning. A *rasika* is a person who is equipped with the knowledge, beliefs and emotional receptivity required to partake of *rasa*. Classical texts have enumerated the qualifications of a *rasika* in considerable detail. In the Hindustānī tradition, the listener is not the passive recipient of a unidirectional musical communication. The *rasika* – individually as well collectively – is an active participant in the process that constantly shapes and reshapes *rāgas* and every other aspect of the musical tradition. By virtue of his connoisseurship, he constitutes one of the pillars of the quality-control mechanism in the musical culture and is as responsible for the trends in the musical tradition as are the musicians themselves. (Also see *Rāga, Rasa/Navarasa.*)

Riyāẓ : *Riyāẓ* is an Arabic word with connotations of practice, toil, hard work, tribulation and penance. The lexical indications suggest two important associations of the word – that the activity tests the limits of human endurance and that it demands a fanatical pursuit of perfection.

Rudra-Vīṇā (also called *Bīn*): A member of the fretted stick-zither family of plucked instruments. A revered instrument with strong mythological and mystical associations. Evolved around the thirteenth century when frets were added to a fretless predecessor. The instrument is associated with the medieval *dhrupad/dhamār* genre of music. It was originally used as accompaniment to vocal performances, but later acquired its independent performing domain. The *rudra-vīṇā* is the principal inspiration – acoustic as well as stylistic – for the plucked instruments in contemporary Hindustānī (north Indian) art music. (Also see *Dhrupad.*)

Saguṇa : See *Sākāra/Saguṇa.*

Sāhab : *Sāhab* is a Hindī word, appended as a suffix to the names of persons addressed with respect. It corresponds approximately to "Sir" or "Esquire" in English. It came into prominence during the colonial period, when Englishmen and persons of high rank were habitually addressed with this suffix. In some religious sects of the subcontinent, the term is also used to refer to/address religious leaders.

Sākāra/Saguṇa (with respect to religious aspirations) : *Sākāra* is Sanskrit for "the one possessed of form". *Saguṇa* is Sanskrit for "the one possessed of attributes". With respect to religious aspirations, the polytheistic Hindu tradition acknowledges the value of idol worship, but regards it as a pathway to the realization of a formless deity, which is devoid of attributes. (Also see *Nirākāra/Nirguṇa.*)

Sampūrṇa : The word is Sanskrit for complete/comprehensive and describes heptatonic *rāga*s (those that deploy seven tones/*svara*s). The description does not double-count a tone/*svara* if the *rāga* uses the natural as well as its suppressed or enhanced microtones. In this classification, the ascent and the descent are considered together. However, *rāga*s may be described by dual classifications such as *ṣāḍava-sampūrṇa* if, for instance, they are hexatonic in the ascent and heptatonic in the descent. (Also see *Auḍava, Ṣāḍava.*)

Saṁvādī : See *Vādī/Saṁvādī.*

Saṅkīrṇa (with reference to *rāga*s) : The dictionary provides the following connotations of the Sanskrit adjective. (1) Narrow, (2) the opposite of generous/ample, and (3) Inferior. Based on allied words *saṅkramaṇa* and *saṅkrānti*, the connotations are: (1) mixed, (2) involving a transition, and (3) infected/corrupted. Considered clinically, these connotations apply to members of *rāga* clusters identified on the basis of melodic affinity. Evidence of their performing history, however, appears to negate the connotation of inferiority as melodic material.

Saptaka : See *Mandra Saptaka, Madhya Saptaka, Tāra Saptaka.*

Saragama : The *saragama* derives its name from the first four solemnization/solfa symbols (*sā, re, gā, mā*) of the Hindustānī scale. The use of solfa symbols as an articulatory device in vocal performance is called *saragama*. Such use is well established in the Carnatic (south Indian) tradition. Ustad Abdul Kareem Khan is credited with initiating its use in *khyāl* performance in the early twentieth century. (Also see *Khyāl.*)

Sarvamānya Svarūpa : See *Gurumukhī/Sarvamānya/Virāṭa Svarūpa.*

Sattva : See *Guṇa* (with reference to artistic values/motivations).

Sāttvika/Rājasika/Tāmasika : This three-way classification of human personalities/tendencies is summarized thus in the *Bhagavadgītā* XVIII.23-25. "Action that is virtuous, thought through, free from attachment and without craving for results is *sāttvika*. Action that is driven purely by craving for pleasure, selfishness and much effort is *rājasika*. Action that is undertaken because of delusion, disregarding consequences, without considering loss or injury to others or self, is *tāmasika*."

Sāttvika : The quality of harmony, balance, goodness, purity, universalizing, holistic, creative, building, peaceful, virtuous.

Rājasika : The quality of passion, activity, neither good nor bad and sometimes either, self-centredness, egoistic, individualizing, driven, moving, dynamic.

Tāmasika : The qualities of imbalance, disorder, chaos, anxiety, impurity, delusionary, negative, dull, apathetic, lethargic, violent, vicious. (Also see *Guṇa.*)

Ṣāḍava : The word describes hexatonic *rāga*s (those that deploy six tones/*svara*s). The description does not double-count a tone/*svara* if the *rāga* uses the natural as well as its suppressed or enhanced microtones. In this classification, the ascent and the descent are considered together. However, *rāga*s may be described by dual classifications such as *ṣāḍava-sampūrṇa* if, for instance, they are hexatonic in the ascent and heptatonic in the descent. (Also see *Auḍava, Sampūrṇa.*)

Ṣaḍja : *Ṣaḍja* is the musicological term for the scale-base, and approximately analogous to the "Key" in Western music. Its lexical meaning in Sanskrit is: "that which is the repository of, and is the source of, six others". The scale-base is of special significance to Indian music because, a musician's choice of the scale-base/tonic/fundamental is entirely arbitrary. Because Hindustānī music is entirely tonal and melodic, every intonation acquires its musical meaning only with reference to the *ṣaḍja* (the tonic). Its corresponding solfa symbol is *sā*.

Śaṅkha (with reference to Viṣṇu) : *Śaṅkha* is Sanskrit for a large conch shell, one of the four items held by the four-armed Lord Viṣṇu, the preserver of the universe, as popularly visualized. It is a horn which cannot produce any melody and emits only a single tone unique to its acoustic properties. It is generally played either as an offering to God accompanying the singing of prayers and drums or during important religious ceremonies. Mythological references also associate the instrument with the declaration of war in the battlefield. (Also see *Viṣṇu.*)

Śaraṇāgata Bhāva : The Sanskrit phrase has three components: *śaraṇa* = refuge + *gati* = movement towards + *bhāva* = sentiment. The phrase describes the stance of a supplicant/ aspirant characterized by surrender of selfhood to the object of his/her attention.

Śiṣya : See *Guru–Śiṣya Paramparā.*

Śehnāī : The word probably derives from Persian *Śāh* = king + *nāī* = pipe. The instrument played in India is, however, almost certainly of Indian origin. The instrument belongs to the oboe family of beating-reed aerophones. It has the status of the most preferred instrument at religious ceremonies and public functions. As such, it could be the single most widely heard instrument in India. In the latter half of the twentieth century, Ustad Bismillah Khan elevated the instrument to the art music platform.

Śṛṅgāra : See *Rasa/Navarasa.*

Śruti : *Śruti* is Sanskrit for "that which is heard". The Indian octave his divided into 22 microtonal intervals, representing the possibility of unambiguous pitch differentiation in terms of vocalized intonation as well as the neuro-acoustic processing.

Śuddha (with reference to *svara*/tone) : The word derives from Sanskrit – *śuddha* = pure. The Hindustānī scale consists of seven natural tones/*svara*s, plus mutations representing either suppressed or enhanced frequencies of five of them. The seven natural tones are called *Śuddha* (pure), the suppressed tones are called *komal,* Sanskrit for "soft", while the solitary enhanced tone is called *tīvra,* Sanskrit for "sharp". The Hindustānī scale deploys *komal*/ suppressed mutations/frequencies of the 2nd, 3rd, 6th and 7th degrees and a *tīvra*/sharp mutation of the 4th. (Also see *Komal.*)

Sitār : A member of the long-necked fretted lute family of plucked instruments. The theory crediting its origins to a Persian instrument called *sehtar* (lit. three strings) and its adaptation in the thirteenth century by Ameer Khusro, are no longer tenable. *Sitār*-like instruments are known to have existed for long in several parts of the country. Latest research suggests that a Kishmiri variant of the instrument was launched into the mainstream by an eighteenth-century musician, Fakir Khusro Khan. In less than 300 years, the instrument has become the most widely studied and performed instrument in Hindustānī music.

Svara/Tone : The word derives from Sanskrit *sva* = self + *ra* = illumination. *Svara* is, therefore, an utterance expressing the entirety of the practitioner's being and has the potential for personality transformation. Though an avowedly subjective expression, it necessarily has certain known and measurable acoustic features. However, the Indian musical tradition also identifies two features which pose conceptual problems. The qualities are *dīpti*, loosely translated as luminosity, and *anuranan*, loosely translated as a resonating/haunting quality. Clarity on these dimensions may have to await either an acoustically meaningful translation of these terms or their recognition as hitherto unknown/unmeasured acoustic dimensions. This brief etymological-acoustic discussion supports the growing realization that *svara* in Hindustānī music does not correspond efficiently to the Western notion of tone or a pitch-ratio relative to the tonic.

The Hindustānī scale has twelve *svara*s, all of which acquire musical meaning only with reference to the tonic, arbitrarily chosen by the musician. These twelve *svara*s have names. But, the existence of standard frequency ratios for eleven of them, relative to the tonic, is debatable. Nor is it clear that their musical values depend upon the existence of such standardized acoustic relationships. There could, in reality, be stronger evidence to support the opposite argument – that their musical value depends precisely on the freedom the musician has to intone them in accordance with aesthetic, rather than acoustic, principles. This is particularly so since, as a rule, Hindustānī music eschews staccato intonation.

This is consistent with the crucial difference between the Hindustānī and the Western scales. The Western scale is an octave with eight fixed points, while the Hindustānī scale is a *saptaka* with seven intervals covering the same tonal distance. Music-making activity in Hindustānī music is focused on the handling of intervals, while Western tradition focuses its attention on handling the tonal points.

The issue here is, in fact, philosophical and cultural more than acoustic. Any cultural manifestation can be held accountable only to its own goals and values. The primary values of the Indian musical tradition are spiritual, with the aesthetic and the sensory being subservient to it. In the hierarchy of music-making goals, the primary place belongs to the generation of *rasa* at the highest possible level of intensity. A musician shapes and reshapes *rāgas* in order to achieve the *rasa* goal. In the process, he also arranges and rearranges relationships between the individual units of melodic expression, the *svaras*. The amorphous character of *rāgas* and the floating pitch values in Hindustānī music are an essential part of a tradition that gives the musician the combined role of a composer–performer, requiring both these processes to be performed simultaneously. The *rāga* and the *svara* both have only ephemeral validity as the stimuli of an interactive process validated solely by its generation of the target emotional response, the *rasa*. (Also see *Rāga*.)

Svarāśrita/Padāśrita/Layāśrita/Arthāśrita : Genres of music are classified on the basis of that element which constitutes the primary target of the musician's energies, with the other being subordinated to it. Since music has four elements, this concept permits a four-way classification of musical genres.

1. *Svarāśrita* (melody dominant), where primary target for musical energies is the melody.
2. *Padāśrita* (composition dominant), in which the composite target of musical energies in the totality of the pre-composed melodic–rhythmic–poetic entity.
3. *Layāśrita* (tempo / rhythm dominant), in which the determining factor in the delivery of musical value is the tempo of rendition, which forges a distinctive relationship between the melody, the rhythm and the lyrics.
4. *Arthāśrita* (interpretative), where the musical endeavour is focused on the musical interpretation of the lyrics. This classification recognizes the interpretation of literary meaning as a musical endeavour qualitatively distinct from the one characteristic of the *padāśrita* genres. Interestingly, this category covers the semi-classical genres because it is

dominated neither by *svara*, nor by *laya*, nor by the *pada*.

Tablā/Pakhāwaj : The *tablā* is a pair of vertical drums, most widely used today as percussion accompaniment in Hindustānī music. It is, historically, as well as stylistically, the successor of the ancient two-faced barrel drum, *pakhāwaj/mṛdaṅga*. Though the name resembles a Middle Eastern drum called *tablā*, the *tablā* is a uniquely Indian instrument. The *tablā* is believed to have emerged, starting from the eighteenth century, as a significant accompanist to the *khyāl* genre of vocal music, and the modern instruments like the *sitār* which required a less intrusive and more delicate rhythmic presence than the ancient *pakhāwaj/mṛdaṅga* could provide.

Tāla : The word derives from the Hindi *tālī* = sound of clapping with the hands. It originated in the ancient practice of keeping time with the clapping of hands or tapping on the thighs to the accompaniment of recitations of Sanskrit hymns. Such a practice was necessary because the hymns were composed to standard metres derived from the literary tradition and their poetic integrity could be preserved only by recitation at a specific tempo. In musical usage, the same function is performed by a rhythmic cycle performed on percussion instruments. Each *tāla* is a rhythmic cycle defined by its distinctive number of beats, sound symbols for percussion impact and beat-subdivisions representing its cadence. Each *tāla* also has a tempo – or a range of tempi – at which it is appropriately deployed. The *tāla* also defines the metric structure of the *bandiś* and regulates the cyclical component of the improvisatory movements woven around it. (Also see *Bandiś*.)

Tālīm : The word *tālīm* derives from the Perso-Arabic word *ilm* = knowledge/science/craft/art. *Tālīm* refers to the process by which an *ilm* – particularly in the arts and crafts – is transmitted from a master to his disciples.

Tamas : See *Guṇa* (with reference to artistic values/motivations).

Tāmasika : See *Sāttvika/Rājasika/Tāmasika*.

Ṭappā : The *ṭappā* is a modern semi-classical genre of vocal music. It owes its inspiration to the songs of the camel-drivers of Punjab and India's north-western frontiers. Originally a folk form, later adopted by courtesans, it was accepted in genteel society by the late seventeenth century. The identifying feature of the *ṭappā* is a vivacious, even mischievous, treatment of melody. The treatment is not only naughty within itself, but also in relation to the beat patterns of the rhythmic cycle.

Tāra/Taratva, Mandra/Mandratva (with respect to *rāgas*) : The Hindustānī tradition divides the melodic canvas into three octaves – lower, middle and higher. The lower octave is called *mandra saptaka*. The middle octave is called *madhya saptaka*. The higher octave is called the *tāra saptaka*. Each *rāga* is assigned a specific region of the three-octave melodic canvas which is its melodic/aesthetic "home". *Taratva* describes a melodic bias of a *rāga* towards the upper half of the three-melodic canvas. *Mandratva* describes a melodic bias of the *rāga* towards the lower half of the three-octave melodic canvas.

Tāra Saptaka : The term derives from Sanskrit *tāra* = higher frequencies + *saptaka* = a group of seven frequency intervals. The term describes the higher octave of the melodic canvas. While the Western tradition considers the scale as consisting of eight tonal points, the Indian system treats the same distance as consisting of seven frequency intervals. Hence, the reference to the scale as a continuum of seven units, rather than eight.

Tarānā : The *tarānā* (etymology speculative) is a genre of vocal music, which uses meaningless consonants as articulatory material, instead of the poetic form. These consonants are drawn primarily from the sound symbols used in the language of percussion (*dha, dhin, tirkit*, etc.) and the plucked lute family of instruments (*da, ra, dir*, etc.). The occasional use of nom-tom phonemes used in *dhrupad* is also encountered in *tarānā* compositions. *Tarānā*s are composed in all *rāga*s and all *tāla*s, and generally performed in medium and fast tempi. The rendition of *tarānā*s is much like the *chhoṭā khyāl*, though usually without virtuoso *tāna*s.

Ṭhumrī : The word derives from an onomatopoetic expression *ṭhumaka*, signifying the sound of anklet bells of a dancer. The *ṭhumrī* is a modern genre of semi-classical music, which originated as an accompaniment to the Kathak genre of north Indian dance, and evolved into an independent art form. The genre subsumes two subgenres – a brisk and lively form called *bandiś ṭhumrī* and a leisurely sentimental form called *bol-banāo-ṭhumrī*. The *bandiś-kī-ṭhumrī* reached its zenith in the mid-nineteenth century and was nearly extinct by the early twentieth century. The *bol-banāo-ṭhumrī* acquired the status of a mainstream genre in the early twentieth century, and is now headed for extinction. (Also see *Bandiś-kī-*

Ṭhumrī, Bol-Banāo-Ṭhumrī.)

Urdu : A dialect of Hindi, the mainstream north Indian language, with a substantial presence of Persian and Arabic vocabulary, but only minor syntactical influence. The dialect is written in the Persian script. The name derives from the Turkish word *urd* = the market in a military camp. This suggests its origins amongst settling soldiers from conquering Middle Eastern armies. Unlike Persian, Urdu never became a language of the feudal courts in India. However, the dialect did trigger off a major literary flowering during the colonial era (nineteenth and early twentieth centuries) primarily through the *ghazal* genre. (Also see *Ghazal.*)

Ustād : The word is Persian for a teacher. In the music world, it signifies a Muslim musician of sufficient attainments to qualify as a teacher. A Hindu of comparable attainments is called a *paṇḍit*. No formalized framework exists for conferring such honorifics to musicians. They emerge through an informal process of consensus building within the community of musicians.

Uttarāṅga Pradhāna : See *Aṅga Prādhānya.*

Vādī/Saṁvādī : *Vādī* is derived from the Sanskrit verb *vada* = to speak. Contextually, *vādī* may be translated as "spokesperson/ representative/protagonist". *Saṁvādī* derives from *saṁvāda* = dialogue. The *vādī* and *saṁvādī* are the two dominant tones/*svaras* in a *rāga*. The *vādī* is the primary dominant, while the *saṁvādī*, generally in the alternate tetrachord of the scale and in acoustic correspondence with the *vādī*, is the secondary dominant tone/ *svara* of the *rāga*. The two, together, form the axis around which the *rāga* exposition revolves. (Also see *Rāga.*)

Vinyāsa : See *Nyāsa/Apanyāsa.*

Virāṭa Svarūpa : See *Gurumukhī/Sarvamānya.*

Viṣṇu (with reference to a deity) : The Hindu pantheon is presided over by three principal gods representing – at an archetypal level – the three primary processes of the universe: Creation, Preservation and Destruction. Bramhā is the Creator, Viṣṇu is the Preserver and Śiva is the Destroyer. Being the preserver, Viṣṇu (along with his various manifestations over the ages) is the most widely worshipped deity amongst Hindus.

Bibliography

Aurobindo, Sri, 2006, *Bhagvadgita: Text, Translation and Commentary*, 3rd edn., ed. Parameshwari Prasad Khaitan, Jhunjhunu: Sri Aurobindo Divine Life Trust.

Ayyangar, Ranganayaki, 2017, *Ragavibodha of Somnatha*, first edn, New Delhi: Indira Gandhi National Centre for the Arts.

Bhatkhande, V.N., 2012 , *Karmik Pustak Malika*, ed. L.N. Garg, vols I-VI, 14th edn, Hathras: Sangeet Karyalaya

———, 2013, *Hindustani Sangeet Paddhati*, Hathras, UP: Sangeet Karyalaya.

Despande, Vamanrao, 1973, *Indian Musical Traditions: An Aesthetic Study of the Gharanas in Hindustani Music*, Bombay: Popular Prakashan.

Deva, B.C., 1981, *An Introduction to Hindustani Music*, New Delhi: Publications Division, Government of India.

Devidayal, Namita, 2007, *The Music Room: A Memoir*, Gurgaon: Random House India.

Hanslick, Eduard, 1891, *The Beautiful in Music*, London: Novello, Ever and Co.

James, W., 1961, *The Varieties of Religious Experience: A Study in Human Nature*, New York: Collier.

Jung, Carl, 1921, *Psychological Types* (*Psychologische Typen*), Zurich: Rascher Verlag.

Langer, Susanne K., 1963, *Feeling and Form*, 3rd impression, Routledge & Kegan Paul.

———, 1957, *Problems of Art*, Routledge & Kegan Paul.

Maslow, Abraham, 1954, *Motivation and Personality*, New York: Harper and Brothers (2nd edn, 1970).

Mathieu, W.A., 1994, *A Musical Life*, Boulder, CO: Shambhala.

McLeish, Kenneth, 1993, *Key Ideas in Human Thought*, New York: Facts on File.

Ortega Y Gasset, Jose, 1959, *Man and Crisis*, London: George Allen and Unwin.

Patwardhan, Vinayak Rao, *Raga Vigyan* (Hindi), vols I to VII: vol. I, 9th edn, 1978; vol. II, 9th edn, 1996; vol. III, 8th edn, 1991; vol. IV, 4th edn, 1959; vol. V, 6th edn, 1984; vol. VI, 2nd edn, 1964; vol. VII, 2nd edn, 1971; Pune: Sangeet Gaurav Granth Mala.

Raja, Deepak, 2015, *Hindustani Music: A Tradition in Transition*, New Delhi: D.K. Printworld (1st edn, 2005).

———, 2015, *The Rāga-ness of Rāgas*, New Delhi: D.K. Printworld.

———, 2012, *Hindustani Music Today*, New Delhi: D.K. Printworld.

———, 2009, *Khayal Vocalism: Continuity within Change*, New Delhi: D.K. Printworld.

Raja, Deepak and Suvarnalata Rao (eds.), 1999, *Perspectives on Dhrupad*, Baroda: Indian Musicological Society.

Ranade Ashok Dā, 2006, *A Concise Dictionary of Hindustani Music*, New Delhi: Promilla & Co. in association with Bibliophile South Asia.

———, 1997, *Hindustani Music*, New Delhi: National Book Trust.

———, 1990, *Key Words & Concepts in Hindustani Classical Music*, New Delhi: Promilla & Co.

———, 1984, *On Music and Musicians of Hindoostan*, New Delhi: Promilla & Co.

Saxena, S.K., 2010, *Hindustani Sangeet: Some Perspectives, Some Performers*, New Delhi: D.K. Printworld.

———, 2009, *Hindustani Music and Aesthetics Today*, 1st edn., New Delhi: Sangeet Natak Akademi and Hope Publications.

———, 2001, *Hindustani Sangeet and a Philosopher of Art*, New Delhi: D.K. Printworld.

Sharma, Premlata, 1989, "Raga Lakshana", in *Nibandha Sangeet*, ed. L.N. Garg, 2nd edn, Hathras, UP: Sangeet Karyalaya.

Stockhausen, Karlheinz, 1989, *Towards a Cosmic Music*, tr. Tim Nevill, Dorset UK: Element Books.

Subba Rao, B., 1956-66, *Raga Nidhi*, vols 1-4, Madras: Music Academy.

Thakurdas, Manikbuwa, *Raga Darshan* (Hindi), vol. I, 1987, Ajmer: Krishna Brothers; vol. II, 1988 Ajmer: Krishna Brothers; vol. III, 1997; Rajpipla: Lakshminath Charitable Trust; vol. IV, 1997, Rajpipla: Lakshminath Charitable Trust.

Wade, Bonnie, 1984, *Khayala, Creativity Within: India's Classical Music Tradition*, Cambridge: Cambridge University Press.

Index I

Personages and Institutions

Index II

Gharānās

Index III

Rāgas

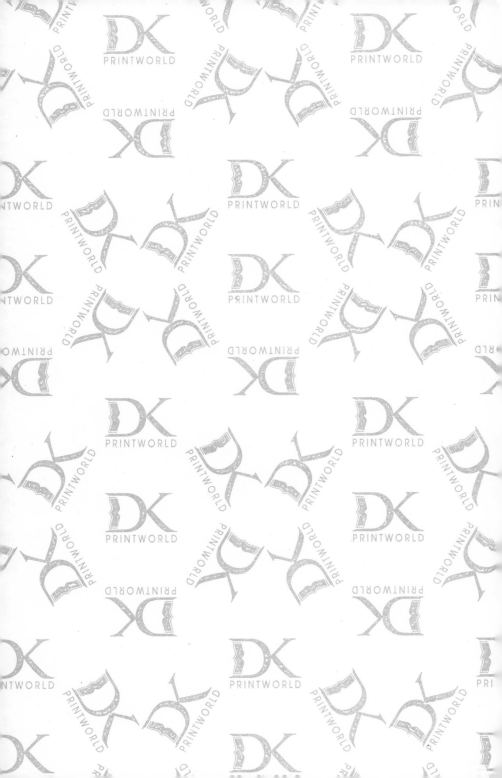